If you listen closely you will hear the spirits sigh
a lesson lost on humans; an enchanting lullaby:
Mercy lies in nature's hands and bound to it we grow.
Of the earth we came to be and of the earth we'll go.

Hall of Mosses

By

Nicoline Evans

Author: Nicoline Evans – www.nicolineevans.com
Editor: Andrew Wetzel – www.stumptowneditorial.com
Cover Design: Dan Elijah Fajardo –
                    www.behance.net/dandingeroz

And a big thank you to everyone who has offered me
support—in all ways, shapes, and sizes—during this entire
process.

An ode to the trees

Chapter 1

Juniper Tiernan stepped off her cottage's creaky porch and into the mist. Visibility through the hazy, post-rain fog was dismal, but she knew what lay beyond—home. The depths of the forest provided more comfort to her than any person or place ever had.

She only had a few days off and it was important that she spent that time in the forest. Her bag was packed: tent, food, sleeping bag, and music. She threw the compact luggage onto her back and wheeled her custom-painted, mint green dual-sport bike out of the shed. Appropriately nicknamed the Jaden Jaunt by locals, she rolled her Yamaha WR250R motorbike to the end of her driveway. Loose rocks slid beneath her boot heels, so she didn't start her bike until she reached the paved road.

Safely mounted, she clipped the Olympic National Park walkie-talkie to her belt—Ranger Clark insisted she wear it—and fastened her helmet.

It began to drizzle again. Not wanting to waste another second, she activated the electric start and revved into first gear. The stormy dew atop the pavement splashed as she raced down Lake Dawn Road toward Hurricane Ridge.

On clear days, the sun cast brilliant shades of green through the overhead leaves, but today she could barely see the road through the fog. The staggered mountain ranges and forest tops were hidden from sight, and instead, she was embraced by the eerie silence of the storm-wrecked woods. She focused on the road's painted yellow line to stay on course.

The concrete trail continued for twenty-seven miles and would take nearly an hour to traverse, but it was the fastest route and led her directly into the open woods. There were dirt trails she'd take once the road ended, but she still had miles left to go.

When the rain began to pool, she eased off the gas. In the woods, the trees would give her shelter, making the ride less dangerous. Wet pavement was lethal; mud was fun.

Her hip buzzed as Clark called her on the walkie. She found a tall evergreen and parked beneath.

"What's up, Clark?" She released the TALK button and waited for his reply. His world-weary voice crackled shortly after.

"Hey there, Juni. Saw the Jaden Jaunt making the trek down Hurricane Ridge and wanted to know where you were headed in this rain."

"The Hall of Mosses."

"You camping out?"

"Yeah, till Friday morning. I have to head into Port Angeles for work Friday night."

"That's five days in the woods. You got enough food and water?"

"Yes, Dad," she teased. Juniper moved to Washington two years ago and the old ranger quickly adopted the role of her over-protective father after dealing with her many reckless — and illegal — motorized romps into the National Park.

"Alright, well, Roscoe and I will be in and out to check on you."

"Don't bother me too much."

Ranger Clark grunted. "You're too comfortable alone in these woods. Sometimes I think you forget how dangerous they are."

"Only if I panic. I know how to forage, how to find potable water without an obvious source. I don't get spooked by animals. Even if I got lost one day, which is highly unlikely considering I've grown to know these woods better than the city I live in, I'd be just fine. I'm better in the forest. I'm at ease with the trees. You don't need to worry about me."

"Well I do, and I always will. I'll be by to check in. Make sure you don't go crazy out there. The trees can't be your only friends."

"They can't?" she teased.

"It's not appropriate companionship. Neither is an old man like me, but it's better than the alternative. At least I can talk."

"The trees speak if you listen. It's a small whisper, but you can hear them if you're paying attention." She paused, realizing she was proving his point about her wavering sanity. She did not truly believe that the trees had voices, but she did believe in their divine energy. "Maybe it's just a feeling I get," she continued, "but it's more substantial than anything a human has ever offered me."

"Gee, thanks."

"You are an exception, of course."

"Yeah, yeah. Just be safe. I'll be around."

"Okay, Pops. See you when I see you."

The radio call ended and she fastened the walkie-talkie back to her belt. She shifted into first gear and reentered the rain.

The hour passed and she found herself at the end of the paved road. There were no hikers or tourists out today, so the

3

parking spots were plenty. She stretched, preparing for the long trail ride. The rain clouds were lifting, allowing her a glimpse of the majesty beneath. The sun peeked through and the massive verdant mountaintops greeted her with love. She closed her eyes and soaked in the quiet energy.

She was alive, despite years of thinking she'd never make it to thirty. One year to go and that old demon would be put to rest. The depression, self-abuse, destructive behavior, and acceptance of toxic relationships derailed her as a young woman, but here she stood now, past it all, breathing freely. Finally uninhibited by the life that used to haunt her. Though some claimed she ran away and never faced her issues, never gave them proper closure, she did not care. She got away—she escaped a devastating fate and the venomous people that kept her trapped. And while the demons living inside her weren't completely dead, she was safe here. Removed from her past, she could finally control the darkness that still lingered inside.

The mountains kept her safe. They would never betray her, never take her for granted. They welcomed her and offered an unwavering sense of security. If she hadn't found herself in the forest, she would have lost herself to the city. The brutal and ruthless nature of mankind was suffocating, and after years of trying, she determined that she could not survive amongst them. She could not continue ripping herself into pieces to keep the ones she loved whole.

Now, she was looking out for herself. She left the pain behind and began anew. Though her decision to leave the Bronx was not selfish, her behavior when meeting new people in Washington was. Her closed-off nature was an act of self-preservation, an attempt to guard her restored spirit. The cycle was sickening, and she was very aware that she had transformed into a self-serving person—similar to those who hurt her in the past—but it was the only way to ensure her survival. She wanted to live past thirty, wanted to be happy and enjoy her life on this wondrous planet.

The forest was her home, the only place she felt safe as she continued to heal. She was stronger now, but the wounds were still raw. There was no doubt she'd grow whole again, she just needed time.

Heading down Whiskey Bend Trailhead toward Goblin Gates, the dirt path was easy to traverse. When she reached Goblin Gates, she walked her bike through a shallow section of the Elwha River, then continued riding on trails she made over the years. Having park rangers as friends proved critical—she got into a lot of trouble when she first moved to Washington. After multiple fines due to repeated offenses, they finally sat her down and saw the devoted passion and respect she had for the park. They educated her on basic survival, gave her a short list of rules, then promoted her from civilian to honorary ranger. Donning this title, she was finally allowed to blaze new paths. Armed with a machete and thick gardening gloves, she hacked her way over the mountains, through the thick trees, and into the Hoh Rainforest. Tourists and hikers had to travel the perimeter of Olympic National Park to get from Mt. Olympus to the Hoh Rainforest Visitor Center, but she cut right through the middle. Now that the path was complete, an excursion that took two days to complete for most people only took her half-a-day.

She zig-zagged between grand firs and western red cedars that stood thirty stories tall, rode over branches that fell from their most recent storm, and splashed through mud puddles. The closer she got to Hoh, the brighter the surroundings became. North of Bailey Range the forest was a dark shade of evergreen, filled with trees taller than most buildings in the state. To the south, the forest turned fluorescent with life. Hoh was an ocean-born forest, home to Sitka spruces, bigleaf maples, and vine maples. The trees here were huddled closer to one another, covered in cat-tail moss and licorice fern. Branches with long, spikemoss curtains draped the forest and the air smelt fresh as dew. Juniper found her usual clearing in the Hall of Mosses and parked her bike. She set up her tent and unpacked her knapsack.

The nearby trees made a tight circle around her temporary home. There were paths to get in, but they were tight. She'd enjoy watching Ranger Clark or Ranger Roscoe navigate this maze on their four-wheelers.

Branches from the trees surrounding her weaved together overhead creating a canopy protecting her from the elements. Rain still dripped onto her tent, but the worst of the storm was over. The sun peeked through the small gaps and cast ripples of brilliant color onto the glade.

Juniper rested on a bed of ferns outside the opening to her tent and stared up at the earth-made kaleidoscope. Its green light danced over her as clouds came and went, and the colors shifted with the setting sun. When her eyes grew heavy from the day's long journey, she crawled into her tent and surrendered to sleep.

Dawn came carrying the melodies of the local American dippers. The high-pitch whistle of the aquatic songbirds rang overhead as they soared toward the Hoh River for breakfast.

Their hungry cries made her stomach grumble. After a quick stretch, she opened her cooler, grabbed a large bag of granola, and drank water out of her canteen.

The day flew by, as did the next, in peaceful solitude.

On Wednesday, Roscoe paid her a visit, as he always did. He was thirty-two, only three years older than her, and he loved nature just as much as she did.

"Juni, are you in there?" he shouted from outside the thick brush that encircled her. His quad could not fit through, so he parked it in the closest spot possible.

"I'm here. There's a walkable path to your left."

He found it, but flailed about in the process, tripping over huckleberry shrubs and thickets of fern.

"Jeez, how'd you get yourself *and* the Jaden Jaunt in there? This is a tight little maze."

"I came around the other side. Been here before so I've already tried your route. It's doable, but only on foot."

"Clearly." Roscoe finally made it into the clearing and brushed the debris off his uniform. He was tall, sturdy, and athletic. Despite his age, his face was still boyish. If he didn't sport bearded stubble, he'd look much younger. His bright, hazel eyes were kind as they scanned over her current adventure.

"How long have you been out here?"

"Since Monday."

He nodded. "What have you been doing to keep yourself entertained?"

"I brought books and music." Her iPod sat next to her, still playing from when she fell asleep with it on. "I don't really need much entertainment out here. Nature provides me with plenty."

"Can I stay a while? I'm on break and Clark is in a rotten mood. Don't really want to head back anytime soon."

"Sure," she answered. To anyone other than Roscoe or Clark she would have declined, but she grew to love them both. They didn't know much about her except that she was an adrenaline chasing biker girl with a deep love for the woods, but they accepted her for that. Despite her guarded friendships with them, they seemed to understand her. Roscoe most of all. She'd known him for two years, and though she hadn't told him a word about her past, he still managed to bond with her on a deeper level. They didn't need to force a connection because what they had was inherent, raw, natural. She often wished to let him in a little more, but the fears from her past always got in the way.

"Did you see the Wolfe brothers on your ride out here? They were bathing in Hoh Lake on my way to see you."

"No, but next time you run into them tell them it'd be nice if they helped me clear the trails we ride once in a while. I understand that they are young, but if they're going to use the paths, then they need to help with the upkeep."

"Message will be relayed. How's the job going?" he asked.

"Eh, alright. It pays the rent and gives me the freedom to live here. The flexible schedule is great, but the job itself is rotten.

The locals are okay, but the unpredictability of the tourists keeps me on edge. I never know who I'll get walking into that bar."

"Luckily this is a little town, barely on anyone's radar. Can't imagine you'd run into anyone you left behind."

Juniper scanned him carefully.

"That's presumptuous."

"Am I wrong?"

"Yes and no." He stared back at her with caring eyes. He loved her, she could feel it, and it felt silly to keep hiding from him. His was the most stable relationship she'd found in a long time. "I did leave a lot of people behind," she confessed, "but I'm not worried about seeing them. I don't like serving people who *remind* me of them. I get nervous that the feelings I left behind might resurface. It's been two years. I feel stronger, but I've never been put to the test. Any real-life reminder might send me backwards."

"You can't live your life in hiding."

"I'm not hiding."

Roscoe's eyes widened. "Then what do you call this?" He raised his arms into the air and Juniper laughed as she realized she was literally hidden in the wilderness of Washington. "I could barely find you, and I am pretty sure you like me okay."

"I get it," she laughed, shaking her head. "This isn't about hiding, it's about connecting with something that makes me feel alive again. I was held together by loose strings for years, I was nothing more than a shadow of the person I knew I could be. Living like that was misery and I often felt I'd find a better life in death."

Admitting that aloud took her breath away. She stopped speaking, afraid of what that admission would mean to Roscoe. She held her breath, waiting for his expression to shift from empathetic to disturbed, but it didn't. He didn't judge her or rapidly change his opinion of her. He loved her just the same.

"Then I'm very grateful you found this forest. You're pretty damn special and missing the chance to know you would have been a great loss."

"Thanks." She felt vulnerable and exposed. Usually they discussed nature, philosophical ideas, and wild, supernatural imaginings, but this was the first time she opened up in a deeper manner. Though he seemed to take her confession well, her mind raced around the thoughts he left unsaid. "It's all in the past. I'm not hiding from anyone or anything. I'm just starting over."

"Nothing wrong with that." He let the conversation fade, reading her anxiety loud and clear. He was honored she chose to confide in him, even if it was only a snippet of the entire story. He gave her a small smile, knowing she still needed distance, and leaned back to grab a fruiting huckleberry branch. "Want some?"

"Sure." She smiled. He shook a few berries off the branch and into her cupped hands. They ate in comfortable quiet and let the rustling trees in the cool spring breeze bridge the silence. She liked his company, but remained guarded and refused to let her mind turn it into something it wasn't. If she did not keep a firm grip on her expectations, she'd find herself spiraling down a hole of disappointment with no clue of how she got there.

Evening crept up on them and Roscoe stood in a hurry at the first sign of the setting sun.

"Clark is going to kill me. I stayed too long."

"Better hurry back then."

"Yeah. How long will you be here?"

"Till Friday morning. Then I have to head back for my night shift."

"Clark or I will come by again tomorrow."

"There's no need for that."

"Well, what if I want to see you again?"

"If you must," she teased.

He smirked and headed back toward the trail. He made it out easier this time and she could hear his quad rev up and race off on the other side of her sanctuary.

Sunset came in shades of pink and orange that bled through the canopy. She rested her head upon a patch of lady fern and watched her kaleidoscope light shift. The wind kicked up as she dozed off. The leaves rustled and swayed in the full moon, making rhythms and earthly melodies through the sky.

Half-awake, voices emerged, in her head or from the forest, she wasn't sure.

<<We've been watching you.>>

The voices called out in discord, speaking over one another.

<<A human presence much appreciated.>>

<<The magic is in you; it's in him too.>>

The rambled, scattered thoughts, neither cohesive nor sensible, interlaced with the words of her dreams.

<<Welcome to the family,>> the most dominant voice said.

Arms made of wood embraced her. They wrapped tight around her and offered the most comforting love she'd ever felt.

<<*We choose you.*>>

Chapter 2

Her dreams were laced with magic. The forest whispered tales of tragedy and wonder, taking her on a voyage as swift as a passing breeze. She soared through the trees, listening to their highs and lows, trying to understand what they were telling her, but their stories were many and the underlying message got lost in the details. When dawn arrived and the sun coaxed her awake, she felt uncomfortable and wary of what she remembered from her dreams. It felt real. Her gut told her not to forget what had happened, not to dismiss the vision, but it was impractical to imagine such a thing possible. Trees could not talk. While their energy was abundant and she could feel them in every breath she took, she never truly *heard* them. Though she often claimed to, it was simply a metaphorical way of explaining her connection to nature. The trees were alive, but never animated. She shook her head trying to snap herself back into the real world. Maybe she did spend too much time alone; perhaps she *was* slowly losing her mind.

Morning came and went. As the hours passed she felt more grounded and less inclined to believe the wild and enchanted imaginings of her mind. It was a lovely notion, trees speaking to her, but it was unhealthy to entertain such a thought. It took every ounce of rationality inside her to let go of the hope that this dream might hold some truth.

Roscoe visited her again that afternoon. He parked on the opposite side of the heavily wooded glade and took the easier path into the center.

"How'd you sleep?"

"My dreams were vivid. They took me on a fantastic journey."

"That sounds fun."

"Yeah, except I woke up wishing it was real."

"Teaser dreams are awful. Hard to snap out of them in the morning."

"Tell me about it."

"At least it was a teaser *dream* and not a nightmare. Those are much worse. Shaking free from one of those is way harder."

"The weirdest part was that the dream started before I was fully asleep. If I wasn't asleep when it began, doesn't that make it real?"

"I find my craziest thoughts come in the small space between being awake and falling asleep. If you lingered there for a few minutes, it was probably just your imagination."

Juniper nodded. She stared up at the trees and willed them to talk, hoping if they did it while she was awake and with company, she'd feel less crazy. If Roscoe heard it too, it would make the fantasy real.

There was no noise except the singing birds and the gust of spring air rustling the leaves.

She let it go.

"Want to walk down to the river with me?"

"Sure," he replied. She put on her shoes and led the way.

They traveled down the small path Juniper made toward Hoh River, and the lush, green foliage encased them as they walked. It took them fifteen minutes to make it to the water and the exertion left them parched. Next to a patch of moss-covered rocks, Juniper plunged her canteen into the river water and then took a swig of the purified water. She then handed it to Roscoe, who finished the jug before refilling it. Juniper was already shoeless and wading through the shallow bend of the river. The water was frigid—summer had not arrived to give it warmth—but the icy trickle across her shins and the cold mud between her toes felt perfect.

"Are you coming in?" she asked him, splashing the chilly water in his direction.

"You're crazy. Spring has barely been here a month. That water is ice cold."

"It feels amazing."

"You are not of this earth."

She laughed. "I'm from Mars."

"More like Pluto. Creatures fond of ice live far from the sun."

"It's really not *that* cold. Your body will adjust, I promise."

Roscoe stood on the dirt riverbank with his arms crossed, his features were sharp and handsome. Juniper tried not to notice.

"I'll drag you in." She began walking toward him through the water. "You better take your shoes off."

He scoffed playfully as she approached. "You're tall but scrawny. Good luck."

She gasped in fake offense then darted at him, rounding him and giving him a shove toward the river.

He shouted playfully as she managed to get him a few steps closer to the water. He kicked off his boots clumsily as Juniper nudged him closer to the berm. He threw his last sock onto dry land as the freezing water hit his skin.

"I let you win."

"Yeah, right. Next time, fight back," she insisted playfully.

15

"Next time, I'll pick you up and toss you into the water. We'll see how warm you think the water is then."

"Warm as a bath." She splashed the water into the air and let it rain down on her. Eyes closed, she didn't see Roscoe move toward her.

He wrapped his arms around her in a bear hug and dipped her body inches from the river's surface. Her long, ash-brown curls landed in the water and straightened with the current. She screamed in surprise, tossing in his grip, but he was much stronger than her.

She stopped her playful struggle and looked up at him with her wide, green eyes. They shared a moment of silence before Roscoe leaned in and kissed her. The air around them swirled and she was sure she heard the trees sigh in unison.

His affection was a bandage on a wound still healing. It was the type of connection she'd been hiding from in hopes to become whole, but here she was, ready to unravel again at its arrival.

The kiss ended and he lifted her. After loosening his grip, he stared at her, trying to read her expression and decipher if he had interpreted her feelings correctly. The kiss felt right, she kissed him back, but now she stood before him impossible to read—walls high and guard up. The energy between them went flat, as fast as it had become flirtatious.

"Are you okay?" he asked, embarrassed.

"Of course I am."

"It just felt like the right thing to do in the moment."

Juniper smiled at him, pushing her fears aside in order to spare his feelings. It wasn't his fault she was plagued by her past.

"It was. You didn't read it wrong. I'm just a mess." She pointed to her head.

He nodded, relieved. She swallowed her anxiety for the moment and splashed him again.

"You're lucky you didn't dunk me. That would've started a river war."

"Oh yeah?"

"Mmhmm."

He laughed, but now his guard was up too. He did not want to hurt her or make her feel uncomfortable, and though she hid it well, he could tell he had.

She wrung the water out of her long hair and walked back toward the riverbank. He followed and sat next to her on a mossy patch of land. Not touching, they rested and watched the sky. It was cold in the shade, but clouds came and went, teasing them with small bouts of warm sunshine. When she shivered, he did not offer his warmth; he was too nervous to go out on a limb a second time.

She dug her toes into the dirt, to stay warm and remain grounded. Their emersion into the soil brought a feeling of peace that she couldn't explain. Having Roscoe next to her enhanced the feeling. She was safe.

They remained in comfortable silence, taking in the energy of the earth around them with eyes closed.

The later it got, the stronger the winds grew. The branches brushed against each other, filling the sky with strange noises.

"I think a storm is coming," Roscoe said in a sleepy voice, breaking their long-held silence.

"I feel it too."

"Want to head back?"

"In a minute." She dug her toes deeper into the soil. The trees above danced and made earthly rhythms with their wind-blown leaves.

<<*Let us in.*>>

Juniper's eyes shot open and she sat upright, looking down at Roscoe in concern. He appeared to be half-asleep.

"Did you hear that?"

He hurried himself out of his daze upon seeing Juniper's new look of alarm.

"Hear what?" he asked, sitting up.

She shifted her gaze skyward toward the trees, their silhouettes swayed against the orange sunset. With a deep breath she shook her head, unsure how to continue the conversation.

"I must have been more asleep than I realized."

"What did you hear?"

She looked down at him and huffed in resignation.

"A voice."

"Mine? I don't recall saying anything, but I've been known to talk in my sleep."

"No, it wasn't you."

He looked at her curiously. "Who then?"

"It must have been an animal. Want to head back?"

"Sure," he stood up first, then took her hand and pulled her to her feet. They put their shoes back on and began the walk back to the glade. They made the trip with heads down to protect their faces from the rough wind and the rain began to fall when they were ten minutes away. It started as a drizzle but soon shifted into heavy precipitation as the world around them became very loud.

Rain pelted Juniper's face as she looked up at the trees. They appeared to be bending in a manner that protected her and Roscoe from the brunt of the storm.

Impossible, she thought.

<<We will keep you safe.>>

Juniper stopped dead in her tracks.

"What did you say?" Roscoe asked over the wild howling of the wind.

"Nothing." Her heart raced. The mysteries hidden deep in this forest were now amplified. "I said nothing."

"You definitely said something," he objected.

Juniper shook her head. "I think it was the trees."

Roscoe took a step closer, gently placed his hands on her cheeks, and looked into her eyes to determine if she was being serious.

"The trees?"

She shrugged, hesitant to repeat herself.

"Let's get back," he continued. They returned to the glade and dipped beneath the woven net of branches. They were soaking wet but had temporary reprieve; the rain merely dripped through the covering.

"I think you should follow me back into civilization tonight," Roscoe stated.

"We can't ride in this."

"You've got a dirt bike, I've got a quad. We'll be alright."

"I want to stay."

"Then I'm staying with you."

"Fine."

They could hear the storm roar around them, but the rain only came into their haven through a few small openings. They dried off, entered the small tent, and snuggled within her large sleeping bag. His body heat provided more than just warmth; it also gave her comfort. He cared for her a great deal and she could feel it every time he was near.

They fell asleep in each other's arms and waited out the storm. The rain dwindled to a light sprinkle and by sunrise, the only noise left was the remaining wind. Without the sun to wake them, they continued sleeping until the voices returned.

<<We aren't a dream.>>

Juniper sat up in alarm, subsequently pulling Roscoe into a sitting position too. She looked at him and noticed he wasn't fully awake.

"Did you say something?"

"No," he mumbled through a yawn.

"It was the trees," she said with a gasp.

"We need to get out of this claustrophobic dome. It's messing with your head." He unzipped the sleeping bag so he could stand. "It stopped raining. Let's head back."

Juniper conceded—she *was* beginning to feel like she was losing her mind.

They got on their vehicles and rode Juniper's self-made trails back to Elwha River near Goblin Gates. The ride took all day and the sun was setting by the time they reached the intersection. When they reached Goblin Gates, they ran into the youngest Wolfe brothers.

"Hey, Juni. Hey, Roscoe." The youngest said with a wave as they parked their vehicles to chat. Noah was small for a sixteen-year-old, but his size did not affect his skilled riding abilities.

"Where are you two coming from?" Wes, his eighteen-year-old brother asked. He stood solid at six-feet and dwarfed his growing brother.

"The Hall of Mosses," Juniper answered. "Have you guys been preening the trails?"

"No, but we plan to," Noah answered, aware that they didn't properly hold up their end of the deal they made with Juniper when Clark gave them permission to ride her trails. "We came after school, but Dedrik and Baxley had to work tonight. They promised to come with us tomorrow, so we will get to work then."

"Alright. If you follow Boulder Creek you'll come across a few old trails I haven't tended to in a while. They are great, challenging rides, just overgrown."

"Then that's where we'll start," Wes responded.

"Fantastic. Why are you stopped here?"

"We just rode up and down Mt. Appleton. You know, that wicked steep trail covered with boulders."

"How'd you do?" she asked.

"Didn't fall," Noah professed with a smirk. "Wes did though."

"Only once, going down, so it was easy to pick up and carry on," Wes retorted.

"That's a tough trail, I'm impressed."

"Yeah, so we are just taking a breather," Noah said, answering her initial question.

"You ought to be headed home now, though," she advised. "The sun is setting."

"We have headlamps," Wes answered while flashing the light on his bike. "We'll be okay."

"Go home," Roscoe stepped in. "You know the rules. I don't want anymore panicked phone calls from your mother."

"Okay, fine."

"And don't take the long way," Roscoe scolded.

"I'm not making any promises," Wes said with a grin.

"See you guys on the trails," Juniper said before she and Roscoe continued their trek home. Upon reaching the start of Hurricane Ridge Road, they stopped to say good-bye.

"Want me to accompany you home?" he asked.

"No, I'll be fine, but thanks."

He wanted to kiss her again, but did not make the move. Instead he smiled and rode off. She sensed his inner turmoil. Part of her wanted his affection while the other part did not want to ruin their friendship, though she sensed there was no avoiding the latter. As his feelings grew they'd eventually need to face the inevitable: try dating romantically or resign to a friendship that would never truly be the same. Deep inside, she hoped this moment came when she was ready for that kind of relationship. She adored Roscoe and would not forgive herself if she ruined their chance to be happy together.

The whole ride back she listened for the voices, but couldn't hear anything over the engine of the Jaden Jaunt. While she could not hear the trees, she certainly felt them. Their tall, looming presence accompanied her every move, and though she was in touch with their energy previously, she felt even more connected now. Out of the woods and approaching reality, she understood that the voices were imagined, but it felt good to pretend that they might be real. Believing that she might be special, in the eyes of nature, gave her a sense of power she'd never known before.

Fueled by the confidence the forest gave her, she breathed easier. She was healing, and sooner than she expected. The pieces of her broken spirit were coming back together—her wounds were now fading scars.

The forest was where she belonged.

Chapter 3

Muddy and in desperate need of a shower, she entered her house and collapsed onto the couch. Old and brightly colored, most people would find it ugly, but she found its odd personality beautiful. Everything in her tiny cottage was bought from yard sales, antique stores, and pawnshops. Her budget was minimal when she arrived in Washington and the furniture, utensils, and trinkets she collected over the years were as unique as she was. Colorful, quirky, and often passed over by other shoppers, she gave a home to the weird and charming objects she found.

The antiquated answering machine on the side table next to the couch blinked. Having no use for a cell phone and wanting to be off the grid, she resorted to a landline phone for emergencies. No one had called her in months.

She pressed the large green button and the recording played. It was her Aunt Mallory.

"Thought you'd like to know your Uncle Ozzie died. He had a heart attack a few days ago. Wasn't gonna bother you with the news since you never answer or return my calls, but Irene insisted. Ozzie loved you." The words sounded like they hurt coming out of Mallory's mouth. She grew harsh again. *"The wake is Monday, funeral is on Tuesday. I don't expect you'll have the decency to show up."* The recording clicked and the message was over.

Juniper shut her eyes and took a deep breath. Her Aunt Mallory and Uncle Ozzie raised her after her parents died when she was twelve.

Seventeen years of toxic friendships and relationships turned her childhood grief into a deep, long-lasting depression, and her Uncle Oz was the only one who noticed her slow decline into a ghost of the girl that showed up at his doorstep so many years prior.

Juniper closed her eyes and fondly recalled the most pivotal moment in her young adult life.

Ozzie insisted that Juniper go on a camping trip with him to upstate New York, just the two of them. She resisted and tried to come up with excuses, never revealing that the true reason for not wanting to go was her anxious attachment to her boyfriend, but he forced her into his truck and took her away.

The drive was long and quiet; he wasn't a big talker. When they arrived at the campsite four hours later, Juniper soaked in the sun and inhaled as much of the fresh forest air as her body would allow. They spent two days together; fishing, barbecuing, and dirt biking. He never said a word about her current mental state—he let the forest take care of that. By the time the weekend was over, Juniper did not want to leave.

"Better now?" he asked during their ride back to the Bronx.

Juniper smiled and nodded. With the push of her uncle, the forest brought her back to life.

She broke up with Damien and left. She said good-bye and expressed her gratitude to her extended family, but they could only see her departure as abandonment. Ozzie was the only one who wished her well.

The answer was clear—she had to go.

Juniper played the message on her answering machine again. Her last shift was Sunday afternoon and she could make the funeral if she booked a flight now.

After a quick shower, she threw her hair into a wet braid and left for work early. With no laptop or internet at her house, she stopped at the local travel agency on the way to book the trip.

They found her a cheap flight and she left with a round trip ticket in hand. There was still an hour to kill before her shift started so she took the Jaden Jaunt on a cruise around town. She drove along the coast of Port Angeles and breathed in the salty air of the Salish Sea. The Strait of Juan de Fuca was filled with cargo ships making afternoon deliveries. Juniper watched the locals working hard and sweating beneath the warm, spring sun. She knew most of them and waved as she rode by. Those who saw her waved back and Jeb McLeer mimed drinking a beer. She answered him with a thumbs up. He laughed and got back to work. She'd be seeing him and many of his co-workers at the end of the day.

Having killed more time than she realized, she headed to work. It was 4 p.m. and Dipper Dive was empty besides the employees and a few day drinkers. Juniper took her place behind the bar, relieved that Misty and Brett had already set up for the happy hour rush. She was alone for the first hour but she'd get backup at 5 p.m.

Carine and Teek showed up at a quarter to, and at half past, the regulars started pouring in. At Dipper Dive, she rarely had to worry about having a tough night with the patrons. They were usually the same, and they all liked and respected her and her co-workers. They were crazy and loud, but never caused her

26

any emotional strife. After two years of serving them their beverages, she grew to like the folks of Port Angeles a lot. They grew very fond of her as well. She never asked for help, but they kept a protective eye on her from afar and offered assistance whenever they thought she may need some.

"The usual?" she asked Jeb.

"Yep."

Juniper grabbed a bottle of Bud Light from the fridge, cracked the top off, and slid it to him. He took a swig as she opened his tab.

"How was your time off, Juni?"

"Good. I went camping. Roscoe Boswald came by a few times."

"Ah, that handsome ranger is keen on ya. He asks about you every time I run into him in town."

"Yeah, he's really nice. It's nice to have a friend who loves the forest as much as I do."

"He wants more than a friendship."

"If you say so."

"I do. Mark my words, it won't be long before he makes a move."

Juniper rolled her eyes and took care of the guy next to Jeb. He didn't need to know Roscoe already fulfilled that prophecy.

"I'm taking a smoke break," Carine informed her and Teek before walking out the back.

"Can you grab the appetizers for seats 101 and 102? Lady at 208 ordered a goddamn mojito," Teek asked Juniper while organizing the ingredients to make the laborious cocktail.

Juniper smirked and headed to the kitchen. She grabbed the plates of hot wings, french fries, and mozzarella sticks, then carefully carried them to the diners. She then noticed that Roscoe and Clark were now sitting next to Jeb in their park ranger uniforms.

"Hey, whatcha guys doing here?"

"Decided to stop in after our shift ended," Clark responded. "How's it going?"

"Good, same crowd as usual. Do you know what you want to eat?"

"I'll have a cheeseburger, nothing on it, and a Blue Moon," Roscoe answered.

"And I'll take a chicken sandwich and a club soda," Clark added.

Juniper entered the order, poured the drinks, and leaned against the bar where they sat.

"Thanks for coming by."

"Of course," Roscoe smiled. "It's always nice seeing you outside the forest."

"You too." She smiled back and Jeb winked at her. She shook her head, half humored and half embarrassed, then tended to a couple whose glasses were empty.

The night passed in a blur as the bar got packed and the orders came in non-stop, but Clark and Roscoe stayed long after they finished eating. They talked to Jeb and his buddy Rick, and Juniper chatted with them whenever she had a free minute. There was a lull in activity around midnight; everyone was drunk and occupied by conversations, darts, pool, or dancing.

Juniper collapsed onto her elbows in front of Roscoe.

28

"You gonna make it?" he asked in jest.

"Two more hours." Then she plopped her head onto her arm. Roscoe rubbed the back of her shoulders for a moment before she stood back up. "And I don't even get a break after my Sunday shift. I have to travel east for a funeral."

"Who died?" Roscoe asked concerned.

"My uncle." She never told him the story of where she came from or how she came to be here.

"I'm really sorry to hear that. Are you okay?"

"Yeah. It's sad, but I'll be okay."

"When is it?"

"Monday and Tuesday."

"Want company? I'll go with you if it will help."

Juniper was taken aback. "Really?"

"Yeah, I have plenty of vacation days that I never end up using anyway."

They both glanced at Clark.

"I'm fine with you taking a few days off. I'll have Cindy come up from Quinault to cover your trails."

"Do you want me to go with you?" Roscoe asked, looking at Juniper with sympathy. She thought it over for a few moments before responding.

"Yeah, actually. I think it would be really nice to have you there with me."

"Okay, count me in. Tell me your flight info and I'll get a ticket."

"Thank you." She was relieved that he'd be by her side. He would keep her focused, grounded, safe.

"Anything for you."

Jeb winked at her again and she rolled her eyes before walking away.

The night ended in a drunken haze for many. Clark left a little after midnight, but Roscoe hung around. At 2 a.m., the patrons trickled out, catching cabs or walking home, and some unwisely drove themselves. Since she opened the shift, Carine and Teek closed up.

Roscoe only had two beers and was sober, so he followed her back to her place on his motorcycle. At the end of her driveway they both stopped.

"Thanks for keeping me company tonight."

"It was fun. I needed a night out."

She gave him a hug. "I'll be on Southwest #236 to LaGuardia. Let me know when you get your ticket."

"Will do."

She nodded and drove her motorbike to the shed in her backyard. Roscoe waited until she was parked and inside before leaving.

She didn't need much sleep and was up with the sun on Saturday morning. She sat on her back porch for hours, watching the stillness of the street's shared lake. None of her neighbors were out yet, though she suspected the kids would be swimming as soon as they woke. She enjoyed the quiet while it lasted. By noon the neighborhood kids were outside, splashing around in the lake. She enjoyed watching their innocent revelry.

She had the later shift. Misty was doing the bar set-up, so she took her time getting ready. Teek was on their shift too, but he strolled in late.

"You stink like whiskey," Juniper noted when he finally arrived.

"Probably because I just drank some."

Misty poured him a glass of water. "Sober up. There's a cruise ship docked in Seattle today and tonight might get crazy. You're no use to us drunk."

"I'm not drunk," Teek said with a slur, "just a little buzzed."

"Lies." Misty grabbed his face and examined his glazed eyes. "What on earth were you doing today?"

"Brett had friends in town from Cali and we were out on his boat."

"Tipsy is one thing, but you're on the fast track to hammered."

"I told you, I'm not drunk."

"You're on your way," Juniper said, picking up the glass of water and handing it to him. "Whatever you drank is catching up to you. Misty and I aren't dealing with the tourists alone. Drink up."

Teek begrudgingly took a sip of water.

"Buncha buzzkills," he muttered as he walked away.

"Frank will freak if he sees him like this on a day a cruise is in town," Misty said, concerned that their manager would fire him. Teek already had too many strikes.

"He will be fine in an hour," Juniper replied. "We just can't let him drink anymore."

"Yeah, good luck to us. He can't stop once he starts, and he's got a bar full of liquor at his fingertips. There's no way we can babysit him once the crowd rolls in."

"Well, we fill him with as much water as we can before then. It's not our fault he showed up like this."

"Yeah, but he's our friend. He'd have our backs if we needed him."

Juniper rolled her eyes. Her co-workers were very close and often spent time together outside of work. They always invited her, but she rarely went. Even so, they cared for her. They spent a lot of time together behind the bar and inevitably became close. Juniper knew Misty was right; Teek would go to great lengths to help her if she ever needed him.

"I'll call Frank to let him know things are good and hopefully stall him from checking in till later," Juniper offered.

"Cool. I'll keep Teek in the kitchen till he sobers up. Are you good on the bar for now?"

"Yeah, I'll let you know when it starts getting crowded. Feed him lots of burger buns."

Misty laughed. "Will do." She laced her arm into his and led their large, wobbling co-worker into the kitchen.

An hour later, a huge party strolled in.

"Misty," Juniper hollered toward the kitchen. "I need you."

She came out of the kitchen and they tackled the new onslaught of orders together.

"How's he doing?" Juniper asked after the rush died down.

"Better. He'll be good to go soon."

"Frank was going to come in an hour ago, but I told him it was dead. He told me he'd come in around ten instead."

"Perfect."

Teek emerged from the kitchen at 7 p.m.

32

"Sorry about that." He scratched his head and squinted his eyes in pain as he took in the crowd around the bar.

"We held Frank off till tonight. You owe us," Misty said with harsh camaraderie.

"I certainly do. Where can I jump in?"

"The guys in section 400 have been rude since they arrived," Juniper said while pointing to the rowdy, college-aged men sitting in the back corner. "I'd rather not deal with them anymore."

"I'm on it."

Tall, intimidating Teek strolled over to their section to check on their drinks. The rambunctious chatter immediately ceased and they drunkenly complained that they wanted the pretty, brunette bartender back.

"The one with the curls and nice ass," one of them slurred.

"Yeah, her," another confirmed, pointing at Juniper. "She's been serving us all night. Send her back."

"If you wanted her to continue taking care of your drinks then maybe you should've treated her with more respect. I'll be tending to your drinks from here on out and if that's a problem, you are free to leave." Teek's voice was deep and menacing. The young men stopped pushing their luck and ordered another round of beers.

Teek returned to the bar.

"I hate college kids," he muttered to Juniper. She smiled in grateful agreement.

Jeb sat in section 200 with the other regulars while the tourists infiltrated the rest of the bar. Most of them were pleasant and in vacation mode, which meant they were excited

33

to be out of their normal daily grind and serving them was enjoyable. They happily bantered with the bartenders, cracking jokes and keeping the mood light.

At 9 p.m., another group of guys walked into Dipper Dive. They pushed their way through section 300 to get to the bar and order drinks. When Juniper noticed them, her heart stopped.

It was Damien.

She shook her head, blinking a few times to readjust her vision, then looked again. It wasn't him, but it looked like him, and the terrifying feeling of him reentering her life shook her to the core.

She darted into the kitchen and retreated to the back corner. Eyes shut, she fell helpless to the panic attack. Her breathing was unstable and her balance was off; the only thing keeping her standing was the wall she leaned against. She opened her eyes but everything was blurry. Tears poured silently down her face as she tried to catch her breath. The feelings she left behind—the pain she tried to forget—had returned. Petrified she might choke on her own terror, she tried to clear her mind. She took slower, more deliberate breaths, hoping to stop her downward spiral, but the harder she tried, the harder the tears fell. Realizing she had no control, she collapsed to the floor and dug her fingernails into her forearm. The pain in her arm helped counterbalance that which was coursing through her entire body; it gave her something new to focus on. As the distraction carried her thoughts in a different direction, her breathing eased and she eventually regained control. When her sight cleared, she rested her sweaty forehead against the cold kitchen wall.

Misty burst into the kitchen and found Juniper on the floor, arm covered in blood.

"What happened? Are you okay?" Misty had tears in her eyes as she raced to Juniper's side.

Mortified and unable to explain her breakdown without sounding crazy, Juniper tried to brush it off as no big deal and wiped her arms against her black pants in an attempt to hide the evidence. But Misty already saw too much.

"Tell me what happened."

"I just had a panic attack. I'm fine."

"You're not fine. Your face is covered in tears and you made yourself bleed."

"It was the only way to snap myself back to reality."

"What caused this?"

Juniper's face constricted as she recalled the trigger and tried to hold back the tears from returning.

"Never mind." Misty pulled Juniper into a tight hug. "It doesn't matter. It's over now."

Juniper accepted her comfort, but only for a moment. She did not like feeling weak and did not want to be a victim anymore. She was stronger than that and letting herself break down was infuriating. Damien wasn't allowed to control her anymore— none of them were. She took a deep breath and swallowed the pain.

"Thank you. Sorry you had to see that."

"Seriously though." Misty's eyes were wide with alarm. "Are you okay?"

"Yes, absolutely." Juniper stretched her face, trying to loosen her expression and release the tension. She wiped her eyes and stood up. "I'll be fine."

"Was it a customer? Do you need me to take a section for you?"

Embarrassed, but wise enough to know to stay away from that guy, she gave another section away. "Section 300. I'll take care of section 100 and the regulars for the rest of the night."

"Deal. Take a minute before you come back out, though. Your eyes are still red."

Juniper nodded. After Misty left the kitchen, she grabbed her make-up bag from her backpack and went into the employee bathroom located at the back of the kitchen. She splashed her face with cold water, waited a few minutes for it to dry, then fixed her make-up. After fifteen minutes, she looked as close to normal as possible. The cuts on her arms were clean, but raw. There was no way to hide them without a long-sleeved shirt, which she did not have, so she hoped everyone was drunk enough at this point not to notice.

She walked out to the bar with fake confidence, as if nothing had happened, and resumed her duties. Jeb was the first to notice the wounds on her arms. He grabbed her wrist and pulled her in to get a closer look.

"What the hell happened?" he spat inquisitively. She had her lie ready.

"There are stray cats out back. One of them got into the kitchen and pounced off a shelf as I was carrying food. It scratched me up real good and knocked the plates out of my hands."

36

"Holy crap." Jeb let go of her wrist. "Frank oughta call animal control."

"He did. I'm sure it will be taken care of soon."

"Sure hope so. You ain't in the business of feeding cats."

Juniper laughed. "That one sure did get a nice, big dinner."

Jeb shook his head and Juniper hoped he never mentioned it to Frank.

The later it got, the rowdier the bar became. With Misty's help, Juniper was able to avoid the guy who reminded her of Damien. Misty didn't know which customer was the trigger, but tended to section 300 so Juniper didn't have to.

Juniper caught the guy staring at her a few times throughout the night, but ignored him the best she could. She began counting down the minutes as closing time neared.

There was only a half hour left before the bar closed when the Damien lookalike made his way over to her section. Very drunk and in good spirits, he squeezed in next to Jeb and began hitting on Juniper. She reminded herself that he was *not* her actual ex and she needed to treat him like any other customer.

"You are stunning. I had to let you know."

"Thank you."

"My name is Brendon."

"Nice to meet you," she responded to his drunken attempts at flattery.

"I kept looking at you, trying to get your attention, but you barely gave me a glance back."

"I'm working."

"Are you working tomorrow?"

"Yes." She wiped down the counter in front of Jeb without making eye contact.

"All day? I'm in town until tomorrow night when our ship leaves port. Can I take you out to lunch before your shift?"

"I work the day shift tomorrow."

"How about breakfast?"

Juniper responded with disinterest, "I appreciate the effort but I doubt you'll remember this conversation by the time you wake up."

"I'm drunk, this is true, but there is no way I'll forget. You're all I've been talking about to my buddies all night. You have to let me take you out."

"No, I don't."

"Please." He faked a sad face and his charm reeked through. He was the kind of guy she always fell for in the past and his presence was making her nauseous.

"Stop."

Brendon protested in a series of ramblings and Jeb took his cue to step in.

"Cut it out, boy. The lady ain't interested."

Brendon took a moment to reassess his approach.

"I'll be back tomorrow, sober, to prove I'm genuinely interested," he said with calm confidence. "I'll show you I'm serious."

She began to protest, but he winked and walked away before she could.

"I'm off work tomorrow," Jeb offered. "I'll hang out here in case he follows through on that promise."

"As if you wouldn't have been here anyway," she teased.

"Hey now, I actually have a few errands to run tomorrow, but I can put them off until later so I can be here for you."

"I appreciate that."

Jeb chugged the last few sips of his beer and slammed a large chunk of cash on the table.

"That should cover it. I'll see you tomorrow."

Juniper counted the money, most of which ended up being a very large tip, then began cleaning her station. Brendon and his friends were already gone and they shooed out the rest of the crowd shortly after.

Teek stayed to help clean up since he was useless the first few hours of his shift.

"What happened to your arms?" he asked, reconnecting with her for the first time since the beginning of the night.

"Minor accident, no big deal."

Misty looked over her shoulder at them, but said nothing.

"Do either of you want to head out? I can stay late since you both did me a solid earlier."

"I can stay," Misty volunteered.

"I don't mind staying too," Juniper added. "We will get it done faster if we do it together."

The cleanup took thirty minutes instead of an hour. They locked up and walked out together. Teek was parked on the opposite side of the parking lot, so he said his good-byes near the door before departing.

"You gonna be alright?" Misty asked once they were alone.

"Yeah. I'll shake it off."

"Okay. You have my number. Just call me if you need me."

"Thanks."

Misty gave her a hug, then got into her car and left. Juniper mounted her motorbike, fastened her helmet, and rode home. She readied herself for bed the moment she stepped foot in her house, hoping that sleep would erase the day's calamity.

It didn't.

Her dreams were horrifying and she woke up multiple times in tears and a cold sweat. By the time dawn arrived, she was ready to give up on sleep. She got in the shower and tried to wash the uncomfortable feelings away. She scrubbed her skin relentlessly, as if shedding a layer would somehow free her from herself. When the water began to sting she snapped out of her destructive mode and buried her face into her hands. She was slipping back into old habits.

Her anxiety shifted to anger. With her guard up in order to protect herself from her own, wild mind, she finished her shower and got ready for work.

She wore a long, black-sleeved shirt under her work t-shirt to hide her self-inflicted scratches. It was almost noon, so she raced to work without drying her hair or putting on any makeup. Brett was already there setting up for the day. Juniper tossed her hair into a wet bun and helped.

Teek was also on shift this afternoon and he arrived shortly after her. The bar wasn't crowded, and likely wouldn't be until the dinner crowd came through. Jeb arrived at 12:30 p.m., asking about her admirer.

"No, he hasn't shown up yet," Juniper said. "Hopefully he won't."

"Got half my errands done this morning, I'll do the rest after dinner."

"Admirer?" Brett asked, overhearing their conversation.

"Last night some guy was begging Juni to let him take her out," Jeb explained. "She said no and claimed he'd forget the conversation by the morning, so he swore to prove his interest by coming back today."

"Might've met your soul mate," Brett joked.

"Not funny," Juniper shot the notion down.

"Roscoe would be terribly upset to learn another man stole your heart," Teek chimed in.

"You're all a bunch of jerks." She tossed a wet rag at Teek's head and they continued laughing at her expense.

Brendon strolled in with a buddy at 1 p.m. He looked even more like Damien in daylight. He was hung over and his self-assured presence was less overwhelming sober. Juniper rolled her eyes and walked to their section.

"You came."

"I'm not one to back out of promises."

"You look like you need a water."

"That would be great, thanks."

She poured two glasses of water.

"I'm still not interested, you know."

"That's fine. Just wanted to follow through." He rubbed his temples and sipped his water through a straw.

"When does your cruise ship leave?"

"In two hours."

"Don't waste your time with me. Have you been to Olympic National Park?"

"Yeah, we drove down Hurricane Ridge yesterday afternoon. It was stunning."

"Yeah, it is," Juniper agreed with a smile.

"Now that I've thoroughly embarrassed myself, we should at least be friends."

"That's fine, except I doubt I'll ever see you again."

He pulled out his phone and handed it to her.

"Send yourself a friend request from me."

"I'm not on Facebook."

"Instagram?"

"I don't have any social media."

He furrowed his brow at her. "Okay. Can I get your cell phone number?"

"I can give you my landline."

Brendon laughed. "Are you messing with me?"

"No," Brett chimed in from the other side of the bar. "She's off the grid."

"Fair enough." He placed his phone back into his pocket. "Well, it's been a pleasure. Hope I didn't annoy you too bad."

"It's all good. Enjoy the rest of your vacation."

He nodded politely then left the bar with his friend.

"You're impossible," Teek said as he walked past. "Poor guy seemed nice."

"He did," Jeb agreed. "Way more tolerable than he was last night."

"I'm not interested. He probably lives nowhere near here."

"Who's to say? You didn't even give him a chance," Brett added.

"Seriously, guys?" she asked, flabbergasted at their sudden disapproval of her reaction to the stranger.

"You didn't have to marry the guy," Brett said. "Just saying you could've been a little more open to it. Could've asked him a few questions and engaged in a conversation at the least. He did make the effort to come back and show he wasn't an arrogant drunk."

"Enough. It's done."

Brett threw his hands up in surrender and dropped the topic. Roscoe walked in a few minutes later and took the same seat Brendon had vacated. He sensed Juniper's tense aggravation immediately.

"What's wrong?"

"Some guy came in to follow-up on his drunken advances from last night."

"He was a perfect gentleman while sober," Teek chimed in.

"He wasn't really even that bad drunk, just a little pushy," Jeb added.

Juniper buried her face into her hands.

"We just thought she could've given him a warmer, gentler rejection."

"I am allowed to be uninterested," she said through her hands.

"Of course you are," Teek agreed. "You're just slamming doors you ought to gently close."

"I really wasn't mean to him," she peered up at Roscoe, who wore a small, amused smile.

"I've felt the ice queen's wrath before," Roscoe said in jest. "I doubt you were mean, but I bet you made this entire bar feel as frigid as Antarctica till you felt comfortable again."

"That's exactly what she did," Brett exclaimed, happy someone described her behavior better than he could. "She froze that guy out so bad, he barely finished his water."

"I certainly caught the chill," Teek said in consent.

"I'm still shivering," Jeb added, aware he was fueling the joke.

"Alright, I get it. It's rag on Juniper day. I will ice this entire building over for the rest of my shift if you all don't stop."

"Take a joke," Brett laughed, rustling the top of her head as he walked behind her. "We love you, Juni."

The conversation ended and Juniper took a few deep breaths before letting it go. It went much deeper than any of them realized and she wasn't sorry for being cold. She'd never apologize for protecting herself.

"Anyway, I got my ticket," Roscoe said, changing the topic.

"Oh, that's great." Yesterday's breakdown and subsequent nightmares flashed through Juniper's mind. She examined Roscoe's warm smile. "I'm really happy you're coming with me."

"I'm excited. I've never been to New York City before."

"Well, my family lives in the Bronx, so it's probably not what you're picturing. I'll make sure to show you Manhattan, though. We should have time for a quick trip there."

"That's fine. It'll be nice to see where you come from."

Her eyes widened recalling her former life and all that Roscoe was in for. "Trust me, you'll be eager to leave after a few minutes with my family. I actually feel bad that I'm about to put you through this."

"I'm sure it's not that bad."

Juniper laughed. "By the time we leave, you'll understand why I like trees more than people."

He shrugged. "Anything that lets me peek inside that brain of yours is fine by me."

"We'll see if you still feel that way by Wednesday."

"Alright, I need to get back to the park. What time should I pick you up?"

"Our flight is at 5 p.m., so how about 3?"

"Sounds good."

He left and she got back to work. Her shift normally lasted longer, but Frank let her leave early so she could catch her flight. She raced home, parked the Jaden Jaunt, and dragged an old suitcase out of her shed. She carelessly ripped all the black clothes from her closet and tossed them into her suitcase, careful to pack enough long-sleeved shirts to cover the cuts on her forearms.

She was still running around her house, throwing things into her bag, when Roscoe knocked.

"It's open," she called out from across the house.

He entered cautiously to the sight of her racing around in a frenzy.

"You didn't pack last night?"

"No," she shouted from her bedroom. She emerged five minutes later in a New York Mets baseball cap and her suitcase in tow. "Let's go."

He checked his bag when they arrived at SeaTac, but hers was small enough to carry on.

"No liquids in there?" he asked, shocked.

"Nope, our hotel will have shampoo and whatever else I need."

"We aren't staying with your family?"

"No way," she said, walking with haste toward the security check. "I got us a room."

"How much was it? I'll pay for half."

"Nope."

Roscoe tried to protest, but she shushed him. "You're doing me a favor by coming. You already paid for your flight, you're not paying for anything else. Don't fight me, you'll lose."

They had fifteen minutes until boarding. Juniper considered filling him in on her past, but every time she tried, she found herself swallowing her words. There was too much to tell and she wasn't sure how to start. The Bronx was sure to resurrect old stories and she'd have plenty of time to explain everything tomorrow, so she relaxed and tried to enjoy the calm before the storm.

Chapter 4

It was nearly midnight by the time they got off the plane and retrieved Roscoe's suitcase. They caught a cab to their hotel in the Bronx, the nicest one she was able to find for a reasonable price, and then passed out in their separate beds as soon as the lights were turned off.

The alarm went off at 7 a.m., giving them a couple hours to shower and get ready.

"You never even told me your uncle's name," Roscoe said, digging for information she hadn't offered.

"Ozzie. His wife's name is Mallory. Their kids are Irene, Zoe, and Ethan, in that order."

"Your aunt and your cousins," Roscoe said, attempting to retain the information.

"Yeah, she is my mom's sister."

Her answer was quick and lacking detail. Roscoe wanted to know more, but was hesitant to ask; Juniper's guard was higher than ever before.

"Will your parents be here too?"

"No. They are dead."

"Oh, wow. I didn't know, I'm sorry."

"Don't be sorry—I never told you. I should have prepped you on the flight, but I was too tired to talk about all of this."

"I understand."

"I moved in with my Uncle Oz and Aunt Mallory when my parents died. I was twelve when it happened and I lived with them until I moved to Washington two years ago."

47

"Okay, got it. Did you move to Washington to get away from these relatives? Or were there other reasons?"

"Both. It was a build-up of things. They were mad that I left, felt betrayed, but I had to. It wasn't healthy for me to stay here anymore. I had to look out for myself."

"That makes sense. I'm sure enough time has passed that they've gotten over it by now."

"No, my aunt still says nasty things whenever she calls."

"Oh."

"Yeah, it's a real loving and supportive situation. I wouldn't worry about the details if I were you. It's messy and complicated and not worth the energy you'd need to expend to try and understand it all."

"I'll absorb it in small doses."

"I think that's wise." She smiled and helped him with his tie.

Juniper wore a black, long-sleeved turtleneck dress to cover the fresh scabs on her arms. Roscoe looked handsome in dress pants and a black button-down shirt. They left the hotel and headed for the funeral home where the wake was being held. Though she feared who she'd see there, she planned to stay for the entirety of both sessions. It was the right thing to do. With Roscoe by her side, she hoped she could easily ignore anyone she did not want to speak to.

They approached the funeral home and Juniper became overwhelmed with memories. She lost many friends, acquaintances, and classmates to drugs, violence, and suicide. Death plagued this town. Though she grew very familiar with the process of death, it had been a while since she needed to attend the ceremonies for one. Now, two years free of tragedy,

48

her former life plagued by death reared to the surface. Faces flashed through her mind as she recalled the many services she attended throughout her life. Her memory worked backwards, starting with her best friend who killed herself one week before Juniper left for Washington, and came to a screeching halt when she recalled her parents. She doubled over to catch her breath. Their faces stained the backs of her eyelids. This memory hurt the worst.

"Are you okay?"

She controlled her breath through pursed lips; too much would send her into a panic attack, making her choke, and not enough would cause her to faint.

"Yeah, I'm fine," she said. "I've been to a lot of wakes in my life. I thought I was a pro, but it all came flooding back at once. I just need a minute."

Roscoe kept his distance and gave her the space she needed to regain her composure. She suppressed the overwhelming urge to run and put on a brave face.

"I'm ready."

They walked into the funeral home to immediate assault.

"Look who decided to come," Mallory proclaimed sarcastically. "You could've called me back to let me know."

"I appreciate that you contacted me, but I didn't feel a return call was necessary. I made the arrangements and came."

"Yeah, well, a little warning would've been nice. Now the entire room will be buzzing about your reappearance instead of remembering Ozzie. You're about to create a damn spectacle."

"That wasn't my intention."

"Yeah, right," Mallory griped. "It always has to be about you, doesn't it? The world revolves around *you* and how *you* feel. Well today, it's about my Ozzie, and if you do anything to detract from that I'll kick you out."

"Understood."

"Who the hell is this?" Mallory asked, finally addressing Roscoe.

"My friend."

Her aunt scoffed. "Don't get too attached. She will run away from you too."

Mallory stormed back into the viewing room. Juniper stood in place with her eyes shut, hoping to maintain her composure.

"What was that?" Roscoe asked, bewildered.

"Your first glimpse of my family."

"Are they all like that?"

"No. But they are all difficult, just in their own, unique ways."

"Sounds fun," he sighed, trying to maintain a strong façade for Juniper.

"Here we go." She wrapped her arm in his and led him into the viewing room.

Just like Mallory predicted, all eyes snapped to Juniper the moment she entered. She didn't want the attention, but wasn't sure how to deflect it.

"Those are my cousins," Juniper whispered to Roscoe, pointing to the three adults standing near the casket. "Looks like Ethan is still on drugs." Ethan twitched and blinked rapidly as he spoke with various guests. "It used to just be weed and cocaine, but his addiction appears to have progressed. The scabs make me think meth or heroin. The two women next to him are his sisters. Zoe is in the black mini-skirt and Irene is wearing red."

"And your aunt thought you were the one seeking attention?"

"Exactly." Juniper was happy he now saw the irony for himself.

The line of mourners grew steadily in size. They spiraled around the room, into the lobby, and out the front door. Her anxiety heightened as she could no longer keep tabs on who was there and who she needed to avoid. Before she could dodge the oncoming attack, the Marone sisters approached.

"I can't believe you had the nerve to come back," Charline spat.

Juniper stood up, unafraid to defend herself. Roscoe stood up too, ready to help her if she needed him.

"It's *my* uncle. Why are *you* here?"

"For Zoe, of course," Tessa replied. "I hope you plan on leaving as soon as the services are over. No one wants you here."

"I can't believe you both still blame me for what happened to Krista."

"Everyone does," Charline seethed.

"She mentioned you in the letter," Tessa added.

"You were her best friend. You should've known."

"I am not a psychic! I had no idea she planned to kill herself."

"If you were a better friend, maybe she wouldn't have done it," Charline seethed.

51

"Maybe if you were better sisters she would've had more people to depend on," Juniper shot back.

"This is on you," Tessa demanded. "She said you were the last person she could stand to lose, yet you left anyway."

"I miss her greatly, but I am not to blame for her death."

"She needed you," Charline seethed.

"Maybe if you had thought about anyone other than yourself you would've noticed," Tessa remarked.

"This is outrageous—I am not responsible for her death. I was a great friend to her. And when I left, it was for *my* sanity, *my* health. I am allowed to take care of myself."

"At the cost of someone who loved you?"

"Get away from me."

Ethan glanced beyond the crowd for the first time and noticed Juniper surrounded by the Marone sisters. He broke away from the grip of those offering him their condolences and intervened.

"Juni," he bellowed, arms open like they were reuniting in the street and not at a wake. He threw his skinny arms around her and gave her a tight hug, taking note of the tension. "What is going on?"

"They are attacking me about Krista's suicide again."

"You can't blame Juni."

"But we do," Tessa replied.

"Have some goddamned respect. She is here to grieve my dad, not to be attacked by a bunch of lowlifes. Please pay your respects and leave."

"Karma will get you," Charline threatened. The sisters walked away, leaving Juniper shaking internally beneath her bravado.

"You okay?" Roscoe asked with an expression of grave concern.

"I'm so tired of this crap. Zoe gave them my number in Washington and they harassed me for an entire year after I left."

"They are sick in the head," Ethan scoffed. "It's obviously not your fault, and it's twisted that they turned it on you. Krista wouldn't have wanted that. I read the letter, she adored you. She didn't blame you, she just said she wasn't as strong as you. You escaped to the other side of the country, she escaped through death."

Juniper's eyes filled with tears knowing that she wasn't too far from having a fate similar to Krista's.

"I should've asked her to follow me to Washington—I just thought I needed to be alone. I had no idea she'd end her suffering that way."

"Don't let their nasty comments get to you."

"She was my best friend. We were a lot alike and I should've known."

"There's no way you could have," Roscoe chimed in, appalled that Juniper was taking the brunt of a burden that wasn't hers to carry.

"I'm still sad about it, and I really didn't want to come here and relive it."

"I'll keep them away from you, don't worry." Ethan kissed her cheek. "I'm glad you're back."

"Had to be here for Uncle Oz."

"I'm happy you came. None of us thought you would."

"How are you? You look too thin." She grabbed his face and examined with concern.

"I'm fine, same as always." He yanked his face from her grasp.

"Same as always?" she asked, knowing he was not into the same stuff he was into when she left.

"Yeah, quit snooping." Ethan was not okay, and they both knew it.

For the first time in a while Juniper felt a twinge of guilt for leaving him behind. They were closest in age and by default, had the closest bond. Anytime he got in trouble or took his partying too far, she was always there to take care of him and help him pick up the pieces. Seeing him deteriorate before her eyes was traumatizing and she couldn't help but feel like it was partly her fault. She loved him, he counted on her, and she abandoned him.

"I'm sorry I left you."

Ethan sighed. "You don't even pick up the damn phone when I call."

Juniper hesitated—she stopped answering Ethan's calls after the fifth time he called on the brink of an overdose. It terrified her that he might die without her, but constantly saving him from himself prevented her from saving *herself* from that life. It was too much and she could not move on if he was always pulling her back.

"I'll get better about it," she promised.

He nodded, and though he wore a tough expression, his eyes revealed his pain. They held years of sadness.

"I really miss you," he confessed.

"I miss you too. Maybe now that so much time has passed you can come visit me. I can show you how much better life is away from this place."

He shrugged. "I don't mind it here."

"This life is going to kill you."

"Leaving would kill me too." His voice became quieter.

"No, it wouldn't," she responded sternly. She was already falling back into the role she so eagerly escaped. She was being strong for him instead of being strong for herself; she needed protecting too, but the sight of his suffering made her forget how easily this place could break her into pieces again. "We will talk more and I will get you through this."

"Who is your friend?" he asked, switching topics.

"Oh, sorry. This is Roscoe," she said, pulling him up from his seat.

"I'm Ethan. Nice to meet you." The stark comparison between the two men was drastic; Roscoe was athletic, clear-eyed, and wore a healthy tan, whereas Ethan was just as tall but fifty pounds lighter, had glassy, blood-shot eyes, and was as pale as the corpse in the casket.

"I'm sorry about your father."

"Me too. He was a good man." Ethan was not interested in talking about his dead dad. "So you live near Juni out west?"

"Yeah. This is my first time to New York."

"I hope you're taking good care of her out there."

"Doing my best."

"Good. I have to get back to my station. We can catch up later. Nice meeting you, Roscoe." He walked back to where his mother and sisters stood. At his reappearance they all glanced in Juniper's direction. She gave a sheepish smile and a wave. Mallory ignored her, Zoe clicked her tongue, and Irene returned her smile with a sad one of her own.

Juniper cautiously glanced at Roscoe to see how he was holding up. His face was paler than usual and his expression blank.

"You okay?"

"Yes. Just taking it all in. I've never seen people behave like this at a wake. They are quite abrupt. If it weren't for the casket I might forget where I was."

"They are a different breed."

"I can see that."

They sat back down and watched as the crowd continued to grow. The Bronx was big, and their community was large and close knit. Everyone came to say farewell to Ozzie; he was a sturdy presence in all their daily lives. Juniper took Roscoe by the arm and snuck out during the break before the second viewing.

"I'll talk to Irene and Zoe later. I need a minute away from all of this."

"Are there any parks nearby?" Roscoe suggested.

Relieved at the wonderful idea, she directed them toward the Bronx Park. It was nothing like what he was used to in Washington, or what she'd grown accustomed to, but it would suffice.

"There's a bench near that pond over there," Roscoe suggested.

Juniper shuddered. "No, I don't go over there." She had no intention of telling him about the time she was beaten, robbed, and raped on her fifteenth birthday, then left for dead under one of the park benches. "There's a river down that path," she offered. "It's really pretty."

"Lead the way."

They found an empty bench along the river. The usual homeless contingent sat along the borders of the park, begging for money. Trucks honked as they drove by, police sirens blared in consistent intervals, and there was a steady, droning hum from the countless voices living in the city.

"This is a really loud place."

"Very."

"I guess I'd also need months of wooded silence to recover from living here."

"Glad it makes sense to you now."

He nodded and put an arm around her shoulder.

"There are a lot of good people here, though. I just got stuck in the wrong family with the wrong crowd of acquaintances. Nothing played out in my favor."

"At least you were smart enough to leave."

She agreed, but stayed quiet. She rested her head on his shoulder and shut her eyes. She focused on the subtle sound of the swaying trees, the darkness behind her closed eyes, and Roscoe's hand on her arm.

She began to drift into a nap when she felt the earth move beneath her. Its vibrations shook her heart and resonated through every nerve in her body.

<<We will keep you safe.>>

Her first instinct was to open her eyes and shake herself out of sleep, but she kept them closed and let the trees continue.

<<*You are our chosen one, our Champion, and with us you are always protected.*>>

She smiled and squeezed Roscoe's hand, which had found its way into hers.

Roscoe shook her awake.

"It's almost three. We need to head back."

They stood and began the walk back to the funeral home. They were a bit early, which gave her time to talk to her cousins. Roscoe found a seat near the back to wait and she approached Irene first.

"Thanks for making your mom call me. I would've been upset if I missed my chance to properly say good-bye to your dad."

"I figured. I know he played a big role in you leaving. He told me about your camping trip after you left."

"Did he tell the others?"

"No, just me. He didn't think they'd understand."

Juniper nodded.

Irene continued, "They were all so dependent on you to help them through their issues. It's amazing how fast most of them caved beneath their burdens without you here to lean on. It really put things into perspective for me. I never realized how much weight we made you carry."

"I should've been firmer in standing up for myself, telling you all when it got too heavy. Instead, I secretly broke apart while holding everyone else together."

"I see that now. I would've called, but it seemed pointless. You stopped picking up. My mom and brother really made it impossible for you to get away."

"They were relentless. Your mom with the guilt-ridden cries of betrayal, and your brother calling me on the brink of death every weekend. I left, but couldn't escape."

"How are you doing now?"

"Much better."

"I'm really glad you came."

"Yeah, I am too." Surprisingly, Juniper found that she meant it. Mallory was terrible, but so far two out of her three cousins weren't too awful to reconnect with. "You seem like you're doing good."

"I am. I left Hank after he sent me to the hospital with a broken jaw. Now that he's gone, I'm happier than ever. I'd really like my kids to get to know you. They need someone like you in their lives."

"I'd love that."

"They'll be at the funeral tomorrow."

"I'm excited to see them all grown up." Feeling better about her relationship with Irene, she let her guard down a little. "I need to introduce you to my friend, Roscoe," she said, shocked at the giddy feeling that accompanied this statement.

"Oh, that tall, handsome man you showed up with? Please do."

Juniper scanned the room, which was now crowded, and her heart sank—Roscoe was talking to Damien.

Chapter 5

"What the hell is Damien doing here?"

"Oh crap. He called a few days ago asking if he could come. We said yes, thinking you weren't going to show up. When I saw you this morning I sent him a text telling him *not* to come because you were here."

All the air in her lungs was stripped. Shell-shocked and numb, she watched her manipulative and vicious past spoiling her healthy and wholesome future. Seeing Roscoe and Damien together put everything into perspective: in regards to people, Roscoe was the best she'd ever known, the best she'd ever experienced, and she would not let anything contaminate what they were building.

"I'm so sorry, I'll tell him to leave," Irene offered sympathetically.

"No," Juniper objected with fierce determination. "I can handle this."

She stormed toward where the men sat. Roscoe wore an innocent and kind expression; he had no idea he was being played.

"What is wrong with you?" Juniper demanded of Damien. He ignored her unpleasant greeting.

"Juniper! You're as beautiful as ever." He stood and tried to give her a hug but she slapped his arms away. Roscoe's happy demeanor shifted to protective as he stood, ready to intervene.

"You were told not to come."

"Right, but that was *after* they already told me I could. I don't believe in uninviting people, especially to funerals. It's tacky."

"You have no right to be here."

"I beg to disagree. I've been friends with Ethan since childhood, I dated you for three years, and unlike you, I stuck around and was in Ozzie's life for the past two years. He was part of my extended family. I have every right to be here."

"Not after what you put me through. Ozzie would be sick knowing you showed up at his funeral just to torment me."

"You give yourself too much credit," he said condescendingly. "I'm here for him, his family, and my friends. Not for you."

"If that were true you would have respected Irene's text telling you not to come."

"Ozzie was like the dad I never had. He'd want me here."

"You are very mistaken," she laughed, confident but manic with rage. "He thought you were trash—a no-good do-nothing bent on taking everyone he loved down in your flames. He's the one who helped me get away from you, in case you didn't know. Helped me realize I deserved better and paid for my flight out of New York. I don't care how well he faked it with you after I left, I can promise you that you are *not* welcome here."

Damien's brown eyes narrowed and pierced through her. "I'm not sure why you hold so much hatred for me. I kept you protected during a lot of rotten ordeals."

"Which I only ever found myself in because of you."

"I never hurt you."

"Oh, really?"

"I never laid a hand on you."

"Which is shocking, considering what you're capable of."

"Watch your mouth," he hissed, looking around to make sure no one was eavesdropping. "I've still got all the pieces to that blackmail, darlin'."

Roscoe took a step closer to her and she grabbed his hand. He continued letting her take care of the situation, but was ready to jump in if needed.

"I'll out you right now, you piece of scum," Juniper threatened.

"Careful what secrets you spill. I'll ruin everything you've built."

Juniper took a breath to calm her rage; she valued her new life too much to risk jeopardizing it.

"I like not having you in my life and I want to keep it that way."

"Then keep your mouth shut."

"Deal. I think we are done here."

"Do you still love me?" Damien asked, managing to sound instigative and desperate simultaneously.

"No."

He eyed her like she was lying.

"I don't," she continued. "And if you try to bother me after I leave I'll *show* you how much I don't love you anymore."

"Is that a threat?" He grabbed her arm and pulled it toward him. She tried to yank it back but he already had her sleeve rolled up. Her scabbed arm was exposed. "You're pathetic," he spat.

"Get off me." She ripped her arm free and rolled her sleeve back down before Roscoe saw the marks.

"Looks like you haven't changed much. Still the fragile, broken girl."

"Stop."

"It's hilarious. You'd have everyone believe I was the cause of all your problems, but you were doing *that* long before you met me and it appears you're still doing it long after I'm gone."

"I never blamed you for anything except the rotten way you made me feel."

"You were damaged before I got you. I never signed up to fix you."

"I never wanted you to 'fix' me, I just expected you to love me."

"See, *I'm* the bad guy." He looked to Roscoe. "Brace yourself. She'll do this to you, too."

"You are horrible," Juniper spat.

"You're so bothered by me," Damien taunted. "It must be love."

"Seeing you here was a terrible accident."

"I think it was fate." He leaned in flirtatiously.

She pushed him away and stepped back.

"Just stay out of my life and I'll stay out of yours."

"Whatever you say, princess."

Juniper shook her head and walked away. Hand still wrapped tightly in Roscoe's, she led them to the empty, back patio.

"I had no idea he was an ex. He introduced himself as a family friend."

"He's a snake."

"I'm not a fighter, but I wanted to punch him so bad."

63

"I'm glad you didn't. That only would've made it worse. He's a psycho, it takes very little to push him over the edge."

"Well, I think you put him in his place. I always knew you were strong, but I've never seen that side of you."

"Hope my crazy side didn't scare you."

"No way, it was sexy," he smiled.

"Sexy? *You're* crazy." The tension in her body relaxed and she laughed.

"Blackmail?" Roscoe scoffed. "I can't believe he was tossing out such empty threats."

"They weren't empty."

"What do you mean?"

She looked around before speaking. No one was in earshot.

"Damien killed a man."

Roscoe's eyes grew wide. "Why?"

"Who knows, he's a lunatic. He started taking dangerous meds a year into our relationship and they sent him on psychotic benders. All his bad personality traits were suddenly amplified and I was too in love to leave, or so I thought—I was never in love, I was paralyzed. When I learned about the murder I wasn't even shocked. I knew he was capable of hurting others; I was living proof of his devious potential. I never got the details about the murder, but I'm sure it was over something stupid."

"But how is any of this your problem?"

"Rumors were flying that I was planning to leave him, which I was, and since the world revolved around him, he couldn't accept my rejection. He plotted and schemed, anticipating the break up. When I told him I was leaving, he threatened to turn me in to the cops. Long story short, he had taken me on a date to the shooting range a week after he committed the crime and had me use the murder weapon. My fingerprints were all over it."

"Wow."

"Yeah. I already wanted to leave, then after learning all of this, I was even more frantic to get away, but he had me cornered. I asked him why he framed me and he said it was because he loved me. The funny part is that I never would have known that he killed a man if he didn't orchestrate that blackmail. He would've been in the clear, with no one to tie him back to the crime."

"But you had no motive."

"I think my prints on the murder weapon would be enough to send me away."

Roscoe shook his head in amazement.

"I had to get out, but didn't know how to leave him without incriminating myself. I grew quiet and numb in our oppressive relationship. I lost all hope, I gave up on life. I was a ghost."

"How long between that and your move to Washington?"

"A year." She looked down in shame. "I still can't believe I let myself feel that way for so long. I thought I deserved it. It's warped and hard to understand if you've never been in an abusive relationship, but despite all the pain he caused me, I would've sworn I was in love. Looking back, I see that I was just too wrapped up in him, too defined by his control over me. I'd been with him so long I no longer knew who I was without him." Juniper took a deep breath, shocked at all she revealed. "That's the first time I've ever said any of that out loud."

"You are safe with me."

65

"I know," she said with a smile. Roscoe made her feel at ease. His patience was saintly and his compassion was amazing. He accepted all of her without judgment, and she found herself falling for him as she opened up.

"You may have felt hopeless and accepted way less than you deserved, but finding the courage to leave outshines all your moments of weakness."

"Thanks," she smiled, relieved that she wasn't holding it in anymore. "I know what I deserve now and I'd never tolerate less again. I'm very grateful I got out, and I have Ozzie to thank for that." Juniper paused. "Sorry this isn't coming at you in small doses."

"It's okay. Does Damien know where you live?"

"No. No one knows my address, just that I live somewhere in Washington."

The door to the patio opened.

"They are about to say some prayers," Zoe informed them, then dipped back inside.

"Better get back," Juniper said, standing and giving Roscoe a kiss on the forehead. She took his hand and led him back into the funeral home.

They sat quietly in the back row as the priest said a few nice words and read the usual prayers next to Ozzie's casket. When he finished, the crowd stood and returned to mingling. Juniper looked to the opposite side of the room and found Damien staring at her. His intent gaze caused her to shiver.

"Let's go," she said to Roscoe.

"There's still an hour left of the wake."

"We've been here long enough."

"Okay. Want to get dinner?"

"Yes, we can go into Manhattan to eat."

"Awesome."

They went back to the hotel, changed into more comfortable clothes, and caught a subway into mid-town. She was able to forget about the day and they enjoyed a fun evening together away from the Bronx. She savored every minute knowing tomorrow's funeral would be grueling. While she was bereaved by the death of her uncle, she found dealing with the living to be far more arduous.

Chapter 6

The funeral service started at 9 a.m., followed immediately by a group trip to the cemetery. Roscoe stayed by her side through it all. After Ozzie was in the ground and everyone said their final good-byes, they went back to Mallory's apartment for lunch. Damien was at the funeral and gravesite, but was not invited to the gathering afterward. Though she was able to avoid interacting with him again, it didn't stop him from staring at her through the entire ceremony. The moment he was out of her presence she was able to relax again.

Mallory ordered pizza, so Juniper and Roscoe took the walk with Ethan to pick it up.

"So, do you miss the Bronx yet?" Ethan asked her.

"Not even a little bit."

"I would've sworn coming back would have left you feeling nostalgic."

"Being here has brought back a lot of memories, but none that I want to relive. I do miss you and Irene, though. I promise to get better about staying in touch."

"That would be nice. We miss you too, my mom and Zoe included. And Damien misses you a ton. Zoe and I went out for drinks with him last night after the wake and all he talked about was you."

"Tell him to let it go."

"I told him that, but it didn't register. He just kept rambling on, no matter how many times I told him you were never coming back."

"Make sure he doesn't do anything crazy."

68

"He's harmless."

Juniper's eye widened in disbelief. "Harmless? Really?"

"That whole ordeal was an accident."

"Framing Juniper for a murder she didn't commit was an accident?" Roscoe cut in, outraged that the threat of someone so unbalanced was being casually dismissed.

"You told him?" Ethan asked Juniper. His expression was a mixture of outrage and horror.

"I had to. Damien was trying to slither his way back to me through Roscoe, so I needed to explain *why* he needed to keep his guard up around him."

Ethan didn't protest. "I just meant the murder was an accident. He never meant to kill the guy. Everything after that spiraled out of control because he was backpedaling and trying to protect himself."

Juniper huffed and rolled her eyes.

"He is rotten."

"I know. I've got your back though, always have."

"Thank you."

When they got to the pizzeria, Juniper was faced with another unwanted reunion. A different ex-boyfriend stood behind the counter, rolling dough and preparing pies. She paused in the doorway and took a deep breath before entering. With her head held high she caught Marco's attention.

"Moving up in the world, huh?" she asked.

"Whoa. Am I seeing ghosts?" he jested. "Who's the lumberjack?" he asked pointing at Roscoe.

"Roscoe. He's with me."

"Nice to meet you." He issued a curt salute from behind the counter. "I'm the guy your little lady used to date."

"Until I caught you in bed with my supposed best friend."

Marco faked a grimace, then laughed. "Awkward."

"How is Larissa?"

"Damned if I know, that ended a few months after it began. She only slept with me to hurt you. I'm just the dumbass that fell for it."

Juniper shrugged. "I needed to get out of that group of girls anyway."

"I'm glad to see you look a lot better than the last time I saw you," Marco commented. Juniper begrudgingly smiled while recalling the memory: she was fifteen pounds thinner and caught in Damien's toxic grip. "It was when we celebrated Zoe's birthday at Mazzine, right?"

"Yup. You were there with Larissa."

"You were already with Damien, what did you care?"

"I didn't," she lied.

"Larissa and I broke up the next week anyway."

"It's all good." She interlaced her arm into Roscoe's.

"I'm sorry to hear about your Uncle Oz. He was a good man."

"No worries, man," Ethan said, offering Marco a handshake.

"Are our pizzas ready?" Juniper asked, hoping to end this unwanted reunion.

"Yup, they're all boxed up," he replied, handing Ethan a tower of wobbling pizza boxes.

"Best of luck in life," Juniper offered Marco as a farewell.

"You too." He then looked to Roscoe. "Take care of her," he demanded.

Juniper reveled in amazement at how time and the arrival of good people helped soothe old wounds. She smiled at Roscoe, who happily returned the smile without knowing why.

"Another winner," Roscoe joked.

"Yeah, I had great taste."

"I like to think your taste in men has improved significantly," he teased and took her hand.

"It certainly has."

Ten pies, eight baskets of fries, and five containers of mozzarella sticks later, they were back at the repass with arms full.

"Think you ordered enough?" Ethan asked his mom sarcastically as he dropped his load on the kitchen table.

"There are a lot of people here," Mallory quipped back.

"You ain't kidding." Ethan knocked the sunglasses from his head back over his eyes and made his way toward the basement. Juniper was sure he was headed somewhere private to replenish his high.

She led Roscoe to a quiet corner in the living room where half the couch was vacant. They sat there in quiet, observing the chaos of the room. Zoe was in high-demand and being pulled in various directions by all the guests.

"She's a lot like Mallory," Juniper whispered as Zoe turned her back to the party and poured herself a vodka on the rocks. "Looks like she gravitates to the same vices as my aunt too."

Roscoe took note but said nothing. He laced his fingers into Juniper's as they sat quietly.

Ethan reemerged from the basement, sunglasses on and sleeves rolled down. His expression was blank and he walked up the stairs with slow and staggered steps. Juniper shut her eyes in disappointment and rested her head against the sofa.

"Juni," Ethan slurred. She opened her eyes and stared at the ceiling. She didn't want to see him like this.

"What?"

"I just wanted to tell you that I love you. I don't think I said that before."

She lifted her head to look at him. He was shaking. "I love you too, Ethan."

He walked away, unable to keep a straight path.

"It makes me want to cry," she confessed to Roscoe, struggling to hold back her tears.

"There's a fantastic rehab facility in Tacoma," Roscoe offered, "Pacific Horizons. He needs professional help and a reason to leave this town. Maybe you can convince him to go."

"He'll never leave."

"He respects your opinion more than you realize. Maybe he just needs to know that you want him there."

"But I *don't* want him there." She buried her face into her hands. "I know it sounds selfish, but I'm so afraid he'll ruin everything I've worked so hard to build. I have a safe place out there, with nothing dragging me down. I know it would be good for him, but it could turn out to be terrible for me."

"After seeing what you left behind, I get it. But I think enough time has passed that you should consider letting some of the people who still love you back in. You're strong enough to help them now, and I hate to break it to you, but I think they need you."

"They always need me. When I was here, after I left, now that I'm back. It's exhausting. I'm sorry if this makes me sound like a terrible person, but I've been through some awful shit too. I still don't know if I ever properly dealt with my parent's death—I never got the chance to. I was thrown into this house and was turned into the maid because Mallory was always too drunk to take care of us or the house, and Ozzie was always out working, and the kids were running rampant around town. And not long after moving here I got wrapped up in the same kind of trouble they were into. It was a mess."

"I know, I just think you'd be surprised how much good helping him would do you. You can't help him while he's living here, that's a vicious cycle no one can break. But if you got him out and away from all his triggers, you may help turn him into the best version of himself."

"Maybe."

"Sometimes I don't think you realize how strong you are."

"Thank you."

She didn't need his validation, she was confident enough to feel secure on her own, but it was nice to have another person notice and value the strength she carried. Unable to fight off his infectious feelings any longer, she let him in with a smile. He felt her open the invisible door, just for him, and he let out a deep sigh, one that sounded as if he'd been holding it in for years. He squeezed her hand lightly with affection and they were suddenly on the same page without any discussion needed.

"When is our flight again?" Juniper asked.

"Takes off in four hours."

"Then let's say our goodbyes and go."

Mallory and Zoe gave her chilly farewells, whereas the hugs from Irene and Ethan were tight and hard to escape. She told them both that they were welcome to visit her anytime and they said they'd consider it. She said goodbye to a few others at the gathering and then left for the airport.

"I can't express enough how grateful I am that you came here with me," Juniper confessed while they waited near their gate.

"It was a little overwhelming, but I'm really happy I did. I feel like I understand you so much better now."

"Sorry if it was overwhelming. I should've warned you about the Damien issue from the start. I didn't realize he'd be there."

"It's alright." He gave her a reassuring smile and finished the last bite of his sandwich.

Their flight was announced over the loud speaker for boarding. After taking their seats, they slept hand in hand the entire flight back to Washington.

Chapter 7

Life returned to normal once they settled back into their daily routines. Juniper had to work Thursday night, so she spent Wednesday beginning some of her long-overdue household projects. She lived so close to the park that Roscoe was able to stop in a few times during his breaks. His continued company was a welcome treat and she was growing more and more comfortable with the idea of him being a steady fixture in her life. It had taken a while, but she finally felt ready to let him in.

After landing in Washington and parting ways, she fretted about how Rhoco would deal with the whirlwind he just witnessed. She wouldn't have blamed him if he chose to distance himself; any logical person would get one glimpse of her baggage and flee, but he stayed. He showed up the next morning with a cream cheese bagel and sat with her for ten minutes before going to work. The trip to the Bronx had not frightened him, seeing where she came from did not alter his opinion of her, and learning about her darkest moments had not changed his feelings. Instead, it seemed to strengthen their bond and solidify his confidence in his feelings for her. As the days went on and he found every excuse to visit her, she realized the crazy trip to New York made him like her more. She was quickly falling for the kind-hearted ranger she'd been pushing away for two years.

She could breathe easier now that her guard was down. Looking back, it seemed silly that she fought his affection for so long, but she needed that time to heal, to learn who he was, inside and out. He was among the kindest people she'd ever known, which was a small, exclusive list that included her parents.

Ethan crossed her mind often. As promised, she made a greater effort to stay in touch with him and Irene. She called them both a few times over the weekend to check in and make sure they knew she was serious about rebuilding their relationships. She spent a long time ignoring them and it felt critical she put forth the initial effort. It was welcomed and audibly appreciated. The more she talked to Ethan, the more she realized Roscoe was right about getting him out of the Bronx. Though it was likely that Ethan would throw her new, peaceful life into an unbalanced whirlwind of chaos as he tackled the long road to recovery, Juniper *was* strong enough to handle it now and it was worth it if it meant saving him from himself. She mentioned the rehab center to him on the phone, but he was reluctant to oblige. He dodged the suggestion every time she brought it up and redirected the conversation with masterful skill. Twenty-nine years of avoiding the truth showed in the artful way he averted her help.

Her weekend shifts at the bar were long but tolerable. There were no more incidents, so the hours passed without alarm. Misty kept a close eye on her whenever they were scheduled on the same shift, but after a few days of seeing she was stable, her protective watch diminished. By Sunday evening, Juniper was eager to make her way back into the forest.

She woke up before dawn on Monday to watch the sun rise over Hurricane Ridge Road. The morning view was so beautiful, she had to continually remind herself to pay attention to the road.

It was mid-afternoon by the time she reached Heart Lake and decided she'd had enough riding for the day. The field around the heart-shaped lake was wide and open; tall mountains surrounded her on all sides and there weren't many people who took the time to find the trails that led to this spot.

It didn't take long to set up camp, and she went for a swim before making a campfire and cooking some soup. The sun set over the trail and Juniper had a front row seat to the majestic display across the evening sky.

Ranger Clark's voice crackled over the walkie-talkie. "Where you camping at, Miss Juniper?"

"Hey Clark. I'm at Heart Lake until Friday."

"That's a far one. The Wolfe brothers were tooling around Boulder Creek all weekend."

"Good. One less set of trails for me to tackle. I'm going to spend some time this week cleaning up the trails around here. I brought my machete and hedge clippers. I might even tackle some of the paths leading toward Hoh if I have time."

"Alright. How as your trip to New York?"

"It was surprisingly okay. Having Roscoe there helped a lot."

"That boy adores you."

"The fact that he's still willing to talk to me after meeting my lunatic relatives says a lot. They tend to scare people away."

"He told me a bit about the trip. The heavy stuff didn't faze him much. He's had plenty of his own trials in life to know better than to let someone's past dictate who they've become."

"He has?"

"Yeah, I'm sure he'll tell you when the time is right. Right now I think he's trying to keep the focus on you."

She wasn't sure how to feel about this. She opened up about her darkest secrets and he didn't share anything personal about himself. Her initial feeling was of disappointment, but then she realized it was the most selfless thing that he could do. Instead of turning her immediate dilemmas into something about him and what he'd gone through, he listened, absorbed, and acted as a solid support system for her. She always assumed he came from the perfect family and never experienced any moments of desperate survival in his life, but now she felt guilty that she never thought to dig deeper.

"I know he's been itching to get closer to you since he met you, but you always kept yourself distant," Clark continued when Juniper went silent in thought. "It's not hard to see why he returned your reservation with his own."

"Of course. I get it. I'm glad he never stopped trying. I think he's become my favorite person."

Clark laughed. "What about me?"

"Yeah, you too, of course."

"I'll be by to visit you, as I'm sure Roscoe will too."

"Sounds good. I'll be here."

The call disconnected and Juniper rested on the blanket in the open field. The sky was clear and the stars were bright. She tried to recall old lessons from her high school astronomy class to determine which constellations hung above her now. She found the North Star and worked from there. After an hour of observation, she realized she was making up her own star formations and naming them from her imagination. Upon declaring one the Fancy Hippopotamus Feast, and bursting out in laughter after doing so, she resigned from this activity and accepted the fact that she retained nothing from high school astronomy.

Finding herself at the mercy of the long week spent with family and work, she passed out beneath the open sky. She woke up covered in dew and surrounded by a family of blacktail deer. Yawning and stretching loudly, the deer took notice of her, but did not run. Unlike most humans, her presence was non-invasive and did not cause them alarm. They continued chomping the long grass, enjoying their morning meal.

Roscoe cruised toward her on his quad, startling the deer and causing them to pause in alarm. Once he parked, turned off the vehicle, and removed his helmet, the deer returned to their breakfast.

"Hey, pretty lady," he said as he made his way to where she sat. "How's it going?"

"Good. It's nice to be back in the forest."

With the bottom of his t-shirt he wiped the sweat off his forehead.

"You up for a swim?" he asked.

"Absolutely." She ripped off her tank top and ran toward the small lake in her shorts and sports bra. Roscoe followed, stripping down to his boxers. They horsed around in the water for a half hour before exiting and drying off on the grass surrounding the lake. The blades were soft under their backs and the sun warmed them with speed. Roscoe rolled over, placed his hand on her face, and kissed her. This time, she felt no desire to recoil. Everything about the kiss felt right.

After a moment it ended and they smiled at each other. He kissed the tip of her nose then pulled her in closer.

"How are you adjusting after last week's trip?" he asked.

"Surprisingly okay. I thought it would be a lot harder. It's relieving to know that I can finally manage how my past affects me. It will always be a part of me and I'm sure I'll slip here and there, but it no longer controls me."

"I'm glad to hear that. I had no doubt you'd come out of it just fine."

"The forest helped me transition back." She turned her head to look at him directly. "So did you."

"You'll always have me."

She smiled and turned her face back toward the sun. With closed eyes she digested his statement with appreciation.

"How are *you* adjusting after learning my dark and melancholy past?"

"I'm fine. I wasn't the one dealing with old troubles, you were. There's no need to worry about me."

"I really thought it would've scared you off."

"Nope. Your dark doesn't scare me."

She nodded, afraid to pry about his past, but desperately wanting to know how his story compared to hers. She wanted to understand how he could possibly accept her baggage without alarm.

He turned to stare at her. "Why did you get quiet?"

"Because Clark mentioned that you've endured a lot too. I want to ask what you've been through, but I don't want to dig at things you don't want to talk about."

"Oh, I have no problem sharing. I just didn't want to burden you with the weight of my past when you are currently managing your own."

"No, I think hearing your story might help me understand why you seem to get me so well."

"Alright then," he began. "My older brother and sister died in a car accident. I was in 8th grade, one year too young to go with them and their friends to the high school football game. Five teenagers died in the crash. My mother couldn't handle the loss. She took to hard liquor to numb the pain and died from her alcoholism two years later. It was just me and my dad from that point on, and he decided to become a recluse after I graduated high school. He moved into the mountains to hide from humanity. I can't imagine it helps him escape all the tragedy, though. I needed people around to distract me, without it I'd have gone mad. I visit him every so often, but he doesn't seem to enjoy my company. I think I remind him of all that he's lost."

Juniper was at a loss for words. "I'm so sorry."

"Yeah, it took me a long time to forgive my parents for giving up on me after my siblings died. They were so blinded by grief they seemed to forget I was still alive and needed them. I got through it though, and I forgave them."

"That's very brave."

"It was awful and tragic, but it was all accidental; a natural and unfortunate chain of events. Yours, I can't even imagine. To have the people I loved and trusted plotting against me and throwing me into dangerous situations; that's a different kind of pain. There was circumstantial betrayal in my past, but none with devious intent."

"Doesn't change the severity of what you've gone through."

"Of course not, I'm just pointing out there are different types of hardships. After going through my own and then learning about yours, it put my own suffering into perspective in the most strange and twisted way. I hope this doesn't come out wrong or make you feel bad, but I'd never trade my tragedy for yours. I'm not sure I would've made it out of yours in one piece."

Juniper laughed, unsure how it made her feel. "I guess that's a compliment?"

"I meant it as one. I've always felt it, but now I know for sure; you're the strongest person I know."

"Thanks. I don't like comparing and weighing our sadness against each other though."

"That wasn't my intention. I'm sorry if it came out that way. I'm not comparing, just like I wouldn't put down your happiness because mine was greater, or vice versa. The point was that we aren't as alone in our grief, anger, or happiness as we sometimes think we are. I was just trying to explain my inexplicable connection to you, but it seems I've done a terrible job clarifying myself."

"No, no. I understand. I'm happy you shared. It does explain our mysteriously deep bond."

"I think so too."

"And to think, there's still so much more to discover." She expressed playfully.

"I look forward to it." He rolled onto his side and pulled Juniper into a tight hug. He closed his eyes and let their lips gently touch. He lingered there for a moment before the contact transitioned into a passionate kiss.

Amazed that she was able to trust a man enough to be intimate again, Juniper embraced this long-avoided connection. Overtop soft blades of grass, their love bloomed. They remained wrapped in each others arms, exchanging body heat and the occasional small kiss. The moment was bliss.

"You are perfect," he said, then kissed her nose. He pulled a nearby blanket over them as the sun began to set. "I have never been happier."

"Neither have I." She smiled. "My heart feels so full."

His eyes glowed at the suggestion of her comment and he kissed her again.

The sound of hikers talking in the distance broke their revelry.

"Oh no," she said in shock.

"Looks like we've got some serious hikers out in the park today. Better put some clothes on," he joked. He kissed her nose then ran to retrieve their dry clothes. They returned to where her tent was set up and got dressed.

"Maybe next time, we can try that swim again without any clothes on," Roscoe said. She raised an eyebrow at him and smirked, but did not respond. He accepted her flirty silence as a positive sign. "I need to get back to my trails. I'll try to come back tomorrow." He replaced their normal friendly hug with an ardent kiss. He held her face like he never wanted to let go.

When he did, he smiled at her one last time before getting on his quad and driving away. She felt liquefied inside, a mush of organs unsure of their function. She collapsed back onto her blanket and smiled at the sky. Everything was going to be all right.

Chapter 8

The trees didn't surround her in this spot as completely as she'd like. She ate dinner, extinguished her campfire, and fell asleep inside her tent. When she woke up she moved her setup to the opposite side of Heart Lake where there was a patch of evergreens clumped together on the mountain's incline. She stayed at the base but felt better being closer to the trees.

Clark rolled up on his ranger quad after lunch to check-in.

"Juniper Tiernan: Lady of the Land, Woman of the Woods, Female of the Forest ... " he trailed off, trying to think of more. "Girl of the Grove, Maiden of the Moorland."

"You're so weird," she said with a laugh in reply.

"How's my rogue ranger doing?"

"If that's me, then I'm doing great," she replied. "I have half a grilled cheese sandwich left if you want it."

"No thanks, I just ate. Crossed paths with Roscoe a few hours ago. He seemed more chipper than usual."

Juniper shrugged, trying not to blush.

"So tell me more about your trip to New York," Clark continued. "I know it was a sad trip, but was it nice to see your family?"

"Um, I don't think I'd use the word *nice*. They are a tough crowd, but I was happy to reconnect with a couple of them. Wakes and funerals are never the ideal settings to see someone again for the first time years, but I think it worked out for the best. It was a controlled environment, not too many surprises during those kind of proceedings."

"Glad going back didn't make you decide you missed living there too much. I'd be sad to lose ya."

"Oh, no way. I'll never miss that place. You're stuck with me."

"Good." He pulled a bag of M&Ms out of his pocket and tossed a handful into his mouth.

"I thought you weren't hungry?"

"I'm not, it's just a snack. You want some?"

"No, I'm good, thanks."

The wind picked up and the trees began to rustle. Juniper became silent, hoping to hear the voices, but none came. Clark sat next to her on the ground, quiet except for the loud crunching of candy.

"I'm glad to be back," she said, honestly. "Everything felt wrong the moment I left. I felt *off*, like I wasn't where I was supposed to be. I feel settled now, at peace. When I'm here I get the sense that good things are coming."

"Well, from what I've pieced together between your tidbits and Roscoe's version of the trip, you deserve a change for the better. And if any place can provide that, it's this forest. It has saved me many times over. I don't think I'd be the man I am if I lived anywhere else."

She nodded. "I certainly wouldn't be who I am today if I hadn't found this sanctuary."

"Are you sure you don't want some M&Ms?" He shook the bag at her.

"Positive."

"Suit yourself." He poured the remainder of the candy into his mouth and stood up. "I need to get back to the lodge. I've got my walkie on. Buzz in any time."

"Will do. Thanks for stopping by."

They exchanged smiles and he got back onto his quad. He drove away just as the wind picked up. She closed her eyes and absorbed the world with all her senses.

The air smelled and tasted fresh, the wind felt brisk on her skin, and the trees were loud with movement. She rested on her blanket and watched their highest branches sway. Focused only on the sight of the trees, she found herself slipping into an entranced nap.

<<Changes are coming, Juniper Tiernan.>> A voice emerged from the swirl of her senses. <<We've chosen you to be the Champion of the Trees.>>

"What does that mean?" she asked in a terrified whisper.

<<You are our representative. You will guide the chosen humans through the fall and aftermath of our reprisal.>>

"Who am I speaking to?"

<<The trees. We carry the voice of Gaia—the Mother to all. Through us, she speaks to you.>>

"Mother Nature?" Her trance wavered at this shocking confession. It was too strange to believe. "Isn't she mythological? An entity humans created in order to put a face to the marvels of our world?"

<<No, she is the creator of all.>>

Juniper took a moment. Hearing voices was not a good sign, but now that she had them talking it was hard not to indulge. "Why do you speak on her behalf?"

<< I am one of many spirits. I am a soul from eons past. I, too, was once a human. I can relate to you, whereas She is a deity of divine light and energy. You aren't ready to be in Her presence. It would overwhelm and possibly kill you.>>

"You were human?"

<<Yes. Upon my death my spirit entered the soil and merged with the earth, letting me live on through nature. I chose the trees. Others chose the water of Earth's oceans, lakes, and rivers, the fire of Earth's core, or the oxygen flowing through Earth's atmosphere.>>

Juniper's heart quickened as her thoughts ran wild. "So my parents may still be alive in the form of nature?"

<<If they were deemed worthy.>>

"What does that mean?"

<<You're letting your human emotions take us off topic.>>

"This isn't possible." Juniper buried her face in her hands and tried to shake herself free from the voices. The trees sighed in collective unison and the main voice returned after a moment of deliberative silence.

<<A human soul is chosen to live on in the afterlife through Earth's environment if they possess a spirit bound to nature. Most people live their human lives connected to Gaia through the places they reside. Many don't realize their love for her until they are struck by dire, human-bound circumstances. You, for example, retreated to the forests after years of suffering beneath the hand of other humans. Others don't realize their love for Gaia until they are dead. Either way if that love and appreciation lives inside them, they are granted the option to continue a life through the element of their choice.>>

"Francis and Celine Tiernan. I am positive they loved nature. What element did they choose?"

<<Even if they were given the choice, it is possible they did not choose any. Some humans cannot let go of the pain from their human lives, even after death has released them from it, and so they choose the infinite dark instead.>>

"The infinite dark?"

<<Outer space—the abyss. Many spirits live there. It's the surest way to break their connection to humanity.>>

"Their death was an accident; it left me abandoned. I'm positive they'd choose Earth, if for no reason other than to watch over me." She felt like she was losing her mind, but her heart couldn't let go of the hope that she might be able to speak to her parents again.

<<It doesn't work that way. We let go of our human lives when we choose Gaia in this realm. Even if they did choose to stay and live on through nature, the bond they had with you while they were alive would be gone.>>

"They would remember me."

<<Of course they would. And it's likely they have checked in on you since their passing, but all human emotion is gone the moment a human soul shifts from body to earth. We are ruled by nature, by Gaia. We have emotions but they are rooted from Earth, not humanity.>>

She was instantly transported back to her twelve-year-old self and couldn't let go of her irrational desire to hear from her parents. Tears poured from her eyes.

"Do you know my parents? Are they with you? Can you connect me to them?"

<<We do not keep our human identities. I only know others by the way their soul feels. >>

Juniper began to sob. The voice disappeared and the trees murmured loudly, their words incoherent amidst the wind. She never expected to feel this low amongst the trees, she'd only ever known them to provide her with hope and optimism. Suddenly, being around them clouded her in despair and the confidence she once had in the forest was disintegrating. The murmuring stopped and all went silent. Just like every human she'd ever grown to trust, the trees were leaving her too.

She wiped her eyes and resigned herself to the inevitable. Her faith in the forest was short-lived, similar to the string of connections she'd formed in her life up to this point.

<<*You are very important to us.*>> The voice returned after a few long and hopeless minutes. Juniper was skeptical now. Everything felt fuzzy and confusing, and she began to consider that this was just a terrifying dream.

<<*The only person who can recall our identities before we died is Gaia. We will speak to Her on your behalf. But if we do this for you, you must promise to let the pain of your past go, no matter the outcome of this attempted reconnection, and accept your role as Champion of the Trees.*>>

"I'll accept that role right now if you tell me what it entails."

<<*You're too emotional. This meeting with your parents may actually be a good thing. It may be the last piece of your past that needs to be settled before you are ready for the greater responsibilities that lie ahead.*>>

Juniper was overwhelmed. She sat with her knees pressed to her chest.

"I am so confused."

<<*Just know that the trees are your ally.*>>

She nodded. As much as she wanted to deny this unnatural happening, her gut found the revelation soothing. There was nothing to fight.

"I trust you," she responded with sincerity. "My faith still lies in the forest."

The voices left and the expected sounds of the forest returned.

Roscoe did not show again until her last full day of camping. Thursday afternoon came and went and he arrived a little before sunset. She hadn't heard from the trees again so it was nice to have his company after a long stretch of strange silence. In the past she could spend an entire week without engaging in conversation before feeling lonesome. Now, after letting Roscoe in and learning that there was magic hidden in the trees, she found that she needed to converse more frequently. It was a sign of healing; the urge to want to speak to another instead of hiding away, locked up tight within herself.

"I see you relocated," Roscoe called out as he drove to her new location.

"I wanted to be closer to the trees."

"It also puts you farther away from the trails. Less hikers, more privacy," he said with a smirk.

"Yeah, but I can still hear them."

"Have there been many more?"

"No, just the few who came by the other day making their return trip."

Roscoe nodded. She remained on her blanket between a semi-circle of evergreens and he sat down beside her. He put his arm around her and they sat in silence for a few minutes. She tensed up, worrying that his presence may hinder the trees from talking. She desperately wanted to hear from her parents.

"Are you okay?"

"Yeah," she answered. "Just a little stressed."

"About what?"

She was afraid to tell him, she still wasn't sure if she believed it herself, but if anyone would make her feel better it was him.

"Where do you think we go when we die?"

He paused, unsure of the motivation behind her question. "Heaven or Hell would be the easy answer, but honestly, I don't know."

"What if I said that every soul had the chance to be reborn into nature? That we could live on through the trees, the ocean, the clouds?"

"I'd say that sounds like my version of Heaven."

"Well, it's the truth. Anyone with a deep rooted love for nature in their hearts gets that choice after they die."

He looked at her quizzically, afraid to ask any more questions because she was talking about speculative matters with irrational conviction. She began answering the next logical question before it was asked.

"Remember when I told you that the trees could talk?"

"Yes," he responded with caution.

"Did you think I was crazy?"

"I certainly didn't think you made that comment with any seriousness."

She sighed. "Would you think I was crazy if I *had* meant it? That I did believe they could speak?"

"Juniper, what are you getting at?"

"They talk to me."

"The trees?"

"Yes."

"I definitely think that's crazy."

"Why?" She maneuvered herself out from under his arm and stared at him with defiance. "You heard them too!"

"When?"

"In the rain. You thought I said something, but I didn't. It was the trees."

"I don't know what I heard, but it certainly wasn't the trees talking."

"Why don't you believe me?"

"Because they are plants! They don't have brains or mouths. They are living, but inanimate. Do they have energy? Yes. Do I believe they are an invaluable resource that humans ought to view with higher regard? Absolutely. But to speak? No. That is impossible."

"They don't speak through mouths, they speak through energy. I hear them in my mind."

"You realize that sounds even crazier, right?"

"They told me I could speak to my parents again," she said in a deflated mumble.

Roscoe paused, realizing where her irrational thinking stemmed from. She was still reeling from the trip home and was reliving the grief she left behind.

"I understand why you'd convince yourself to believe something like that, but it isn't possible."

"Never mind."

"I'm not trying to dismiss this conversation, but I'm not sure how I'm supposed to jump in like this topic isn't insane."

"I would've thought it was insane a few years ago too."

"I've worked in this forest for years. I lived near it my entire life. I have never heard a tree speak." He rubbed his temples in frustration. "The last thing I want to do now is push you away. Can you show me?"

Her face tightened and she wished for a way to prove her claims, but she didn't know how. She shrugged.

"I want to believe you," he offered sympathetically.

"I swear there is magic in nature."

"I don't doubt it, I've just never seen anything solid. I only know how it makes me feel, which is a powerful magic all on its own."

She nodded, understanding the sensation he spoke of. "There's more to it, though. Maybe you just needed to be told the truth so that you could be open to it when it happened. If your mind doesn't conceive an event as possible, it'll never be ready to accept it, even if it's happening all around you. Maybe your perceptions of reality are blocking you from experiencing the truth."

"Maybe."

"Do you think I'm crazy?" she asked with fear in her eyes.

"No, I think you've been through a lot and the stress you've been suppressing is coming out as wild hopes."

She nodded, afraid her weird outburst would make him withdraw. He sensed her worry.

"You can't scare me away." He smiled. "I'm here till the end."

She smiled and kissed him. She wasn't sure *why* she was hearing things, but she was driven to determine whether the voices were real or fake. She could no longer remember the day in the rain clearly; maybe it was just the whistling wind that they heard. Maybe Roscoe was right and she was projecting her grief in a manner of delusional hope. Though his logic made sense, she couldn't force herself to believe the voices weren't real. Until she had solid proof she would keep her revelations private. Jeopardizing her relationship with Roscoe after all the progress they made wasn't worth the risk. She finally found a pocket of happiness with him and she refused to lose it over something that might be a product of reliving old sorrows.

Chapter 9

Roscoe stayed with her through the night. When they woke in the morning, he seemed in good spirits and did not bring up their conversation from the previous day. Though she knew he hadn't forgotten about it, he acted as if he had. They ate breakfast and talked about safe topics: work, the weather, their summer plans.

"When are you heading back into town?" he asked.

"Within the hour."

"Alright. I'm going to head to the lodge and get ready for my day on the trails." He leaned in and gave her an affectionate kiss. She could feel his love for her radiate as their lips touched. "Have a good night at the Dipper."

"Thanks."

Once her tent was folded up and her bag was packed, she stood in the open space between the trees, hoping to hear from the trees one last time before she left. Whether it was her parents or the voice she'd heard before, it didn't matter, she just needed the reassurance that she wasn't going crazy.

She heard nothing.

Resigned to the silence, she departed.

Juniper purposefully took the trail leading toward Lake Mills, hoping to run into one of the Wolfe boys. That was their main spot and they often congregated there when they weren't riding trails. To her luck, Dedrik and Baxley were tinkering with their dirt bikes next to the lake. She rode up, parked nearby, and sat on the ground to watch them work.

"This stupid bike keeps jamming," Dedrik complained at her arrival. He and Baxley were the oldest of the Wolfe clan. "And I don't make enough at the auto body shop to buy a new one."

"Can't they help you fix it?" she asked.

"They've tried, but it's gotten to a point beyond repair. Every time we patch it up, it just falls apart again. They told me to stop bringing it in."

"I say you sell it for parts, then use that money to buy a new bike," Baxley said without looking up.

"That's not a bad idea," Juniper said in agreement.

"I'd never get enough for this piece of junk, and I don't want to be without a bike."

"Maybe your parents will give you a loan and you can pay them back over time," Juniper recommended.

Dedrik shrugged, too aggravated to continue entertaining their suggestions.

"Question for you both," Juniper said, redirecting the conversation drastically. "You spend about as much time in the woods as I do. Have you ever gotten the sense that there is more to this place than what we can see?"

"What do you mean?" Baxley asked, looking up with an eyebrow raised.

"I don't know how to explain it except to say it's some form of magic."

"This place is full of magic," Dedrik answered without pause.

"Really?"

"Of course. I don't think it's the typical kind of magic we picture in our heads, but it's just as powerful in its own way. It's nature; it's overwhelming. Every time I can see the mountains in the distance, or whenever I ride amongst the giant trees, I am reminded of how small I am. This place sets me right and puts my ego in check. I used to be real trouble in high school, and this forest reminds me that I am *not* invincible and that I ought to be grateful. Being alive is a miracle and this forest is a testament to that."

"Do you mean like gnomes and fairies?" Baxley asked, his face still scrunched with scrutiny.

"No," Juniper scoffed, "I meant something along the lines of what your brother just expressed."

"I feel connected to this place on a deep level too," he offered. "It's my second home. I'd protect this park with my life if I ever needed to."

"So would I." Juniper wasn't sure how to ask them if the trees had ever spoken to them. "Do you think this forest protects us too?"

"Sure," Dedrik answered. "We are safe from most people here—society has lost all touch with their innate survival abilities and most couldn't survive a few hours in the woods, let alone days."

"Are you in trouble or something?" Baxley asked, concerned.

"No, no. I'm fine. I just feel extra connected to the trees lately, and was wondering if either of you felt the same."

They both shrugged and Dedrik answered, "Not any more than usual."

"It's probably crazy, never mind."

"You're not crazy," Dedrik offered with a smile. "The rest of the world is. We are the lucky ones. I feel sorry for the fools out there who think their cities offer a fulfilling life. Their happiness is fake, or at the least, limited. Humans don't flourish under metal and pavement. We were designed to breath fresh air and live off the land. I don't care what anyone says; you're not fully alive living inside manmade boxes. It's just not possible."

"Agreed," Baxley seconded his older brother's opinions.

Juniper was relieved they didn't ask her to explain what she meant in any more detail.

"Can't say I disagree," she stated. "I used to live in the Bronx. City folk don't know what they are missing till it's shown to them. And while they might adopt an appreciation for nature, I don't think many would be able to adapt to a life surrounded by it after enjoying so many years of easily accessible convenience and luxury."

Baxley shrugged. "More of it for us, then."

Juniper smiled. "Okay, I'm off. Thanks for clearing the paths along Boulder Creek."

"No problem. See you soon, Juni," Dedrik said as she got on her bike and rode off.

Her conversation with the Wolfe brothers had taken longer than she thought, so when she got home, she had to get ready for work fast. When she arrived at the Dipper, Misty and Brett were antsy to leave their shifts. Carine and Teek would join her soon. There were a few customers in the bar but not many. The hour passed fast and Teek strolled in minutes after she finished wiping the counters and refilling the napkins and straws.

"Hey, Juni. How's it going?"

"Slow."

He looked around the bar as he threw his backpack under the counter.

99

"I'm kind of shocked not to see your hometown admirer here."

"Hometown?"

"Yeah. He came in the past two nights. Brett and I thought he was the same guy from a few weeks ago, that one from the cruise ship, but it was a new one. Said he was from the Bronx, tried reaching out to you first, but we all know how awful you are with technology."

Juniper tensed. "Did he say his name?"

"Damien."

Her face twisted with fear.

Teek's expression sunk; he hadn't expected such a devastated reaction from her. "He seemed real nice, he definitely adores you. Spoke of you like you ruled the freaking sun. He didn't give me any negative vibes."

"He's an ex-boyfriend. He's one of the primary reasons I *left* New York."

"Oh man, he made it seem like you were long-lost friends. That you'd be excited to see him. He was hoping to surprise you and I got the impression it would be a happy reunion."

"No. He is dangerous. He played you. What else did you tell him?"

"Just that you like the forest."

"Did you tell him where I live?"

"No, only that you were camping and that you'd be back to work this weekend."

"So he'll be showing up tonight," she said, more to herself than to Teek.

"I'm so sorry. I had no idea."

"It's not your fault." She ran her hands through her hair in panic. "Do you have Roscoe's cell phone number?"

"Yeah," he handed her his iPhone. She stared at the icons blankly. The last time she had a cellphone there were actual buttons.

"Jesus Christ." He snatched the phone and found the number for her. When he handed it back it was already dialing. She waited, hoping Roscoe would answer.

"Hello?" Roscoe sounded surprised.

"Ros, it's Juni."

"What's wrong?" His shock turned to worry.

"Damien is in town. He came into the bar last night looking for me. He made himself sound like an old friend, so Teek and Brett told him the next time I'd be here."

"He found you? How?"

"I have no idea."

"Why didn't Ethan warn you?"

"I've only talked to him four times since I've been back, and he was loaded for two of them."

"But they're best friends, wouldn't he realize that Damien was gone?"

"I don't know. Maybe, maybe not. They are grown men, I doubt they are worried about the other's constant whereabouts. If Ethan is wrapped up in his own problems, anyone or anything unrelated to gaining his next score is at the bottom of his list of priorities."

"He was supposed to keep an eye on Damien."

"He's an addict. If you don't recall, they're notoriously unreliable."

Roscoe groaned over the phone.

"It doesn't matter," Juniper continued. "I just need to handle it."

"What are you going to do?"

"Tell him to leave."

"And what if he doesn't?"

"Then I'll threaten to get a restraining order against him."

"If you want one of those you'll need proof that he has actually threatened you. Being a crazy ex doesn't warrant legal intervention."

"I'll get Ethan to testify that he joked about hiring a hit man. That should back Damien off."

"What if it doesn't scare him off and only angers him further? What if he then tries to remedy the situation on his own? He's a wildcard, he could tear your whole world apart."

"What else am I supposed to do?" Her voice shook as she tried to hold back her tears of frustration.

"I'm not sure," Roscoe offered sympathetically. "Why not talk to him and see why he came here in the first place? If he approaches you with calm, rational conversation, maybe you can get him to *leave* calmly too."

"Let's hope it's that simple."

"I am working until 8 p.m., but I'll come by as soon as I'm done. You'll be okay."

"I know I will, I'm just aggravated."

"I understand. Can I talk to Teek?"

She handed the phone back to Teek, who was wearing a look of horror.

"A hit man?" Teek said as soon as he had Roscoe's ear.

"Yeah, this guy is unhinged. You need to keep her safe."

"I will. I feel like an idiot for telling this creep anything."

"Trust me, I understand. The guy tricked me into a friendly conversation while I was in New York. I had no idea he was a threat until Juniper stormed over and cursed him out."

"The dude is a scary good actor."

"Yeah, well, now he's here and no one knows what he really wants. He might show up before I get there tonight. I'm sure she won't ask for help. The fact that she called me is a miracle, and I have no doubt she can mostly handle him on her own, but just promise me you'll step in if she needs you."

"Absolutely." They hung up, but Juniper had her hand out.

"Can I have your phone again?"

"What for?"

"I need to call my cousin."

There were only three working phone numbers she had memorized: Mallory and Ozzie's house, Irene's work line, and Ethan's cellphone.

Ethan picked up.

"Who is this?"

"Ethan, it's Juniper. I'm on my friend's phone. Damien followed me."

"What?"

"How did he know where to find me?" she asked.

Ethan groaned. "He's such an ass. I accidentally told him while I was plastered one night. I made him promise to forget the info, but he's a goddamn rat. He swore he wouldn't seek you out. I had no idea he was headed there. If I did I would've warned you."

"I should've never told you where I work."

"I'm so sorry."

"Thank God I didn't give you my home address."

"Please don't hate me," he pleaded.

"What does he want?"

"I don't know. He went M.I.A. after the night I let the info slip."

"You were supposed to be keeping an eye on him."

"I know. I'm sorry. That's my bad. I've been wrapped up with work."

"I don't know what to do."

"Just stay calm. When you came back it stirred up old feelings. He misses you."

"I told him at the wake that I was not interested in rekindling anything, ever."

"Maybe he just needs to hear it one last time before he can let it go. Maybe this is just for closure."

"He's a goddamn psycho. Do you really believe he came out here just to be told 'no'? Or that he'd simply walk away if I didn't comply? He doesn't accept rejection. He doesn't know how to live in a world that doesn't revolve around him."

"I know. Just stay with friends and see what he does. Don't let him get you alone."

"No kidding."

"Keep me in the loop. I feel awful and will do whatever I can to help."

"Thanks, Eth."

"Love you."

"Love you too."

She handed the phone back to Teek and he ended the call.

"You gonna be okay?" he asked.

"Yup. Now I'm just biding my time till the devil arrives."

"Sorry again."

She sighed. "It's fine."

She didn't want to talk about it anymore. There was nothing to be said that would make her feel better, nothing she could do to remedy the fact that her past had finally caught up with her.

Chapter 10

At 7 p.m., Damien entered. Teek noticed first and intercepted.

"You said you were a friend."

"I am," Damien replied, defiant.

"You're an ex she wants no part of."

"Let her tell me that."

Teek's chest expanded as he contained his rage. Juniper caught the exchange from the corner of her eye.

"Stop," she demanded as she stepped between them. She looked up at Damien with outrage. "Why did you follow me?"

"After seeing you again, I realized how much I miss you and how wrong I was for all that I put you through. I wanted to apologize, in person, for everything." He was sweating and breathing heavily. He could barely hold eye contact with her between his darting gaze.

Teek stayed close.

"You want to apologize?" she asked.

"Yes, I'm sorry." Damien's hands were clenched into fists.

"Fine. Apology accepted. It's ancient history. Now please leave."

"No." He stepped in closer. "I want to make things right. I want us to try again. I promise it will be better."

"Absolutely not. I'm done. I've moved on. No chance in hell I'm going backwards."

Damien's face contorted with fury but he didn't make any sudden movements.

"Let me try. I'll prove to you I'm serious."

"I'm not interested," she insisted.

"Juni—"

"She said no." Teek stepped in. Damien glared at him with glazed eyes. If Juniper hadn't been standing there he surely would have pounced and initiated a brawl. The customers sitting at the tables near them noticed the altercation and began to listen. Aware that he was causing a scene, Damien backed away toward the door.

"I'm not giving up. I'll make you love me again."

He left and the onlookers returned to their meals, forgetting the anticlimactic incident quickly. Juniper took a deep breath and exhaled slowly.

"He's lost his mind," she stated.

"What are you going to do?"

"I'm not sure."

Teek's phone rang and an unsaved number popped up on the screen.

"That's Ethan," she said, grabbing the phone. "Ethan, it's Juniper."

"I'm coming," Ethan declared.

"To Washington?"

"Yes. I'm catching a flight in the morning. I'll be there tomorrow afternoon."

"Good. He just stopped by my workplace saying he was sorry for all the pain he caused me and that he wanted to make it right. I firmly told him I wasn't interested and that I didn't want him to try, but he didn't care. He left saying he'd make me love him again. It was like he couldn't hear me at all; like he interpreted what I said completely wrong."

107

"That's because he's on all kinds of prescription medicine right now. I told Zoe about our conversation and she filled me in. He's been seeing multiple therapists and is on a lethal mixture of antidepressants and antipsychotics. I did some research on what he's taking and I'm shocked he's still alive. It's worse than any prescription cocktails he's cooked up in the past. You need to stay far away from him. He's delusional and unstable."

"Great."

"I feel so guilty. This is all my fault."

"We can't change the past."

"Don't go home. He can't know where you live."

"I won't."

Ethan sounded clearer than usual. "I won't let anything happen to you."

They exchanged good-byes, then she handed the phone back to Teek and filled him in on the update.

"I need a restraining order."

"Do you have the grounds to file?"

"I have no hard proof, but once Ethan gets here he can act as a witness and relay the whole hit man nonsense to the police. That has to be enough."

"Hopefully."

Roscoe showed up at Dipper Dive five minutes after eight. There was nothing for him to do except catch up on the day's events. He offered for her to spend the night at his place and she accepted.

Two more days until she'd be lost in the woods again—Damien would never find her there.

She and Roscoe spent Saturday afternoon together in his backyard, waiting for Ethan's arrival. Teek called Roscoe multiple times to check-in, and by noon all her co-workers were filled in and calling to see how she was coping. While she appreciated the concern, it made her grateful she didn't have a phone. Their frequent calls made it impossible for her to get a moment without worry.

When they picked up Ethan from the airport, he was still high from whatever he took before boarding. Juniper wondered how long he'd last here in Washington without his fix. Knowing him, he'd find locals who'd hook him up real fast. She tried not to worry about that and just focused on the great relief she felt to see him again. While she felt safe with Roscoe and Teek and all her co-workers, having someone from home who truly understood Damien, her past, and the world she came from helped ease her nerves. Ethan was savvy to this type of crazy and knew how to handle it.

"I am so glad to see you," she said as she gave him a huge hug.

"Same, cuz. I missed you the moment you left."

"You know how dangerous Damien is. How on Earth could you let such personal details about Juniper slip?" Roscoe asked, outraged.

"I feel horrible. I'm going to fix it though, don't worry."

"Maybe you'll like it here." She shrugged. "Maybe you'll find something worth staying for."

"I'm here to keep you safe while I collect that asshole and return him to where he belongs. I'll escort him back to the Bronx and make sure he stays out of your hair for good."

"That's fine, but if you think you could live a better, healthier life here with me, you're welcome to stay."

He eyed her with a twinge of annoyance. "We're not getting into that."

She dropped the subject; junkies never liked talking about their vices. Especially with people who wanted them to kick their habits.

They all agreed it was best to hunker down in Roscoe's Port Angeles townhouse. Ethan unpacked before accompanying Juniper to work. He hung out at the bar for her entire shift. Damien never showed.

After closing the bar with Misty and Carine, they all walked outside together.

"That's a good sign," Juniper said in reference to the no-show.

"Quite the opposite," Ethan objected. "His absence is troubling. Leads me to assume he's plotting."

"Plotting what?" Misty asked.

"Not sure. But I have no doubt he's been creeping around, watching from afar. He's probably hidden in a nearby shadow right now."

"Creepy." Carine shivered.

"Tell me about it," Juniper groaned.

Misty and Carine departed separately and Juniper and Ethan left together.

As she steered Roscoe's borrowed car out of the parking lot, the headlight of a motorcycle appeared down an alley. Ethan noticed first.

"Don't go to Roscoe's."

"Why?"

"I think Damien is following us."

"Where should I go instead?"

"A hotel."

She took them to the Port Angeles Hyatt. The motorcycle trailing them followed them into the parking lot.

"We'll go in and wait it out in the lobby. I doubt he'll follow us in."

"Will he be mad to know you're with me now?"

"Probably."

"I want to file a restraining order against him, but I need your help."

"How so?"

"I don't have any hard evidence that he has threatened me, but you could testify that he confided in you that he planned to have me killed."

Ethan rubbed his brow. "I'm not sure a piece of paper is going to do much good."

"It's better than nothing."

"Maybe, but I think doing that might make it worse. I need to get him back to the Bronx, off these meds, and back to normal. He is unhinged; taking this issue to the authorities will only fuel his deranged obsession."

"Fine, but if it escalates any further do you promise you will do that for me?"

"Yes." He grabbed her by the shoulders and kissed her forehead. "Whatever it takes."

"Thank you."

They entered the hotel and found a couch at the back of the lobby that was mostly hidden behind a pillar. Ten minutes after they entered, Damien came in through the entrance. Ethan grabbed her and they ducked behind the large pillar.

Damien went to the front desk and spoke with the concierge for a few seconds before getting angry and storming out.

"Must not have gotten the information he was hoping for." Ethan smirked.

Juniper collapsed onto the floor in relief. Another night free of crisis and one more day before she was safe in the forest. She hadn't told Ethan her plan to escape among the trees yet, but she would tomorrow. She hoped he would join her. She had a feeling the forest might heal him, might soothe his addictions and give him a reason to stay here in pursuit of a better life.

Chapter 11

Roscoe waited for them at his townhouse, angry that they were out of touch for so long after her shift. Ethan's phone was on silent and he hadn't answered any of Roscoe's concerned texts or calls.

"He followed us to the Hyatt," Juniper explained as she entered and gave him a kiss. "We hid in the back of the lobby and watched him enter and go to the front desk. We assume he asked for the room we were staying in, but the concierge wouldn't divulge the information and he stormed out."

"We need to involve the proper authorities," Roscoe said.

"No," Ethan objected. "The cops will make everything worse. I can talk sense into Damien."

"I will kill you myself if this turns out badly for Juniper," Roscoe threatened.

"I won't let him get to her," Ethan promised.

They resigned to sleep, and tackled Sunday as it arrived. Roscoe went to work and Ethan accompanied Juniper to her afternoon shift at the bar. Frank was in, training long overdue new hires.

"This is my cousin, Ethan," she introduced them. "He's visiting for a while so I hope it's okay that he hangs here while I work."

"Why would I care?" Frank retorted.

Juniper rolled her eyes and began setting up her station. Brett came in a half hour late. Frank scolded him, using him as a bad example for the new employees. Brett took the punches in stride and helped set up the bar.

The day began smoothly, not too many customers and no drama. Frank led the new employees around the establishment like little ducklings, leaving Juniper and Brett alone. Soon, the trainees were behind the bar with them, learning drinks and getting acquainted with the set up.

Ethan took a break from his iPhone games after his phone began buzzing nonstop. Juniper looked at him in question but he did not indicate that it was anything concerning her. He got up from the bar without saying anything and went outside. She could see him talking on the phone through the window. There was a brief rush of orders and when she looked back out the window for Ethan, he was gone.

She waved Brett over in panic.

"My cousin is gone. I need to go outside to check on him."

"Sure, we're slow. I've got it covered."

Juniper raced outside to find Ethan and Damien arguing at the back of the parking lot. She ran toward them, hoping to break up their altercation.

"You're supposed to be my friend," Damien shouted at Ethan.

"I am, but she's my family. She'll always come first."

"She's left you to rot time and time again. You think she'd do the same for you?"

"I know she would. You're medicated and unstable right now. You are a danger to her. I will not let you hurt her."

"Stop!" Juniper yelled, inserting herself between the two large men. "That's enough."

"Get out of the way." Damien shoved her, knocking her to the ground. Ethan lunged, grabbing his old friend by the neck.

Damien threw a hard punch that connected with Ethan's nose. Blood poured down his chin.

"If you think I'll let you snitch on me you're sorely mistaken. You should've held those cards a little tighter to your chest." He struck him again.

"You're a coward," Ethan panted as they brawled. The words came out slurred and his eyes darted around in confusion. The blows were taking their toll and the world now spun in circles around him.

Juniper began shoving Damien, trying to break his grip of Ethan.

"Let him go!"

"A restraining order? Really?" He walked backward, towing Ethan in a chokehold.

"Only if you didn't leave. I won't do it, just let him go."

"This jerk is supposed to be my best friend. How'd you convince him to act as your witness? To provide the cops with outside proof?"

"I didn't have to. Your crazy behavior was enough motivation."

"It's your fault this escalated. Just like last time. You act so innocent but you're the real pot stirrer. Causing drama then dipping from the scene to keep your hands clean."

"What are you talking about?"

"Everything! Our whole relationship. You ruined me. Made me look like the bad guy who pushed you away. Turned me into a monster that everyone hates. I came here to make things right and look what you've done. Made me out to be the villain again."

"You've done that all on your own."

"No, this is your fault." His grip tightened around Ethan's neck and her cousin's face turned purple.

"Let him go now and this won't get any worse."

Damien's rage caused his entire body to tremble. The chemical mixture coursing through his body distorted everything: her voice was lined with static, his vision was double, and he couldn't keep up with the speed at which his mind was processing the situation. His senses were heightened. Each second felt like a slow step through quicksand, their every move was magnified as if it were being viewed through binoculars. She took another step closer to him but he saw it as an attack. He swung around, dragging Ethan with him by the neck.

Now she pounced.

Once attached securely to his back she began pounding the side of his head. After a few slams he finally released Ethan to deal with her. Before he could, Ethan caught his breath and rammed his shoulder into Damien's sternum. Juniper jumped off Damien's back and let the men catapult past her.

They fought relentlessly. The motivation for their fight quickly escalated from being about her to being about everything they'd ever fought over through their decades of friendship. Damien fought Ethan into submission, then stood over him and pummeled his face with aggression. Juniper sobbed and launched herself back onto Damien in an attempt to make him stop, but he was doped up with medication and barely felt her blows or kicks.

Damien was so lost in his fury it took a few minutes for him to gather his wits and realize what he was doing. Ethan was curled in a bloody heap beneath him and Juniper was on her knees sobbing next to his body.

Damien became rigid.

"What is wrong with you?" she exclaimed.

"This is your fault."

"You killed him!" she sobbed.

He shook his head. "He's just knocked out. He'll come around."

"He was knocked out two minutes ago, but you kept going." She collapsed onto her cousin's chest, hugging and crying onto his beaten body. Ethan's eyes shot open and he inhaled as much air as he could swallow. Shocked and confused, his body went into a fit of sobs as he gasped for every ounce of oxygen he could get. No matter how hard he tried he couldn't catch his breath.

She stood and ran toward the bar to call 9-1-1 but Damien chased her down before she reached the door.

"No way you're turning me in for this."

"What is wrong with you? He needs medical help!"

"Not at my expense."

"Let go of me," she screamed. After a moment of struggle, she broke free of his grasp and ran toward the bar. Brett was now at the door, assessing the scene in horror and stepping out to take action.

"Call an ambulance," she hollered. She pointed to Ethan. "My cousin needs help."

Brett ran back into the bar to call the police as Juniper pulled out of the lot on her motorbike. Though Damien gave chase, she had a small lead.

It wasn't enough. The Triumph Roadster he rented was too fast. He was on her tail within minutes and she wasn't able to shake him.

She wasn't sure where to go or what he expected to achieve by following her. Did he plan to take her out too, just like he had done to Ethan? Or was he just on a psychotic warpath with no clear purpose or end goal? When he began ramming into the back of her bike she realized that he wanted her dead.

Instinct led her to the forest. His bike would not ride well there and maybe she could lose him on the trails.

When she reached Hurricane Ridge it turned from gravel to dirt and she began putting distance between them. The dust kicked into his eyes and his wheels held less traction. After almost skidding out and launching himself over the edge of the mountain, he slowed and followed her at a safer distance. It was a single road with no turn offs, so it didn't matter how far she sped ahead of him; she couldn't lose him until she reached the forest.

The wind picked up as she reached the end of the road. Her frantic and scared energy radiated into the sky and swooped down over the trees as a distress signal. They swayed in ominous defense. Though the sky now looked as though it might rip apart and destroy everything beneath it, seeing the weather behave in congruence to her current emotional state calmed her nerves. Deep down, she knew nature was on her side.

She hit the first trail with speed, aware that Damien's roadster would struggle on this terrain. The moment he entered the woods her suspicion was proven correct. He decelerated immediately and almost fell at the first turn. When it began to pour his chase slowed even more. Juniper was a skilled rider and the rain was not a problem. She did her best to keep her wet hair out of her eyes as she sped forward. Damien was losing her and his distant howl of frustration was followed by a blast of thunder. The clouds covering the trees made the forest darker than night; only their headlights and taillights were visible. Damien tracked her red taillight with miserable accuracy. Though he could no longer ride his bike with ease, he was still managing to keep up.

Juniper drove faster. The slick mud and her dim headlight turned her progression into a reckless and dangerous slide down the hill. She hit a rut that turned her front wheel unexpectedly and caused her to fly over the handlebars. Ignoring the new pain, she stood up and ran. Deeper into the forest and away from the approaching headlight.

Everything was dark but her feet seemed to know where to step. She didn't question her body and let it lead based on instinct. The forest guided her now, still, it was hard to determine the source of her newfound direction. It wasn't coming from her—she couldn't see anything through the pitch-black shadows of the trees—but she carried onward with inexplicable confidence.

Her bike blocked the trail and forced Damien to pause in his pursuit. Part of her believed for a moment that she was free of him, that the chase was over, but her momentary relief was promptly squashed the moment she heard an engine rev. A small light returned to the trail and grew in brightness as it got closer. She never imagined she'd feel safer cloaked in darkness, but the luminous return arrived with alarm. She ran faster, but the bike was on her in seconds. It blasted her with harsh light and defeat—she was caught.

"You're done," Damien shouted over the engine and the roar of the wind.

She ignored him and kept running. He let her expend her energy, following her at slow speeds. The chase turned pathetic and he openly mocked her by letting it continue. Watching her futile attempt to escape fed his ego. Seeing her struggle beneath his newfound control of the situation was intoxicating. She was powerless, just like she used to be, just how he liked her.

She fell to her knees, completely out of breath. He stopped the bike a few feet away and left her in the spotlight of his bike's headlamp.

He was a shadow as he approached; she couldn't see anything past the light.

"What do you want with me?" Her mind circled around Roscoe, willing him to come, praying he'd sense her distress. She cried out to him in her thoughts.

Damien remained silhouetted, knowing that her inability to see him would heighten her fear.

"Obviously, you are incapable of reason," he shouted over the pouring rain. "I came here in peace. I came here with good intentions, but you turned my amicable visit into a freak show. You've turned my honest attempt to reconnect into something poisonous. You are the root of my woes, and I don't want to suffer anymore."

She heard the threat. Soaking wet and covered in mud, she tried to catch her breath so she could run now that he was on foot, but she was spent. Kneeling with hands buried in the sludge of the trail she surrendered.

She kept her head down, not wanting to see the blow before it came, hoping it might hurt less if it arrived without warning, but when the crack of the strike echoed through the sky, she felt nothing. She turned to squint through the glow of the headlight toward the sound that came from the treetops. It was a screech, one of true horror, and it came from Damien.

Another snap of the whipping wind and his howl abruptly travelled in the opposite direction. She stepped out of the light and looked up toward the noise, hoping to determine what was happening. It was still too dark to see much, but what she *could* see was otherworldly.

Damien was being tossed among the trees like a ragdoll, branch to branch, seemingly at the trees' discretion.

She pinched her arm twice to make sure she was not dreaming, but the scene continued. As sinister as it was, and as unnatural as she should have found it, she felt relieved.

Numb to the vision of Damien's slow and gruesome murder, she stood like a statue, watching the brutal scene without emotion. Rain fell with relentless momentum, cleansing her as it cascaded down. The cool water acted as an agent of serenity as she felt her greatest demon expel from her body and dart toward the murder in the sky. Its shadow wrapped around Damien as he flew between boughs. His screams accompanied the thunder and lightning like a ghostly melody. The rain acted as steady percussion. She found herself swaying, dancing with dead eyes beneath it all. He was stripped from her, taken up and away, leaving her lighter than she'd felt in years. Stunned at her new buoyancy, she smiled amidst the terror.

The rain softened to a drizzle and the clouds parted. It was early afternoon and the sun was finally allowed to reemerge. Hazy light shone on the forest, warming her saturated body with fresh spring heat. She looked for Damien.

It took a few minutes but she eventually found him speared to a tree limb that was sixty feet high. Blood showered the ground as his body drained. She ignored the twisted guilt she felt at his bizarre demise and walked up the trail toward her bike.

She examined the forest around her. In the light of day, the trees moved as she always knew them to, but there was no mistaking they were capable of much more than a simple sway. They *were* animated; they were more alive than she ever dreamed.

"Thank you for saving me," she announced into the sky.

She waited a moment hoping to receive a response, but there was none.

Everything went blurry as the reality of what she just endured caught up. Her energy was depleted and her body was breaking down. As her vision began to fade, a cool breeze crossed her path, causing her to halt.

<<*Your survival is ours to protect, dear Champion.*>>

She nodded in gratitude before blacking out. The horrific aftermath still hung above her, dead by the hand of nature.

Chapter 12

When she came to, she was in Roscoe's arms. He was carrying her into the hospital—she recognized the emergency room.

"Where's Ethan?" Juniper asked with a pant as she forced herself awake. She tried to wiggle her way out of Roscoe's arms but his embrace was firm.

"Juni, calm down. You'll hurt yourself further."

"I'm fine, put me down."

"No, you're not. I found you unconscious in the forest."

She looked around in confusion. Teek, Misty, and Carine were sitting in the waiting room.

"Put me down!" Her outburst worked and Roscoe obliged.

"What are you guys doing here?" Juniper asked her friends.

"Brett filled us in, he's still at the bar," Misty explained.

"I need to see Ethan," Juniper repeated.

"Where's Damien?" Roscoe asked.

"Didn't you see him when you found me?"

"No."

"He's dead."

"Dead? How?"

"You wouldn't believe me. Where's Ethan? Is he okay?"

Roscoe shook his head and there was a long pause. Tears filled Juniper's eyes before he answered.

"He didn't make it."

Juniper stared back at him. The emotion she didn't feel for Damien's death came pouring out with doubled intensity for Ethan.

"He has to be okay," she objected. Frantic tears fell.

"The head trauma was too significant. He died in the ambulance," Carine explained. "We waited here, hoping this would be your first stop."

"Where is he? I need to see him."

"It's been a few hours. They had to bring him to the morgue."

"This isn't possible." She wiped the tears from her face with angry force. "He was going to get better. I had him thinking of a better future. It can't end like this. He never got a second chance."

Her friends watched with sympathy as she struggled to accept this reality, but had no words of comfort to offer.

"He wasn't supposed to die. Not for me," Juniper sobbed as she fell into Roscoe's arms. "I ruin everyone I love."

"You do not. Stop it," Roscoe demanded. "It was unfortunate circumstances and timing. If he were still here I bet he'd tell you he'd do it again if it meant your survival."

"I'm not that important that anyone should die on my behalf."

"It's not your fault."

"It's Damien's," Misty chimed in. "This lands on him."

"You're grieving," Carine added. "You'll see the situation clearly in a few days."

Her friends huddled around them and turned their embrace into a group hug. Amazed that their affection made her feel better, she let herself drown in the warmth of their compassion.

She wasn't sure how long they stood there, or when the hospital transitioned into Roscoe's townhouse, but when she reassessed her surroundings, she was on his couch wrapped in a blanket.

She sat up, thoughts clouded and memory faded. The smell of marinara simmering caused her stomach to grumble. She looked over her shoulder to find Roscoe in his kitchen cooking.

He caught her bewildered stare, finished stirring the sauce, then made his way to sit next to her.

"How are you doing?"

"I am so confused."

"You've been asleep for a few hours. I think the shock of it all knocked you out."

"Remind me of everything," she requested with tears in her eyes.

"Ethan passed away this afternoon."

She nodded and the tears fell.

"You told us Damien is dead too, but never said how."

These words came as a punch to the chest. She recalled the chase through the forest, she remembered how the trees saved her from Damien's wrath.

"Can you tell me now?" he coaxed.

She shook her head.

"Why not?"

"Because you won't believe me."

"I promise that I will."

Juniper shook her head. "I have to show you."

"Where?"

"In the woods."

He glanced out the window at the setting sun, then back at Juniper.

"In the morning. We can sort it out then."

She nodded, still exhausted from the trauma.

"How did you find me?" she asked.

Roscoe hesitated. "Your voice came to me in a thought. It's weird, I know, but I heard how scared you were, and somehow I sensed your location. I didn't try to make sense of it, I just had to find you. I'm not sure how to explain it now. I'm just grateful it happened."

Juniper did not respond. She remembered calling out to him in her thoughts, but never imagined they'd actually reach him. She suspected it had something to do with the trees.

"I'm grateful too," she said with a smile. They relocated to his bedroom and Juniper fell asleep in his arms.

When morning came, they got dressed and headed toward Olympic National Park. At the end of Hurricane Ridge Road, Roscoe followed Juniper down her man-made trails. They weaved along the dirt paths, over exposed roots and through dense sets of trees. When the path opened wider they rode faster and memories from the previous night assaulted her senses. Juniper tried to keep them contained, tried not to be overwhelmed, but it wasn't easy. She replayed the supernatural events that took Damien's life in her head, appalled by her callous acceptance of the brutality. It was gruesome, unnatural, and disturbing. Then she remembered the trees had done it to protect her from certain death. A wave of familiar security washed over her and it overpowered the shame. She was connected to them, they were loyal to her; she wasn't sure why or how, but she cherished the bond. Recalling this made the rest of the ride to the murder scene less daunting. The trees were on her side.

When they arrived, Juniper parked Jaden Jaunt and circled the area with eyes glued to the higher branches. Roscoe followed suit, hesitant and troubled; he couldn't wrap his mind around the direction in which she searched.

A few minutes in, Juniper's breathing became panicked and her pace quickened. She couldn't locate the body.

"He was here, I swear."

"Up in the trees?" Roscoe asked.

She didn't answer. Instead, she walked closer to the tree she was certain Damien had been speared to. There was blood on the branch, blood on the trunk. Her eyes followed its trail down the side of the tree. She circled the tree and before her eyes hit the ground, she tripped over a soft lump and landed on the other side.

It was Damien; cold, lifeless, and covered in moss. Small vines and roots stemmed from the earth and tangled over his body. Juniper looked toward the branch he hung from last night, which still pointed toward the sky. She looked back at his body, which had a clean hole through his stomach. There was no indication that his weight tore through the wound and caused him to fall. It didn't make sense.

She looked at Roscoe perplexed. He returned her stare with horror. Refusing to step any closer, he talked to her from a safe distance.

"You need to explain what happened here."

"When Ethan started breathing again after the knockout, I tried to run into the bar to call for medical help, but Damien stopped me. I relayed the message to Brett and ran for my bike. Damien followed me on his. I couldn't lose him on the roads because his bike was faster, so I headed here thinking I'd dodge him through the trails. It started pouring and I got too confident and crashed. I tried to run but he caught up. I was out of breath and couldn't run anymore. He said I was the cause of all his troubles, all his suffering, and that he didn't want to suffer anymore. I couldn't see anything. The storm made the forest pitch black and he had the headlight on me like a spotlight. I was blinded, but I knew he came toward me for the kill." She paused. "Then it got strange."

Juniper broke eye contact with Roscoe and stared at the ground as she verbalized the rest of the story.

"The sound of a whip cracked through the sky, so loud it rivaled the thunder. Damien's screams followed. I stepped out of the light, and once my eyes adjusted to the dark, I saw Damien being tossed through the air, tree to tree. Each toss was accompanied by an earsplitting snap of the branches batting his body. When he finally went silent the rain stopped and the clouds separated, letting the sun cast light on what occurred. That's when I saw Damien's body impaled on that branch." She pointed at the bloody branch sixty feet above them.

Roscoe shook his head in disbelief. "One, he'd still be up there if any of that were true. Two, you're asking me to believe that trees are responsible for this ruthless carnage. Look at his body!"

"Yes, look at it. It's covered in earth after one night. How it is already being taken over by roots and vines and moss?"

It was a freakish sight and Roscoe had no words to justify the way the earth claimed the body. It appeared as if the trees were trying to hide the evidence.

"I don't know. If he was spiked to that branch, how did he end up down here? There are no tears in his wound."

"I'm not sure. That part confuses me too. Maybe the branch bent and dropped him."

"Juniper, this is insane."

"That's why I brought you to the scene instead of trying to explain it at your place."

"It still doesn't make sense. It doesn't add up. I'm a ranger here, I'm responsible for reporting this, but I can't repeat these claims to any authorities—it sounds like delusional gibberish. I need the truth."

"That is the truth!"

"No, it's not! Trees don't kill people. If you did this, just fess up. I have no doubt it was in self-defense."

"I didn't kill him," she sobbed. "I was prepared to die last night when all of this happened. It's crazy, I know, but it's the truth."

"They are going to arrest you for manslaughter," he shouted in frustration. A brief moment of agitation passed between them before he accepted that she had no alterations to her version of the truth. "I'll come up with a believable story for you. Help me rip him from the ground."

They stripped the vines off his body, wiped the moss off his skin, and pried his limbs out from under the strong hold of the newly formed roots. He propped Damien's body up against a tree and planned to come back for it with a larger vehicle.

"Let's go," he said curtly.

"I need a minute. I'll be close behind."

"I'm not leaving you here alone, not after discovering all of this. I have no idea what the truth is and I'm not leaving you alone to warp it anymore. It's for your own good. If you stay with me, at least I'll know it wasn't you if this situation manages to get any weirder."

She didn't appreciate his lack of trust or demeaning tone, but she kept her frustration to herself. Despite being flustered, rattled, and asked to believe in the impossible, Roscoe was still trying to protect her.

They rode the trails back to Hurricane Ridge Road and toward the office where Ranger Clark spent most of his time. All threats gone, Roscoe let her depart on her own.

She needed to grieve Ethan's death, needed to figure out what the trees wanted from her. The only way to achieve either was by spending some quality time alone in the woods.

She called Irene before leaving. It was the first time she repeated Ethan's fate out loud. She began to weep the moment the words left her lips.

"What do you mean he's dead?"

"Damien killed him."

"How? Why? They were best friends, I don't understand."

"Damien followed me here. I told Ethan and he came out to help me deal with the situation. It escalated and Damien beat him senseless," she explained through her sniffles. "The head trauma killed him."

"This can't be true."

"I'm so sorry. I feel responsible. I should've dealt with it on my own."

"Stop it. Then you'd likely be dead instead. Neither one of you should have suffered. Where is that scumbag? Locked up, I hope?"

She paused before answering. "He's dead too."

"From the same fight?"

"No, from a death-race on motorcycles through the forest. I crashed and blacked out, and when I came to, I was already recovered by a park ranger and told the news about Ethan and Damien."

"Well, I'm glad Damien's dead. He brought nothing but heartache and pain to everyone who had the misfortune of meeting him."

"It's all so confusing. I just miss Ethan. It shouldn't have happened like this. He liked it out here. He might've had a chance to try again in a new city."

"Don't let those thoughts tear you apart. I'm coming out to see you and accompany Ethan's remains back to New York. I can't make it out until Thursday, but I'll tell the rest of the family."

"Thank you. I don't think they'd receive the news well from me."

"They wouldn't. They'd blame you."

"I'll mourn him here with you, if that's okay. I can't go back to the Bronx again."

"Absolutely."

"I'm sorry."

"So am I. Love you, take care. I'll see you early Thursday morning."

"Okay, love you too."

They hung up and Juniper tried to force the tears to stop. The harder she tried, the faster her sorrow fell. Caught in a full-fledged panic attack, she succumbed. She was curled on the floor in a matter of minutes, unable to catch her breath and choking on her tears. There was no longer a single source for her pain, just an overwhelming loss of control. Everything hurt and she was submerged beneath the weight of life's collective grief. Despite the heaviness, she got to her knees and tried to see through blurry eyes.

She had to get to the forest.

Chapter 13

Bags packed, house locked, she departed. The wind dried her tears as she drove toward the woods. She avoided the trail where Damien's body waited to be retrieved and headed south instead. The trail leading to Moose Lake was long and unpaved, but easy to follow.

She took her time getting there, letting the cruise soothe her. There were people hiking along the way, not many, but enough to cause her pause. It wasn't customary to see motorbikes on the trails; they were allowed in certain spots, but not all. Due to her friendship with the rangers they granted her full access to the park, as long as she kept them informed of her whereabouts via radio and respected the hikers on foot. She slowed down whenever she needed to pass hikers—to minimize the trail of dust her bike kicked up—and waved. Most people didn't mind. Still, she always steered her bike off-trail whenever possible to avoid their path completely.

She veered off the main trail and headed down the steep switchbacks that led to Moose Lake. When she reached her destination it was vacant of tourists. People still walked along the trails encircling it, but they were far away and none strayed toward the water. Once it got darker all hikers and distant voices would be gone and she'd truly be alone.

She assembled her pop-up tent in the lush meadow and readied herself for sunset. It was a beautiful sight from the valley where the lake sat, one of her favorites. Subalpine trees sheltered her in all directions and the colors of the sky were visible above their highest branches. This was the perfect place to heal.

The sun began to dip toward the western horizon and the sky swirled with orange and pink light as it sank behind the mountain. The moon illuminated the night and Juniper observed the countless stars in wonder. Thousands were visible without the competition of manmade light.

Her eyes darted back and forth between the stars, drawing pictures, counting futilely, trying to locate the North Star. Though she was still, the consistent eye-motion left her hypnotized. It sent her into a peaceful trance and she imagined Ethan greeting her parents among the stars. The thought stirred her memory and she recalled the possibility that their spirits might live on among the trees. She sat up, wondering if that notion had been a dream or reality.

The trees surrounding her were silhouettes in the moonlight, noiseless shadows of the night. Besides grieving the loss of Ethan and coming to terms with Damien's death, she wanted an explanation. She needed to know the full extent of nature's magic and what it intended for her.

She rested her head back on her blanket and hoped for a tree spirit to speak to her again. It felt crazy to her logical inclinations, but her wild imagination craved for these moments of fleeting whimsy. It was hard to decipher if they were real— they always occurred in moments of half-slumber or during states of high-emotion, both of which were known to cause hallucinations.

She let the overwhelming sight of the stars lull her to sleep. When she awoke, there was no memory of voices or conversations with the trees, just a deep slumber that was sorely needed. Perhaps it was for the best, and maybe the trees knew it, too.

It was Wednesday and she'd need to leave before nightfall for Irene's arrival Thursday morning.

Most of her mourning would be done with Irene at the morgue, but coming to terms with it beforehand was helpful. She did not want to have another meltdown, especially not in public. She still did not trust that others could love her through the tough times, so she did her best to keep her moments of weakness hidden.

The day was brisk but bright. She wore a sweatshirt while she soaked in the silent sun.

Halfway into a nap, the quiet was broken.

<<*Do you believe in us now?*>> the trees inquired.

"I always believed in you," she answered, surprisingly unafraid that she spoke aloud to the trees without trepidation. "I just don't understand what you want from me."

<<*We want you as our willing Champion.*>>

"What does that mean?"

<<*The end is coming, but Gaia is not ready to give up on her favorite creation. Humans have potential; there is good buried beneath the war, hate, and destruction; beneath the callous disregard for the world that provides them shelter. She wants to give mankind a second chance.*>>

"The end?"

<<*Earth must start afresh. You've been chosen to represent the forests: the trees and the flora. All foliage and vegetation.*>>

"What would I need to do?"

135

<<You must listen. As chosen Champion, we will speak to you only. We will guide you through the ruin and lead you on to better days. You, in turn, must lead those who have chosen to follow you into their renewed existence on Earth. This new life will be one of appreciation, respect, and loyalty, and where the inhabitants of Earth show genuine care for nature. You will be the leader of the new land.>>

"Leader? Have you been observing me at all? I am a recluse; I don't do well with other people."

<<You will excel. We have no doubt. You and six others have been chosen as Champions. You will work closely with them, when the time comes, as your territories are heavily overlapped.>>

"There are others?"

<<Yes, they are in charge of different regions and functions. Right now, they aren't your concern. You must focus on finding your Second. A mate to guarantee the continuation of the population.>>

"Excuse me?"

<<We believe you've already found him, though he needs convincing.>>

"Roscoe?"

<<Wouldn't he be your choice?>>

"Of course," she responded with confidence, "but I don't think I'll ever convince him."

<<You must find a way. Each Champion must have a Second. We chose the Second for all the others, but time is short and you must choose and convince your own.>>

"You picked who they would spend the rest of their lives with?"

<<It's a meeting of worlds. We chose a Champion for each element, then a Second in a different region of the globe.>>

"Why so far apart?"

<<To keep small pieces of each unique culture crafted by mankind alive. Despite what it will feel like when the end arrives, nature does value the heart of humanity. Some Champions are tasked to unite with their Seconds now, others are waiting until after the cleanse. In the end, love is not the goal. Though we suspect these unifications will result in deep affection, it is not necessary. They are simply tasked to combine followings and govern their elements as a solitary unit.>>

"Does my situation screw things up for the trees?"

<<Not at all. In fact, we are excited to see how your element evolves due to the fact it will be rooted in love.>>

"Love," she repeated in a whisper. She *did* love Roscoe. "I'm about to become the local loon."

<<Do whatever it takes, time is running out. The process began years ago as we searched for our chosen few. Surely you've noticed the influx of tsunamis, large-scale hurricanes, teams of tornados, and earthquakes of large magnitude. These events shook the human population, but did not completely devastate. You were the last missing piece and now that we have you, we can truly begin.>>

"What does that mean?"

<<Our attacks will be greater and carry with them finality. The Champions and their followers will be the only survivors once our task is complete.>>

"Whoa, hold on. What?" The purpose of her role as Champion was finally sinking in.

<<It will begin with floods, hurricanes, and tsunamis tearing through the South Pacific in volumes uncharted by mankind. Our Ocean Champion is prepared.>>

"Something like that will happen here?"

<<We will warn you when the time comes. In the meantime, you must convince your Second to join you and gather a following of humans you trust; humans who will obey you as you abide our lead.>>

"Good luck to me," she responded sarcastically.

<<Whenever you feel small or fear you might fail, remember that the earth is on your side. Out of millions, Gaia chose you. Never forget that.>>

She supposed that was meant to make her feel better, but it only added pressure to the high-demands she couldn't fathom achieving.

<<We're watching over you, Little Blossom.>>

Her heart seized as she felt the spirits depart. Her father was the only person who ever called her that. Her parents were with her and all doubt she had vanished.

Renewed faith in the trees and determination to make them proud threatened to burst from her seams. She had to focus and mentally restrain her thoughts so she didn't combust beneath the wide array of emotions she suddenly felt.

She wasn't sure how she'd manage to lead a group of modern day humans into the end and convince them to trust her as she navigated them through a new world, but her parents had faith in her and their confidence was all she needed.

Chapter 14

Juniper packed her belongings as the sun started to set and made it back to Lake Dawn Road before nightfall. A message from Irene let her know she booked a red eye and that her ferry from Victoria, BC would dock in Port Angeles on Thursday morning. Juniper tidied her home for her cousin's arrival then fell asleep.

Morning arrived and she finally got up after hitting snooze on her alarm four times. She brushed her teeth, combed her knotted curls, and raced to the MV Coho terminal. The Black Ball Ferry had already docked and Irene stood at the bottom of the platform with her suitcase and a smile. Juniper parked her bike illegally and jogged toward her cousin. Irene buried her in a loving hug.

"It's so good to see you," Juniper said.

"You too. I apologize if I'm a little out of it for a few hours. I'm still coming down from my pain meds."

"Why are you on pain meds?"

Irene examined Juniper as if the reason was obvious.

"Ethan. I couldn't be alone with my thoughts that entire trip. I had to numb them or I would have lost my mind mid-flight."

Juniper's eyes filled with scared tears. Irene had issues with pain pills in the past; they warped her into a thief and a liar. She hurt a lot of people during her dependency on the meds and hearing that she'd reverted back to an old vice to handle her brother's death was terrifying.

"I don't like it," Juniper stated, choking back the tears. She didn't want to cry, but she couldn't swallow the upsetting notion that another loved one was suffering because of her. Ethan died on her watch; he'd still be alive if he never traveled to Washington. Now Irene was falling victim to the unyielding clutch of an addiction she beat years ago, all because Ethan died trying to protect Juniper. It all fell on her shoulders.

"I don't like it either, but it's the only way I know how to deal. I promise it won't be a lasting thing. Just till the grief settles."

Juniper shook her head but said nothing more. There was no use arguing, Irene was too stubborn to listen. She'd either fall back into old habits or keep her word and kick the meds the moment she no longer needed them. Time would tell. All Juniper could do was watch over her and be there to catch her if she fell.

Juniper scanned her cousin's luggage. "I was going to call you a cab, but since you fit everything into a backpack I can bring us both to my place on my bike."

"Well, I'm only staying until tonight. My return flight is another red eye. It leaves at midnight."

"Oh, okay. Do you want to relax at my place for a little while before seeing Ethan? Or do you want to do that now?"

"Let's go there now. I need to make sure they have all the arrangements for the transportation of his body in order. I don't want to handle that later in case something goes wrong."

Juniper understood and helped Irene onto the back of the Jaden Jaunt.

They headed to the hospital mortuary. Upon arrival, they were directed to the room where Ethan's body waited and the Undertaker prepped them on what to expect. No amount of warnings or words of encouragement could prepare either for the sight of their loved one lying cold and dead. His face was swollen, bruised, and covered in abrasions. The force of the blows fractured his skull and pieces of bone made their way into his brain, which caused the hemorrhaging. Post-mortem, his skull was misshapen and unfamiliar. Seeing him like this intensified their grief. They held each other as they adjusted to the sight of Ethan in this condition.

"I want him cremated," Irene decided. "I wasn't sure what the right choice was, but after seeing him I think that's best."

"I agree."

Irene left to relay her wishes to the Undertaker and together they made arrangements with the chosen funeral home in the Bronx for direct transportation of the ashes. There was nothing left for them to do at the mortuary, nothing more to say, so they departed and spent the remainder of the day at Juniper's home.

The sun reflected off the silvery pond in her backyard, dancing as ribbons in the hazy afternoon light. The view from her porch was soothing after their emotional day spent at the hospital.

"It's peaceful here," Irene said with eyes closed, absorbing the sunlight that covered her face.

"I wish you'd consider moving here."

"I'd love to," she said, not thinking of all her responsibilities back home.

"So, why don't you?"

"I can't relocate my kids. They are settled in New York."

"They are still young. They're resilient. I have no doubt they'd adapt."

"They're city kids. Dragging them out here would be traumatizing. The change in pace would derail them. They've been through enough because of me and I don't want to send them on any additional tailspins."

"Plan a visit. See if they like it without mentioning you might want to move here."

"I'll think about it."

Juniper accepted that answer as the best she'd get. According to the trees she still had time to persuade her loved ones to relocate. Irene and the kids would be better off with her, regardless if the end was truly on its way. The Bronx was not safe. Their family had been there too long; there was too much bad blood and too many toxic ties rooted deep into the streets of that city. Irene knew it too.

"I feel like he is here with us," Irene confessed with forlorn hope.

"He is. I can feel him in the breeze."

Irene smiled at this thought as she took greater notice of the cool air. They sat in silence, listening to the birds chirp their springtime songs in celebration of the forest's rebirth. Though it was ironic that they grieved the loss of life while nature celebrated its return, the juxtaposition proved healing. All was not lost. Ethan may have left his human body but he lived on through the earth. Juniper knew this as a fact and Irene felt comfort in this notion as a metaphor.

The rest of the afternoon flew by and they rode into town for dinner. They enjoyed a nice meal and Juniper gave Irene a tour of Port Angeles. It was nice to have a loved one nearby after all that just happened; she treasured their time together.

Night passed as fast as the afternoon and suddenly she was at the airport hugging Irene good-bye. It was hard to let go, and watching her cousin board the plane was even harder. The world was forcing Juniper to return to her old routine but that no longer felt right. Everything was changing. It was time to start making moves, time to rearrange her life and start anew. This time, her new beginning stemmed from a place of peace; from the world she created in the forest. She could build something great from this vantage point. She believed in herself and the task placed upon her by the trees, now she just needed to rally those she cared about to follow in her faith.

She went to the library the next day before work to research all that the trees had told her over the past few weeks. The only item that had any context behind it was the name Gaia. It was the name given to Mother Nature in Greek mythology. She was the mother to all; creator of Earth and the entire universe. It was fascinating to consider there might be truth to the ancient myths. Or maybe it was just a name that stuck over the eons. Either way, Mother Nature existed in some form; be it visible or veiled, tangible or ethereal, out of human divinity or something otherworldly—this immortal deity was real.

The rest remained a mystery. There were no solid belief systems or findings explaining the trees' insight on the choice given to humans after death: living on through earth, bound to Gaia, or having an afterlife free of all earthly bonds in space. This concept was foreign and she found nothing online to verify these claims. To her, the lack of findings validated all that the trees proclaimed. It was original content; nothing she crafted from information she'd seen and forgotten, nothing made up by other storytellers in the world. It was novel, unique, and unprecedented; something only an authentic source could relay.

The tree called her Little Blossom—her father would never lead her astray.

She went to work, ready to start selecting the people she wanted by her side. Roscoe, of course, her co-workers, who had become like family over the years. There were a few bar regulars like Jeb that she'd try to bring along. Irene was a very important member of her recruitment. Not only because she was family but because she had a long distance to travel, kids to bring with her, and it would take a lot more work to make her believe the trek was worth the hassle. She wasn't sure when she'd see the Wolfe brothers next, but they were certainly worthy of rescue.

Roscoe came into the bar wearing a weary look of defeat.

"I'm so torn," he said, collapsing into an empty barstool. There weren't many customers at the bar yet, so it was safe to talk.

"About what? Believing me?"

"I want to, it's just insane."

"I know it seems insane, but it's the truth."

"I wish there was a way you could show me."

"I have no evidence to verify what happened to Damien, but I can prove that the trees speak to me."

"How?"

"Well, now that I've accepted the task they assigned me, maybe they'll speak to me with you present. Then you can hear them too."

Roscoe looked up at her with uncertainty but did not object.

"When?"

"My last shift is Sunday afternoon. We can go camping that night or head into the forest Monday morning. Your call."

"Sunday night it is. I really want to believe you, you know that, right?"

"Yes."

"Okay, good."

He left and Juniper tackled her shift. Jeb kept her company during the rush. Anytime she felt overwhelmed or in the weeds, she took a moment near him to catch her breath and take in his friendly face. This job was a means to an end, and that end was on its way. Once she convinced Roscoe, she'd work on the others.

Sunday night arrived and she waited for Roscoe at her house before heading into the forest. A stormy week was forecasted, but she didn't want to cancel their trip. She needed to show him proof and he was open to its delivery. She led them down the Lillian River Trail, and he followed her along the wet and winding paths. It took them through a lowland before leading them up into a montane forest with primitive trails and slick, mossy floors. They did not travel far before finding a suitable place to set up camp.

There was enough overhead foliage to protect them from the brunt of the rainfall, but it didn't keep them or their surrounding area dry. It would be a wet few days and Juniper hoped this didn't prevent the trees from speaking.

With ponchos donned, they placed their packed tarps in all necessary locations: atop their vehicles, on an open piece of land where their tent would fit, and above the area they'd be residing. Once all tarps were in place they began assembling the tent. After finishing the grunt work they bundled up in sleeping bags inside the tent.

After a few minutes of relaxed silence, Roscoe addressed the most pressing issue.

"The situation with Damien is taken care of."

"What did you tell them?"

"That he chased you down, you crashed and blacked out, and that I found you unconscious and him dead. We concluded that he must have crashed too and his body catapulted from his bike into a low-hanging tree branch."

Juniper sighed. "I'm glad it's settled and off your shoulders. I would've taken the heat for it."

"I know, but your story would have landed you in a psych ward. I wasn't letting that happen on my watch."

"Thanks. I still wish you believed me though."

"I think you're still suffering from some serious distress. I'm not sure you can presently distinguish up from down, or real from fake."

"Thanks for your confidence."

"You said your truth, I'm saying mine. I think this trauma needs to settle and everything will make better sense once we're through the worst of it."

"And what if after this camping trip you hear what I've been hearing and change your mind about my current state of sanity?"

"Then I'll apologize and we will take it from there, but I'm not counting on that."

"I'm worried the rain is going to get in the way."

"Trees can't talk when it's raining out?" he asked, swallowing his sarcasm the best he could.

"I'm sure they can. I probably should have told them you were coming and that I needed them to let you in," she mumbled to herself. "But they know I need you on board, that you're my choice. Maybe they'll gather my intentions for bringing you here without me having to say it out loud."

"I'm your choice?"

"Yes, as my Second."

"In any other context I'd be elated. Two weeks ago I'd have kissed you for saying that. Now, I'm completely freaked out."

"Don't be."

"Did *you* choose me? Or did the trees?"

"I did. They just told me I needed a Second and pointed out the obvious. I guess they've been watching us. They like you too."

Roscoe collapsed onto his pillow. "This is absurd. The trees *chose* you? They *chose* me? They *like* me? What is all of this about?"

"I really wanted you to believe me before I explained any more. It only gets crazier."

"Great."

There was a moment of pause before Juniper continued. "Let's just say it has to do with saving the planet."

"From what?"

"Humans."

His eyes widened in fear.

Juniper continued. "We would be representing the good left in humanity; that which Gaia hopes to save."

"Is this some bizarre Noah's Arc-styled nonsense? Pairing up mates in order to start over?"

"I really want to wait until you hear the trees for yourself. Once you feel the magic you'll understand."

"If I hadn't liked you so much, for so long, I'd be gone already."

"I know. I'm sorry. It took me a while to accept this strange reality too. But I don't want to be alone; I want you by my side."

"I'm giving your brand of crazy a try. Just be patient, and don't get your hopes up because I'm out the moment it crosses the line."

"I understand."

"Can we talk about something different?" he asked. "I want what we used to have back, what we were on the verge of a few weeks ago. We were so close to having something good before being launched into this downward spiral of lunacy."

"You do understand how important what I'm telling you is, right?"

"Juniper, it's too much."

"Fine. What do you want to talk about then?"

"How was your visit with Irene?"

"Wonderful. And healing. I'm hoping to get her and the kids to move out here soon."

"That would be nice."

"I just don't have much time to convince her." Juniper was playing out the scenario in her mind.

"Huh?"

"Well, it's starting in the South Pacific, then through the other six territories in an order I'm not privy to yet. I'm not sure how long that will take, but I need her close to me when it's our turn."

"Hold on, what's starting?"

She looked at him with surprise at all she had revealed. It was too much too soon.

"Everything. I just need you to trust me, and trust that I'll tell you everything the moment you believe."

"This is insane."

"You already think I'm crazy. I'm not letting you think I've totally lost it. Bits and pieces will translate better."

He lifted the hood of his rain jacket and left the tent. She was alone and unsure if her plan would work. If the trees didn't come through, she'd never convince him.

The day remained dark under clouds, and the trees stayed quiet. All she heard from them was the rustling of their leaves. Roscoe came back a few hours later, right before nightfall. He was sopping wet when he reentered the tent, and soaked everything near the entrance. He stripped down to his boxers and she handed him sweatpants and a long-sleeve shirt from his duffel bag. He carefully unzipped the tent enough to place his wet jacket into a large garbage bag. He then dried off in a towel, changed into warm clothes, and got back into his sleeping bag.

"Do you feel better?"

"I'm fine," he responded, grouchier than before.

Juniper took this as her cue to give up until tomorrow. She rolled over and closed her eyes. She didn't want to talk to him either.

They fell asleep in separate sleeping bags, but halfway through the night he pulled her closer to soothe her bout of shivers. His body warmed hers and she fell back asleep.

The tent's temperature elevated as morning approached. The rain had stopped, leaving everything dewy and humid. Juniper tore her socks off and fell back asleep.

Moments later Roscoe began tossing around, groaning and grimacing from whatever swirled inside his dreams. Juniper did not notice until his flailing collided with her shoulder, jolting her awake.

"What the hell?" she asked, eyes still closed. His inaudible mumbling continued.

She rolled over to look at him through half-closed eyes. He was having a nightmare. Realizing she could not help him, she placed a comforting hand on his forearm and tried to return to her own dreams.

A few minutes later Roscoe ripped his arm from her caring touch and clumsily backed away from her, tangled in blankets.

"What did you say?" he demanded.

Half asleep, Juniper struggled to process the situation.

"Nothing," she replied.

"That wasn't you?"

"What wasn't me?"

"What you just said!"

"I didn't say anything," she yawned. She let her thoughts settle and wrap around where they were and why. "It was probably the trees."

He unzipped his sleeping bag and backed away from her.

"This is crazy."

"They are harmless."

"It didn't feel harmless, it felt very creepy and dangerous."

"Creepy, sure. But dangerous?"

"My dreams last night were horrifying. I saw the worst of humanity played out from the trees' point of view: the holocaust, slavery, all of our wars. I was in the trees, seeing the humans as *they* did, feeling what *they* felt as they observed the worst of our past. They hate us, resent us for taking over the planet like a debilitating virus and killing them with no remorse along the way. The emotion they shared with me was violent: bitter disgust and abhorrent rage. They want the planet back."

"Or maybe they just want us to help them make a shift in how humans treat nature. We've had long conversations about this before, we both agree a change needs to happen."

"Yes, but being threatened *by* earth, *by* the trees? Feeling the wrath we've caused them, the deep and irreparable pain? They did not give me the impression they planned to forgive the human race."

"Then why would they confide in us? We are human."

"I'm not sure."

"There are six others, plus each of their Seconds. Fourteen total. Plus any followers they gather along the way."

"There are more people who can talk to the trees?"

"No, I don't think so. I was chosen for the trees. I'm pretty sure the others were selected for other elements, like water, fire, air. Eventually all Champions will work together to rebuild human life on the planet. We are tasked to make it better than it is right now. To build a society that respects the planet and does not craft a life based on its destruction."

"We are nobodies. How on earth would you, or me, or any other 'chosen' individual, sway the engrained lifestyles of billions of people? We've been trying to help for years. So have other people. It's a culture shift, an alteration to our way of thinking as a species, something that needs to happen gradually. And I believe we are on our way, but it'll take time."

"It would be after the purge, when there are less of us."

"Purge?"

"A clean start. They are reclaiming the planet, setting it back to how it was before we got here. I imagine some remnants of our history here will remain, but the majority of our established routine will be wiped. No going back, so we'll need to start anew. That's when we change the way we exist on this planet."

"So, genocide by the hand of nature?"

Juniper paused. "I agree, it sounds harsh, but we don't own this planet. We are guests here and we've been awful. It's tragic because a lot of good people will die, but we have no say in the matter. We aren't in control, we just grew to believe we were."

"I totally get and appreciate all those sentiments in metaphorical terms. Realistically, it's savage."

"I don't know what to say. It took me weeks to come to terms with it, and I fear this will make me sound barbaric, but isn't that what this planet needs? We have spread across the globe like a crippling disease. Earth is dying beneath the vast sores we've created; beneath the vile pollution we relentlessly make. The human race will go extinct regardless. Now it's just a matter of whether the planet dies along with us. This cleanse gives us a chance to save both."

"They said nothing about a takeover. They only showed me how much they hate humans."

"I think they were just showing you their side, trying to explain why it needs to be done. They knew I'd explain the rest. They want our help. I'm sure they didn't mean to scare you."

"Maybe the voices I heard were just part of the nightmare. You didn't hear it, maybe it didn't really happen."

"I was sleeping."

Roscoe buried his face into his hands in disbelief.

"I need you to believe," she pleaded.

"There are so many reasons why I can't, why I don't *want* to. I still think we are feeling the aftereffects of trauma. We both need time."

There was a new tension between her and Roscoe. He was on edge, freaked out by the seemingly impossible truths that just smacked him in the face. Despite the facts being displayed right before his eyes, he still refused to see. Juniper was more open to it, possibly because she was desperate for something bigger: a worthwhile quest to embrace that was larger than her own troubles, a way to forget her trivial worries, a way to balance out old regrets with new, meaningful purpose. She always believed in magic, and now that it was slowly revealing itself to her through nature, she couldn't help but be drawn to its existence. She wanted to believe, whereas Roscoe was scared to.

They spent the afternoon trying to pretend like things were normal, but the effort was strained. By twilight, Roscoe could no longer fake it.

"I think I'm done. I'm going back to Port Angeles. I have the night off and I need to spend it someplace familiar."

"I understand."

"Maybe it'll make more sense tomorrow."

"I hope so." She did not want to lose him.

"Sorry I freaked out before," he said, hoping to leave on a positive note.

Juniper nodded. He wasn't sorry for his disbelief; he was sorry for making her feel small. She appreciated that he valued her feelings, but it didn't change the fact that he chose society's entrenched perception of reality over her offering of something different, something better. She wasn't going to force him to believe in the magic if he'd rather ignore it. Denial was his burden to bear. When he came into acceptance she'd welcome him happily, but until then she'd let him have his distance.

"The mysteries of the forest are endless," she offered with a smile. "And if the end is coming, at least we have each other."

He smiled uncomfortably, unwilling to engage in anymore talk about an apocalypse. "You'll always have me," he said. "Even in the moments I find you utterly terrifying."

"Gee, thanks," she laughed, relieved to hear he still cared for her. "Who knows, maybe a few more camping trips and you'll be best buddies with the trees."

"I think we both need a good night's sleep." Roscoe put the topic to rest. It gave him a crippling sense of inferiority, like all control was lost and he was an insignificant pawn in a deadly game.

Juniper dropped the subject, gave him a hug, and they parted ways hoping it would all make sense soon.

Chapter 15

Coral Belawan, Champion of the Ocean, stood at the back of the catamaran headed for Antarctica. A four-boat fleet followed, each with nearly a hundred passengers. Her older brother, Gus, stood beside her. As ferry operators in Australia, they had access to the boats when the monsoon started. Coral had accumulated a decent following over the five years she was given to recruit, and it was time for them to find safe ground elsewhere.

The waves were volatile as they sailed away from their home and she watched them grow in size with a troubled heart. The first tidal wave arrived twenty minutes into their trip. It traveled east to west, covering the width of both New Zealand and Australia. All her loved ones were with her now, but it didn't ease the guilt she felt for those left behind. The ocean spirits promised they had the means to save those who were pure of heart and connected to the earth, but she wasn't sure how.

Nature tore across the land, demolishing everything in its path. Between the floods and the impact of the waves, imagining anyone had survived felt overly optimistic. She let go of hope as the second, third, and fourth sets of waves ripped across the region. Living through such destruction was impossible. There'd be no life left in the South Pacific after the storm passed.

She shifted her gaze west and saw Zander's small fleet of boats making their way south. He hailed from Barbados and was able to wrangle a decent following from neighboring countries in the Caribbean. She hadn't met him yet, but knew him well. They spoke often through the ocean spirits that connected them telepathically. She grew to love him dearly and eagerly anticipated their first encounter. The love she felt for him felt true, even at a distance, and she hoped it translated once they existed together in the new world. Their connection was pure, untainted by society or human limitations. It was a bonding of souls, a union grown from the purest source.

Her heart broke for those lost, and for her homeland further north in South Kalimantan, Indonesia, but yearned for her soul mate—her Second. At first she thought the whole thing impossible: ocean spirits, nature connecting her telepathically to a man across the globe, the end of the world. But the more time that passed, the more she could not deny her new reality. Strangers were coming to her from neighboring islands saying they heard her name in answer to their prayers. People she'd never met from Fiji, Guam, French Polynesia, and Cook Islands found their way to her in Australia, claiming they heard her voice in their dreams. When the ocean told her there'd be floods in New Guinea, there were. They said a hurricane would tear across Hawaii; it did. She could no longer fight the truth: the world was coming to an end and she had a duty to uphold.

Her family's ferry line had a franchise operation running in the Caribbean, so she got Zander a job there and guided him as the ocean directed her.

The wreckage before her now was unreal. Though she knew it was coming, she never properly imagined the devastation. Before the first wave even hit, she heard the screams of terror from miles away. The voices crying out echoed into the afternoon sky. There were houses and cars floating in the water, far from where they originated. Skyscrapers along the coastline cracked in half at the first impact and were sucked into the surge, disappearing from sight in seconds.

Everyone on the catamaran remained quiet as they sailed away from the storm. The eerie silence lingered as they watched mortality rain down. The ocean around them remained calm, keeping them safe from harm, and its serenity contrasted what they witnessed with drastic irony—it was the apocalypse, yet they cruised freely from the end.

When the screaming stopped, so did the collective breath the survivors held. Mournful whispers and the sound of crying replaced the booming wail of death. They grieved the lost souls together, huddled in small groups and bundled under winter coats and blankets. The air grew colder the closer they sailed to their destination. It grew quieter too. Though rain and waves still lashed across the South Pacific, the scene grew smaller the farther away they sailed. The sky dissolved from gray to blue and eventually they lost sight of the storm completely.

The moment the view of the wreckage was out of sight, Coral burst into tears. The weight of what she was part of finally hit her. She fell to her knees at the back of the boat, crushed by the burden, soaked in shame. A few of her followers ran to her side to comfort their bereaved leader.

"Could I have done more to save others?" she asked, desperate for validation.

"No," a man from Samoa said. "You saved so many. Look around. Without you, we'd all be dead."

He was right. She stood and put on a brave face. This was not a time for weakness; she had to be strong for those she led out of the ruin. She returned her sight to Zander, whose boats were now much closer. Soon, she could collapse into his arms in private; until then, she had to radiate bravery.

As their fleet approached the shore, they pulled in the inflatable boat that was towed behind their catamaran and loaded it with their pre-packed survival kits. Since they could only tow one inflatable Zodiac each, there would be quite a few trips back and forth. The ocean was on their side, so time was not an issue. Each of the five Zodiacs was steered by the most skilled survivors and it took the entire afternoon to get everyone off the larger vessels.

The continent was mostly vacant besides a few scientists who were bunkered in research labs. Coral took out her handheld GPS computer and plugged in the coordinates 68°34'35.3"S 77°58'9.2"E. The location of the Davis Station appeared on the screen and she led her followers there. With Australia gone, the facility would remain permanently vacant and it was a safe place to make shelter. Over time they'd expand upon it, or find other vacant research stations to inhabit, but for now it would suffice. The walk was long and treacherous, but they made it without injury. The moment they arrived, everyone got to work at making it a suitable home. People selected sleeping quarters, others designated jobs to themselves and those around them. Coral watched, pleased that her following was determined to work together to survive.

The ocean told her the next attack would take place across Europe and Asia. She wasn't sure of the details, just that she had

159

to remain hidden until the entire planet was cleansed. There were plenty of radios, so she hoped to secretly intercept updates.

She stepped back outside and inhaled a large breath of the freshest air she ever tasted.

Hello, Coral, Champion of the Ocean.

The voice came from no particular direction. She looked around for a moment before realizing it was in her head, similar to when the ocean spoke, but this wasn't the ocean. The accent sounded Nordic. The voice was crisp and audible over the harsh, snowy winds. She tensed, unsure who now spoke to her.

I am Aria Cecildottir, Champion of Air. Welcome to my home away from home.

"You're human?" Coral asked aloud. "Where are you?"

The Base Camp of Mount Everest, but I'm from Hof, Iceland.

"How are you speaking to me?"

Through the air. When you're in my element I have easy access to you, and the air's presence is strongest in Antarctica.

"I haven't learned how to do that with the ocean yet."

You had a natural disaster to escape. I'm sure that's next on their list of lessons.

"Well, it's nice to meet you, Aria. Do I have to speak out loud in order for you to hear me? People are going to think I am crazy."

No. In time you will learn how to answer through your mind's voice.

"That's good. We are all safe in Antarctica. How are things on the mountain?"

Fine so far. I made contact to update you on the current situation. I am in direct contact with Sahira Dayal, Champion of the Mountains. As you may know, our elements are next. Sahira is stationed in Switzerland with my Second. Though her accent was thick she spoke fluent English. *I am at the top of Mount Everest with Monte Bram, Sahira's Second. We are anticipating the next purge. We will convene the moment it's complete. I was informed by my element that you arrived safely in Antarctica and I wanted to welcome you. The spirits of the air reside all around you.*

"Will they talk to me?"

No, only to me. Just as the ocean will speak only to you. But I am only a thought away if you ever need their assistance or mine.

"Thanks. The sentiment is returned."

I will keep you informed of the happenings here. We are at a safe altitude and Sofyla Yurchenko, Champion of Soil, is scooping up her Second in Saudi Arabia. I don't know much about them yet except that they'll weather the storm in the caves of Africa with Eshe Ahikiwe, Champion of the Core, and Zaire Nzile, who is the Second of the Fresh Water Champion.

"I'm never going to remember all these names."

It'll get easier once you start speaking with the other Champions directly. Is your Second with you?

"He's still getting his people off their boats. I'll meet him shortly. I'm quite excited."

I understand. I still haven't met Erion. He's riding out this portion of the cleanse in the Swiss mountains with Sahira. No one really lives in Antarctica so they found my partner in Canada. From the conversations we've had, I don't think I could have been better matched.

161

"Same. I'm positive Zander is my soul mate."

There's something to be said about connecting through nature. The universe knows what it's doing.

"I sure hope so. Why did they make you leave your countries if the cleanse won't hit there?"

I wondered the same thing. They said we had to be with the Mountain's Champion and Second if they were to survive. I guess direct communication with the air spirits is critical during an attack like this.

"Did your people follow you there?"

Most of mine stopped their journey at the Swiss Alps. They are safe with Erion; he gives me consistent updates. Only my family followed me all the way to Nepal. I don't know what's in store for those left in Iceland and Canada, but I am grateful I was able to save a significant amount of people.

"I thought it would be hard to get my people to follow me to Antarctica, but they seemed to sense the end was coming. The moment the monsoon came they boarded my boats, no questions asked."

The elemental spirits only speak with their chosen Champion, but I believe they subconsciously reach into the minds of others who have strong bonds to nature.

"I agree. Half my followers are strangers who traveled from islands all over the South Pacific to find me. They weren't sure why or how, but they managed."

Impressive.

"Yes, well I have to get going, but please stay in touch. We are in the dark down here."

Of course, Aria promised, then her presence disappeared.

Coral suddenly felt much better. She no longer felt so alone. There was another out there with the same burden as her; the same responsibility to execute. Another strong female championing the human race through the apocalypse. She returned to the chaos inside Davis Station, reinvigorated and proud to embrace her role as leader. She would not fail her people, the other Champions, herself, or Gaia.

Chapter 16

Jeb barged through the front doors of the Dipper Dive halfway into Juniper's Friday night shift.

"Turn on the news," he demanded.

"What channel?" Brett asked while locating the remote.

"Doesn't matter."

He flipped from ESPN to ABC and live footage of a natural disaster was being covered as breaking news.

Jeb began to explain. "A set of tsunamis tore through the South Pacific. Australia, New Zealand, Indonesia, Philippines, all those islands in between; they've been wiped. The waves ripped through them all."

"Holy crap," Brett said in awe as he watched the footage play out on screen. The waves hit the land repeatedly. The cameras missed the first round, but captured the continued beating via helicopter.

"It doesn't look natural," Jeb commented. "The water is moving with intention, like it has control over where it goes."

Juniper was in utter shock; the trees' predictions were actually happening. She stayed quiet, too flabbergasted to speak.

"The newscasters are saying there won't be any survivors," Jeb stammered, relaying all he'd heard up to this point. "There might've been some after the first wave, but not now. The entire area has been obliterated."

"Did they say how many people populated that area of the globe?" Brett asked.

"Indonesia has 250 million. The Philippines have about 100 million. They'll mention the total number again."

"No survivors?" Brett asked again to confirm.

"So they think."

"That is a lot of death."

Juniper felt sick. Even if she had tried to reach out to authorities to warn them about this disaster, who would have believed her? How could she have explained her source? The best she could do was try to save as many people on her end as possible.

Roscoe burst into the bar. He glared at her with alarmed disbelief and she nodded, answering his unasked question. He collapsed onto a bar stool and stared up at the TV screen with a look of horror.

She walked over to him, hoping they could have a quiet conversation while Jeb and Brett bantered.

"I feel guilty by association," he said.

"So you're saying I'm at fault?" she asked, appalled at the accusation. "What would you have had me do? Tell them the trees warned me that this was coming? *You* didn't even believe me—do you really think strangers would have taken me seriously?"

"No," he surrendered. "But I wish you'd tried."

Juniper groaned. "I wasn't even totally sure what the warning meant. Plus, I would've looked like a lunatic."

Roscoe shrugged. "Maybe, but it would be worth it if it meant you could save others."

"So you believe me now?"

"I guess I have to."

"You need to believe in the trees, believe in nature. It's essential."

"You want me to accept that this supernatural massacre is a good thing? I don't understand how you are okay with it."

"I'm not, but we have no say in the matter. We cannot stop it, so we might as well ready ourselves for what lies ahead. I do have faith in nature and I trust that we can rebuild our lives and thrive on the other side of this catastrophic end."

"I need to call my dad."

Juniper nodded. She didn't want to press the issue of belief further. The trees chose her because she believed without proof, without any indicator that there was truth behind the faith she felt in the forest. Her love was abundant and pure, stemming from genuine intent and authentic allegiance. She felt safe in nature, she felt the love returned in small, sincere ways, and through this she found herself in allegiance with the trees. After they saved her life, she realized how much depth there was to her previously light-hearted loyalty to the forest. There was something solid in which to place her faith, something wholesome and purposeful in which to believe. Despite the gruesome manner in which this new reality was beginning to unfold, her alliance with nature did not feel wrong.

In this notion she'd remain steadfast.

The bar did not get rowdy this Friday night. Instead, there was a somber feeling of companionship amongst the bartenders and patrons. The TV stayed on the live broadcast all night and everyone watched with hurting hearts, grateful they were not alone to receive this grave news. Gratitude for life filled the bar and its large presence was overwhelming. Seeing so much death made those far from the wreckage thankful to be alive. Juniper felt their grief in crushing surges, and it terrified her that she might not be able to save them all.

She tried to hush the fear.

The weekend passed with speed and she made her way back into the forest. The more time she spent surrounded by human civilization, the further she felt from her newly accepted purpose, and the more it felt like she had made the whole ordeal up in her head. She needed to talk to the spirits of the trees; she needed an explanation, clarification, validation. Anything to remind her this wasn't a weird dream.

The weather was dry, but the trails to Happy Lake Ridge were long and formidable. The loose rocks and narrow trails always tested her riding skills. Though treacherous, the ride was therapeutic. Challenging herself was healing and settled the nerves that had surfaced at the announcement of the South Pacific tsunamis. When she reached a relatively flat section of Happy Lake Ridge, she set up camp facing west.

<<Welcome home,>> the trees said in unified harmony.

"Thanks. It was a tough weekend. I saw the purge of the South Pacific. That's what will happen all over the globe?"

<<Yes, just in different manners.>>

"What's next?"

<<The air spirits have been gathering the massive pollution of China, India, and the Middle East into an expansive fog, while simultaneously working with the water spirits to cool the air of Asia and dump thousands of meters of snow over the Himalayas. All of Asia and Europe are in its range. It's a collaborative effort of avalanches, an

167

arctic freeze, and unbreathable air. I suggest you avoid the news next week if the tsunamis caused you grief.>>

"Are you sure this is necessary?"

<<Unfortunately.>>

"People are being saved?"

<<By our Champion of Air and Champion of the Mountains, yes. Humans from various countries in their regions are already stationed near the top of Mount Everest and Mont Rose. They will ride out the devastation at safe altitudes.>>

"How far will it reach?"

<<North to South, Russia to Sri Lanka. East to West, Japan to Ireland.>>

"That's millions of people."

<<Yes, it will be one of the larger attacks.>>

"When will it be our turn? How will it happen?"

<<We will keep you informed. How is your progress with your Second?>>

"Well, he believes me now, but whatever dreams you placed in his head have him terrified of your intentions."

<<It was our attempt to explain why we must excavate the planet of most human life.>>

"I get it, but it backfired. Now he thinks if he stands by me he'll be a guilty party to the extinction of the human race."

<<It's not an extinction. Gaia loves humans too much to eliminate them. This purge, being chosen—it's a second chance.>>

"Roscoe doesn't see it that way. He said the visions he received felt like nature hated mankind."

<<Bring him back to the forest. We will speak to him this one time in order to remedy our misstep.>>

"When do I meet the other Champions?"

<<Possibly never. But you'll begin communicating with them when you're ready. You'll know them well soon.>>

Juniper took a deep breath. "How many people do you think I can save?"

<<However many you can recruit to your side. If they believe, they will follow.>>

"When is the attack on Europe and Asia happening?"

<<Next week. It will be slower than that on the South Pacific and will take two to three weeks to complete.>>

"I see. Roscoe heard you speak to him in his dreams before the tsunamis, but didn't believe any of it to be true until he saw the South Pacific unfold. I suppose I'll need to do that with the rest of them and accept that they'll think I'm crazy for a while."

<<You must do whatever you think is best. It is your duty to gather a following to endure the purge in your region. The less people you have, the harder it will be to survive the aftermath. You need able hands and sharp minds when you attempt to rebuild your humbled civilization.>>

Juniper said nothing more. There were no words to express her emotions, no questions to ask that could justify or rationalize the torn feeling in the pit of her stomach.

After a few minutes of silence, she felt the presence of the trees fade. They were still with her, just farther away. It was nice to feel alone again; she needed time by herself to come to terms with her role as an accomplice. She wondered if the other Champions struggled with the same moral dilemma when they were first recruited.

Sunset came in a blaze of glory and left the world in darkness at its departure. The moon was hardly visible and her surroundings felt strange. Paranoia washed over her. She shivered and crawled into her tent, hoping to hide from whatever dangers lurked in her vicinity, imaginary or real.

The following morning arrived with a brisk breeze. It didn't feel like spring and she hadn't packed like she would have during the winter months. Her tent was vented, her sleeping bag wasn't insulated, and she didn't dress appropriately. If it didn't warm up she imagined she'd need to head home sooner than anticipated. But maybe that was a good thing; she *should* be there convincing Irene to return with her kids, and she still needed to persuade those she cared about in Washington to follow her lead. She wasn't sure how much time she had left.

She dug her walkie-talkie out of her backpack.

"Heya, I'm halfway down Happy Lake Ridge if you want to come visit."

"Hi Juni," Clark answered via his direct line. "I'm buried in paperwork today but I'll give Roscoe the heads up. It's awfully cold this morning. Did you pack proper gear?"

"No, I should've checked the weather. My mistake."

"I'll tell Roscoe to bring some extra blankets and socks."

"Thanks."

"You okay otherwise? Roscoe's been acting weird."

"Yeah, I'm fine. I do need to come in and see you soon though. I have a lot of updates to share."

"Stop by anytime. For you, my door is always open."

"Thanks. I'll try to come by before the weekend."

"I look forward to it."

The conversation ended and she hoped Roscoe would visit. There was a chance he might choose to stay away. He no longer seemed comfortable in her company, especially in the presence of trees.

Afternoon arrived with warmth, which Juniper was thankful for. The trees did not speak but she was certain they sang through the entire day. Their choral tune accompanied the cool wind and noisy animals. It was a hum in layered harmonies. The sound was ethereal, unlike any she'd heard before, and though its tone was spooky, she was not afraid. The longer the song continued, the more it echoed off the surrounding mountains, reverberating like a choir in a grand church hall. The growth was slow but steady, building until the entire forest was flooded in the sound. Juniper was so lost in the enchanting melody she did not notice Roscoe's arrival.

"Heard you were cold," he said, carrying an armful of blankets.

She snapped her head in his direction and let the song of the woods fade to the back of her awareness.

"I am, thank you."

He tossed her the blankets and she threw on two extra pairs of socks.

"I'll be honest," he confessed. "I did not want to come."

"Well, I'm glad you did."

"I can't stay long."

"That's fine."

They sat next to the fire Juniper built. Roscoe put an arm around her beneath the comforter they shared and pulled her in closer. She nuzzled her head onto his shoulder.

For a few moments they sat like this, pretending nothing had changed, that there wasn't an enormous tension residing between them. When the trees spoke, all pretenses of normalcy were lost.

<<*Welcome back, Roscoe.*>>

His spine went rigid as he scanned the sky frantically for the source.

Juniper tried to calm his nerves. "It's okay. I promise."

"You heard that too?"

She nodded.

<<*We did not mean to frighten you when we spoke to you through your dreams.*>>

Roscoe buried his face into his hands. "This is what I was avoiding. I'm not crazy, I know I'm not."

"Avoiding the truth doesn't make it go away," Juniper encouraged. "Be open to the improbable just this once. It's magic; an awe-inspiring gift that you really ought to accept."

"I can accept the magic in nature. I just can't accept that this so-called magic is out to kill us all," he hissed.

The voices of the trees answered in unison. <<*Gaia loves humans too much for a complete extinction.*>>

"Who is Gaia?"

"Mother Nature," Juniper answered.

<<*Your race is being given a second chance. We understand your hesitance to accept this strange reality—we were once human too—but it's crucial that you do. Juniper has chosen you as her Second. She needs you.*>>

"You were once human?"

"I hadn't gotten that far into the explanation," Juniper cut in before the trees could freak him out anymore.

<<Better that she explains it,>> the trees responded. <<Take care, Roscoe.>>

The wind lessened and the voices were gone.

"This is absurd."

"Maybe, but it's our reality."

"I can't sit back with this information and watch millions of people die. The guilt will eat me alive for the rest of my life."

"Do you understand why they are doing it?"

"Yes, but it doesn't change the fact that millions of good people who are victim to the world they were born into will die along with those who cause the actual damage. There's no way you, or any of the other Champions, can save every good soul on Earth."

"I can barely fathom gathering a following here. I really need your help."

"I'm going to help on behalf of mankind, not Gaia or whoever. I will save as many people as I can. I'm starting with my dad, then I'll work on Clark and my other friends. I have a feeling most won't oblige till the end is upon us."

"I'll talk to the trees, see if they can help in any way."

"Just keep in mind that *they're* the ones trying to kill us. I think we ought to stay objective when it comes to our trust in them."

"They saved my life. Damien would have killed me if it weren't for them."

"Maybe so. Maybe they have some bizarre love for you, but that love does not span across the board. They have no bond with humans elsewhere."

"I'm the liaison. I am the bridge connecting humans to nature. They love me. And through me, they love those I love."

"So I better not piss you off, huh?" His bitter tone was unlike any she'd heard from him before.

"No, I didn't mean it like that. They only hurt those who hurt me. They are my protectors. Please stop blaming me. I didn't choose this."

"But you're choosing to be an active party to genocide."

"I cannot stop it! My hands are tied so I'm doing the best I can to minimize the damage." She shook her head in frustration. "But I can barely get you, the guy I love, to be on my side. Not sure how I'm supposed to convince others who I have less of a connection with to believe me so that I can save them."

Roscoe groaned. "I need to balance your whimsical faith with some logic or else we are screwed. I will handle what we've been dealt in my own way. With reason and empathy, with a sound moral code."

"I don't want people to die either," she said in a low voice, bruised by his resistance. His emotional response to this situation always painted her as the bad guy and it was wearing her down. "I just can't control situations that are beyond me, I can only adapt."

"You work on your people, I'll work on mine. Keep me posted if they tell you anything else." He went to his quad without giving her a chance to respond. She wasn't even sure if she wanted to tell him more. She contemplated whether or not to mention next week's attack on Europe and Asia, but feared if she did, he'd be sent into a worse tailspin as he tried to fix a situation he could not control. Even if they reached the mainstream media, no one would heed their warnings. They'd never take them seriously—the people in power didn't even take scientists with highly-esteemed awards and years of experience seriously. They'd be fighting a battle they couldn't win.

In reverse, if she did not tell him he'd be furious with her when the events began to unfold. He'd surely realize this was part of the bigger picture they were now a part of and he'd feel betrayed that she had not confided in him.

The choice was heavy.

She tried to forget about it and worry about herself. She had a lot on her mind and worrying about his feelings or their relationship was a distraction. The fate of many lives rested in her hands, and if she did not handle the upcoming weeks properly she could wind up alone in the end.

The trees sensed her worry and returned.

<<*You will never be alone.*>>

"I will if I don't get people to believe me. You said so yourself."

<<*Trust in us. All will not be lost.*>>

"And if I don't get anyone to listen to my warnings when it's our turn?"

<<*Fear not, Little Blossom.*>>

"Dad?" Her eyes brimmed with tears.

<<*We do not see bodies; we see auras, we see souls. Yours is the brightest green we've ever seen. Just as our Champions of other*

elements shine brightest in other hues. The less a human is connected to Gaia, the less they glow. Many humans are a dull shade of gray. Just because there are only seven Champions does not mean there are not others out there worthy of our mercy. We will not overlook them when we strike.>>

She nodded, accepting the relief this revelation gave. This news would be well-received by Roscoe and might help him adjust.

<<You still need a solid following with unshakable faith. It's imperative the surviving humans of the trees listen to you. You are our only mediator; you will become their only salvation in the new world. If they do not trust in you and abide your lead, they will perish. Not by us directly, but at the hands of the environmental shift. The world will be dangerous. We will be guiding you through your survival and only those who follow will endure the first few years.>>

"I see."

<<We have faith in you.>>

Their presence faded and she sensed her returned solitude. This ordeal grew heavier each day. She realized how much she needed Roscoe on her side; the weight was too great to carry alone. Without him she was sure she'd be crushed beneath this burden.

Chapter 17

She hurried home Friday morning, hoping the time apart gave Roscoe room to breathe. She needed him to recover from the shock so he could hear her out with a level head.

"Roscoe, it's Juni. Where are you?" she said into the walkie-talkie.

It took a few minutes for him to respond.

"I'm home," he yawned. "I'm on the afternoon shift."

"Can I come over?"

"Sure."

She sped toward his townhouse, and when she arrived, the door was already unlocked. She entered to find Roscoe half asleep on the couch.

"You were right, I need to do more. Can I borrow your email account?"

"Yes, but for what?"

"I'm going to email the climatologists of each news station. Can you help me? I'm really bad with the internet."

Roscoe was happy to help and together, they searched for the contact info of the weathermen on every major broadcast network. They were only able to find the generic email addresses, which would likely land their email into the abyss of the internet, but it was the best they could do. Juniper comprised an email stating that she knew the tsunamis were coming and that the next disaster would be avalanches across Asia and Europe, followed by an arctic freeze and toxic fog.

"Really?" Roscoe asked as she typed that part and Juniper nodded. The email made her look crazy, but she hoped they'd remember it after the avalanches began and would take her seriously when she warned them of the next attack. She wondered if this defeated the intentions the trees had for her to find a worthy following, but she wouldn't be able to live with herself if she hadn't tried to reach the masses.

"Do you think they'll believe me?" she asked after sending the email to fifteen different contacts at eight major stations.

"No. The email addresses we found all started with the word 'info', which means they get thousands every day and that the account is probably monitored by an intern. I have a bad feeling it will get lost amongst all the others, and even if it is seen, they'll probably delete it after reading the first sentence due to the volume they're sifting through." Roscoe rubbed his brow in frustration. "I see what you meant when you said you'd feel like a lunatic. It felt easier to reach an audience in my mind, but now that we are actually trying, I realize how far away they are. I don't imagine we will get a response."

"I'm happy we tried."

"So am I." His mood seemed to lift despite his continued skepticism.

"I have good news," she blurted, ready to move on to the next order of business.

"Oh yeah?"

"You said you were worried about all the good people we wouldn't be able to save. Well, if these emails aren't taken seriously, the trees have a way to save more."

"Is that so?" he asked skeptically.

"They see people in colors, hues that represent their auras, and they can tell just by looking at a soul if they are a decent person or not. They told me they planned to spare those individuals."

"Are you sure they aren't bluffing in order to get me on board and to make you feel better?"

"It didn't feel like a lie."

"Well, considering how helpless we are in this predicament, I guess we'll just have to wait and see. I sure hope it's the truth."

"It is," she responded with overflowing optimism. "I'm sure it is."

"Have they said yet how they plan to exterminate the majority of us on this side of the planet?"

"Not yet, but they told me the details of the next attack."

"Right. The avalanches and what not. How do they plan to spare humans from that? If they haven't already climbed to the tallest mountains, they'll surely die."

"I'm not sure. Maybe those spirits can control who the air touches; maybe the snow can quickly melt around those caught who shouldn't be."

"Insanity." His bad mood was returning. "No one survived the South Pacific tsunamis. Were there no outlying people there worth saving?"

"Maybe they washed up someplace else and reports haven't surfaced yet."

Roscoe rolled his eyes. "Okay, enough. Thank you for the update. Let's move on from this, shall we?"

"I really wish you'd stop talking to me like that."

"Like what?"

"With such disdain."

"This whole ordeal is irritating. I obviously have reason to believe you, but just because I have some proof doesn't make it easy. This is madness."

"I need you. I can't do this alone."

"I'm not going anywhere, I just need space." The guilt he felt for continually losing his temper with her showed. "I'll come around. Give me time."

She gave him a half smile and left. There was nothing more to say.

Misty and Carine were scheduled to work with her that night. She hated going back to bartending when she had more important work to do, but these were her people and she was determined to save them.

Their shift started off slow and they spent a lot of time watching the news. Jeb was with them and provided his never-ending commentary on the post-tsunami reports.

"I'm telling you, it's climate change. It's finally appearing in scales we never imagined," Jeb said for a third time.

"Maybe," Carine said. "Or maybe it's just some freak occurrence."

"There's never been a death toll so high." Misty shook her head.

"It's a damn tragedy," Jeb added with a look at Juniper. "You're quiet, what's on your mind."

"I feel strange," Juniper answered honestly.

"Why's that?"

She hesitated. "Because I knew it was coming."

The girls looked at her with skepticism and Jeb raised his eyebrows.

"I'm not sure what you mean by that," he said.

"I'm going to tell you something, but you have to promise to listen with open minds. After I tell you I need a vow of patience, and if what I say comes to fruition, you must believe everything I tell you after."

"What the hell is happening?" Misty asked in bewilderment.

"Do you all promise?"

They all nodded their heads in agreement and Juniper went on.

"Mass avalanches are next. Every mountain range across Europe and Asia is targeted and the surrounding areas will be buried."

"It isn't even winter there," Carine retorted cynically.

"I check the BBC every day," Jeb responded. "All of Europe is experiencing abnormally low temperatures."

"What do you mean they are *targeted*?" Misty asked with a look of mistrust.

"I can't go into those details yet. Just know that avalanches are next, followed by an arctic freeze and a creeping fog of densely polluted air that will sweep the remainder of the region. The devastation will surpass the tsunamis."

"First off, you're crazy and I don't believe you could possibly know this," Carine quipped, "unless you have some secret degree in climatology you never mentioned before."

"I don't."

"Right," she continued. "Secondly, if you knew this to be true, why on earth are you telling us and not someone who could actually do something about it?"

"I was still being convinced before the tsunamis. I wasn't sure if they would really happen, but now that they have, I believe my source. I sent out emails to some news stations, but I doubt anyone will respond. I sound crazy. And the reason I'm telling you is because there's a lot more to come and I want to save you."

"Save us?" Jeb asked.

"I can't say anymore or I'll lose you. It only gets weirder. I need you to believe me before I lay out the details. You all have become my family here in Washington and I want you by my side in the end."

"The end?" Carine asked.

Misty put the back of her hand against Juniper's forehead.

"She doesn't feel hot," she told the others.

"I'm not sick or crazy. You all promised to listen with open minds."

"It's pretty demented to be predicting such travesty," Carine stated without sympathy. "Millions of people will die if what you're saying actually happens."

"I know. I don't want it to happen. I'm just trying to clue you in now so when I tell you the rest later you'll actually believe me."

"Okay, this is crazy. We heard you. If it happens we'll know that you called it." Carine rolled her eyes and walked to the other side of the bar to tend to a patron.

"I'm really bothered," Misty said, her face tight with discomfort. "This isn't cool, Juni."

"Sorry," she offered as Misty turned away. She looked to Jeb, who glanced back at her with concern. "I'm not crazy," she insisted.

"When is this all going to happen?"

"Next week."

"Alright then. I really hope you're wrong, but if not, I expect a superb explanation."

He sipped his beer and Juniper walked with her head down out the backdoor of the kitchen. She needed to be alone. She needed fresh air. She needed *someone* to believe her.

The weekend passed and she made her rounds disclosing her crazy secret. She told Brett and Teek, both of whom turned her information into a joke. They ragged on her throughout their entire Saturday shift. Roscoe was in charge of telling Clark, and Irene took the news with great concern. She feared Juniper wasn't handling the aftermath of Ethan's death well and begged her to see a grief therapist. Juniper agreed in order to calm her cousin down, but also made Irene promise that she'd move to Washington with her kids if her predictions about the next large-scale natural disaster came to fruition. Irene made the promise, not taking the commitment seriously, but Juniper rested easier knowing that the most important people in her life were in the loop. They all thought she was insane, but they'd come around once the truth unfolded. She just had to be patient.

Monday rolled around and she headed to the forest. The trees did not scrutinize her sanity as her friends did. All she could do for now was give her loved ones space until that shift occurred.

The forest was wet after a weekend of rain. Though there was a break of sunshine, the forecast predicted harsh storms beginning Tuesday and lasting through Friday. She packed appropriately and set up her water-ready campsite the moment she found a suitable spot near PJ Lake. The ride down was lovely, laced with huckleberry patches and meadow clumps. Deer grazed the hillside, acknowledging her arrival but not fleeing in fright. She was a welcomed friend here.

The space around PJ Lake was a cozy nook buried within the wide mountain range. Brushy avalanche chutes were surrounded by giant silver firs that cascaded down the basin and surrounded the fresh water. The lake was fluorescent turquoise in the spring sun and the wild flowers surrounding it were brightly blossomed. Purple asters and burnt orange columbine decorated the lakeshore, making the landscape look like an exquisite painting. Juniper hoped the forecast of rain was wrong because she wanted to enjoy this view all week.

She laid a blanket near the edge of the lake and made herself a picnic. She snacked on granola and apples while watching the water. The jumping trout were out and she tried to count how many she saw. Evening arrived and the air filled with the sound of croaking frogs. Their song joined the hooting owls and rumpus insects. It was a peculiar discord, but soothing all the same.

The rain arrived mid-slumber. She awoke in her tent engulfed by the clatter of the storm. The air was wet and chilly, so she put on an additional sweatshirt to stay warm. A quick look out the tent's ventilated pockets and the picturesque view of PJ Lake was gone. Everything was shrouded in gray and blurred by the fast falling rain. She cozied up in her sleeping bag and listened to the sound of the sky falling. She had brought a book to read, but did not find the urge to interrupt this moment. With eyes closed she let the noise consume her.

Come out.

A voice emerged from the onslaught of rain. Juniper's eyes opened.

Come outside.

It did not sound like the trees. The voice sounded closer, more human. She peered out the vented pockets of her tent, looking for the source.

You cannot see me, Juniper.

The voice had a thick Brazilian accent.

"Who are you?"

Dip your toes into the pond so I can hear you better.

"It's pouring out there."

My message is important.

Juniper was no longer taken aback by the strangeness of any given situation; she was over the shock. So she stripped down to her underwear, sparing her dry clothes, and entered the rain.

The rain hit her bare skin like icy spikes and she tried to ignore the sting. By the time she reached the pond she had adjusted to the prickly sensation. She sat on the wet, mossy lakeshore and placed her feet into the water. It was surprisingly warm.

My name is Marisabel Rios. I am the Champion of Fresh Water.

"You're a *person*?"

Yes.

"How are you speaking to me?" she asked, spitting out the rain that fell into her mouth as she spoke.

Through the lake and the rain. Just as you use the trees. Don't you speak to your Second this way?

"No. He lives in my town. We talk the normal way. You know, with our mouths."

Well, that's fortunate. My Second lives in Egypt and I have yet to meet him. How'd you get so lucky to have yours nearby?

"The trees let me pick him. They said they found me so late there wasn't enough time for them to select my Second."

Marisabel huffed in annoyance, but kept her thoughts to herself.

I hope you have chosen wisely. His role is crucial in the upcoming months.

"I did." Juniper's defenses were up. She wiped her wet hair from her eyes and sat up straight. "Why did you reach out to me?"

First, I wanted to let you know that our Champions of the mountains and air are safe, as are their Seconds. That cleanse will begin its unraveling tomorrow. I also wanted to check on your progress. Rumor has it you're struggling.

"I'm doing just fine. I didn't have months, or years, like the rest of you. The trees sprung this on me a few weeks ago."

I'm not here to attack or criticize you. I'm here to offer assistance. You and I will be teaming up after the last battle. I want to be friends.

"We will?"

So I am told.

"Do you have a large following?"

186

The current count is 250.

"How on Earth did you get so many people to believe you? Everyone I've told so far thinks I'm crazy."

Once I deemed them worthy, I showed them the power of the river. Submerged and holding hands I was able to speak to them through their minds. I showed them what I know, showed them what is coming. With the power of the Amazon coursing past us I transferred my feelings and beliefs to them. You need to do the same.

"How does that translate to trees? I can't submerge a person in a solid object. Am I supposed to get them to climb a tree? Find a tree with a large hole and crawl inside? They'll only think I'm crazier."

The forest is a wooded ocean. I imagine just being there, surrounded by miles of trees, is enough to communicate telepathically.

"Even if it is, I have no clue how to do that yet. I still can't control where and when I speak to the trees."

That, you'll never control. They will always hold that power.

"Will they teach me how to speak to other humans through them?"

Perhaps. It came naturally to me, but others needed lessons. I suppose water is easier to manipulate than rocks or fire or trees. Once you learn how to do it, you need only imagine what you want your connected source to know. If you feel it, they'll feel it too.

It was amazing how clearly she heard Marisabel through the torrential rain.

"So how are you talking to me? We aren't touching."

Yes we are. The rain has drenched you and your toes are in the lake; that water is connected to my soul. My voice echoes inside every little raindrop; it is carried through the lake and into your mind.

187

"You can talk to anyone in a body of fresh water?"

Theoretically. I can hold a full conversation with you because we are equals; both chosen Champions of nature. Others, I can only speak to in images or passing thoughts. They never realize I am there; they don't correlate their sudden feelings, inspirations, or imaginings to me. The only other humans I can have fragmented conversations with telepathically are those whose auras are already bound to the element of water, specifically fresh water. I send out generic messages every so often, hoping others might hear me. A large portion of my following arrived that way.

"How do I do that?"

Let your bond with the trees swell inside you, then say what you want them to know. The key is to believe wholeheartedly in your message, and to trust that it is being delivered.

Juniper shook her head in disbelief. Another seemingly impossible task. Many sarcastic comments popped to mind, but she held her tongue. She did not want to come off as cynical.

"I'll try."

You'll be fine. I'm here if you need me.

"How do I contact you?"

Fresh water and compelling conviction. Believe you'll reach me and you will.

Juniper felt her chest contract with anxiety. It was a lot of uncertainty, a lot of pressure.

Until next time, Juniper of the Trees.

A brief tingling sensation trickled down her skin from where the water's surface touched her calf muscle to the tips of her toes. She hadn't felt the presence arrive, but she certainly noticed its departure. She yanked her feet out of the water with haste and stood. The storm tore through the sky and cascaded down with ruthless strength. The rain created a distorted view of her surroundings and she found it hard to see. With her arms wrapped around herself, she inched her way back to the tent. She shivered beneath the second tarp covering the tent and could no longer ignore the cold water that soaked her body. In an attempt to avoid contaminating the inside of her tent with this awful chill, she unzipped the door wide enough for her arm to fit, grabbed a towel she left near the entrance, and wrapped herself in its dry fabric. The wind was harsh, so she quickly wiped as much water off her skin as possible and dove inside.

After swathing herself in dry clothes and blankets she took a moment to breathe. She replayed the conversation with Marisabel in her head repeatedly, hoping to make better sense of it. It felt ridiculous every time. The voices, the connections, the power; it still felt bizarre. It was so much simpler when her bond with the trees remained undefined. Back when her connection to the forest was uncomplicated and effortless. The trees used to keep her company, but now they only caused her grief. She hoped that when the truth revealed itself to her friends their faith would be restored. Maybe then they'd realize she was trying to protect them. All she could do in the meantime was stay confident. When the time came, they'd need her, and if she believed she could save them, so would they.

Chapter 18

Trapped in a tent for three days was not how Juniper liked to enjoy nature. Come Thursday, she was ready to head home. The rain dwindled to a drizzle and she was able to pack up her belongings without getting drenched. Before leaving, she decided to try to send a message out to other like-minded people across the globe. She placed her hand on the nearest silver fir, closed her eyes, and let her bond with the trees consume her. Once she felt the connection coursing through every inch of her body, she spoke.

"My name is Juniper Tiernan. I live in Port Angeles, Washington. If you can hear me, please listen. I am real. My voice is not a dream or hallucination. I know this seems crazy, but I promise it's not. You are not losing your mind, you've been chosen. If you can hear me, you've been given a second chance. The world as we know it is about to end and you need to abandon your homes and head toward Washington State. If you join me in Olympic National Park, you'll be safe. I can help you survive." She felt silly talking to no one, but carried on. "I hope this works. I hope you can hear me. I don't want to face the end alone."

She opened her eyes to the sight of the endless forest. Her message felt empty. She could not feel anyone on the other side. The attempt was futile.

She pushed the failure to the back of her thoughts and mounted her bike. She refused to give up; she'd save Roscoe and the others, even if they fought her along the way.

The slope up to the main trail was muddy and she had to be careful not to slip down the steep mountainside. She drove slow and moved along the path with deliberate care, exhausted by the time she reached the main trail.

Hurricane Ridge was vacant as she sped toward Lake Dawn Road. Her house was in sight when the first sneeze arrived. She parked her bike and ran into her dry sanctuary. The house was chilly so she cranked up the heat before stripping off her wet outfit and replacing it with dry clothes. The fleece lining of her sweatpants warmed her body as she curled into a ball beneath the comforter on her couch. She watched the rain through the French doors leading to her backyard and was grateful to be inside. It fell loudly on her roof, making her tired. It was only 5 p.m., but she fell asleep and slept through till Friday. She awoke when the sound of loud banging came from the front door. She got up with the blanket still wrapped around her body to find Roscoe standing on her porch.

"You're soaking wet," she said after letting him in.

"Yeah, well, it's raining."

She grabbed him a towel and he dried off the best he could.

"Are you okay?" she asked.

"I can't stop dreaming about you, and while I'm awake, my thoughts spin around images of you. Sometimes, I swear I hear you speak to me. There is something between us that I can't deny. I've been trying to put space between us, but I can't, and I'm realizing that I really don't want to. I thought distancing myself from you would protect me from the downfall of all this craziness, that maybe if I let you go I wouldn't end up with a broken heart, but I now see how foolish that is. I am drawn to you, I am meant to be with you. I cannot fight it anymore."

She blushed despite the hurt she felt that he tried so hard to leave her. Even though he made an attempt to abandon her, he didn't, and there was great reassurance in his return. He loved her, flaws and all.

"I'm not staying long," he continued, "but you should know there was a devastating avalanche in Mongolia. Another in Russia shortly after. Not only is the snow burying everything at the bottom of the mountains, but these avalanches are carrying an arctic chill that is freezing everything within a 50-mile radius of the run out zone. Thousands of people have died."

"It's begun."

"I've been away from the news for a few hours but I imagine there have been more."

"I assume so. They said every mountain range in Europe and Asia would suffer this fate. Once the towns around the mountains were buried, the toxic fog would roll through to take out everyone else. Have we received any response emails?"

"No. No one has written back."

"I figured."

"I'm on your side. I'm sorry it took me so long, but I needed the time. I care about you, I know you're a good person and that you didn't wish this on the world. I'm not okay with any of this, but we need to survive and save as many people as we can."

Juniper flung her arms around his neck. "Thank you," she whispered with great relief.

"Sorry I made this harder on you."

"It's okay."

He kissed the side of her head and she let go.

"Have you had any success convincing the others?" he asked.

"Not much. I was hoping to run into the Wolfe boys, but I haven't seen them in a while. I have a feeling they'll believe me."

"What about your work friends?"

"No. I told them about the avalanches and they all thought I was demented. Not sure how they'll react tonight when they see me. I think they are going to be scared."

"Probably, but they'll come around, even if it's at the last second. Maybe that's what we need to start planning for, how to save everyone in the last moments. You have to find out how they are attacking our area."

"I'll try. We have time, though. They are phasing us out last and they still have a lot of land left to cover."

"It's nature we are talking about. One swift move and millions are dead. We probably have less time than you realize."

"I'll do my best to get some intel."

"Okay, Clark is going to be pissed if I stay too long. There were campers out in this rain and we've spent the last four days keeping an eye on them."

"You mean I'm not the only crazy person who hides out in the forest during a rainstorm?"

They both laughed.

"They're Floridians," Roscoe replied, "and they said that they are used to the rain. When I suggested they vacate the forest, they refused." He shrugged. "Hopefully they got a hike in during the drizzle this morning."

"That's devotion," she said. "Bet they're the type of people we're meant to save."

"I hadn't thought of it like that."

"Offer them a trip back to the park. Once I get a date from the trees, you can send them air miles."

"Not a bad idea. Alright, let me go." He pulled her in for a loving kiss. His energy was back to normal and he embraced her like he had a few weeks ago, like she was the woman he'd grown to love before all this chaos unraveled.

He left and she got ready for work. Everything was falling into place. The doom she felt hours ago was washed away and replaced with uncontrollable hope. Roscoe was finally willing to work as her partner for the greater good. With him, the task felt less daunting. With Roscoe on her side, she no longer felt alone.

Chapter 19

Base Camp of Mt. Everest, Nepal, Asia

The snow continued for two weeks. The blizzard fell relentlessly over the entirety of Europe and Asia, which made the newly blossomed spring landscape vanish and return to the harsh winter that just passed. The temperature was frigid and everything was iced over; the air and water spirits were working hard to ensure the mountain purge succeeded.

At 17,600 feet, Aria Cecildóttir, Champion of the Air, sat with Monte Bram, Sahira Dayal's Second, in their large group tent. The trek up was foreboding and they lost many along the way, but those who survived now rested. Everyone was still adjusting to the altitude change and learning to breathe minimal amounts of oxygen. Aria had a few years to study the climb up Mount Everest and even had the chance to attempt it once. She only made it to Camp III at 21,300 feet, but learned valuable information along the way. She was confident she'd succeed in helping those around her survive.

The air spirits told her they'd need to climb higher to outlast and evolve properly, so she had plans to acclimatize her following once the purge in their region was complete. For now, they were at a safe altitude.

Everyone with her now was recruited by Monte, except Aria's family. Her mother, father, and twin brothers followed her from Iceland to Nepal, while the rest of her followers climbed Mont Rose in Switzerland to wait out the attack with Sahira. Aria wished she could have stayed there too, but it was essential for Monte to have a Champion with him. They'd be lost in the aftermath without one of nature's correspondents.

They had numerous tents set up along the Base Camp of Mount Everest. No one spoke English except Monte, so she felt out of place and was grateful that her immediate family followed her there, otherwise she'd have been totally isolated.

"Have you talked to Sahira?" Monte asked as he approached her and her family, who sat huddled around a weak bonfire. He wore a Jinnah cap and a parka lined with Tibetan wolf fur. "She isn't answering my thoughts."

"I spoke with her yesterday. The avalanches were supposed to start this morning."

"Why hasn't our mountain been affected yet?"

"I'm not sure. This isn't my element. The air spirits aren't in charge of this attack."

"Call out to her. I need to know that she's okay."

"Maybe their mountain has avalanched. Maybe she is busy taking care of the people there. She will reach out to us when it's time. You need to worry about protecting us. There are a lot of people counting on you."

"Yes, but I cannot help anyone if Sahira doesn't tell me how. The mountains won't speak to me, they only talk to her."

"Did she tell you what to do when our avalanche begins?" Aria asked with a shiver. She was used to snow, just not at this elevation or in such quantity.

"Just to be at the top of the mountain when it happens. I'm not sure if there's more I need to know."

"Sahira won't leave us stranded."

The earth shook the moment she finished her thought. A rumble came from the center of the mountain as a rush of cold air whipped their faces. They buried their exposed skin beneath the clothing they wore, waiting for it to pass. It tore past them for five minutes before dwindling.

"Was that it?" Aria asked, shaken but ready for action.

"An earthquake," Monte said with a look of terror. "It has begun."

He hurried to the edge of the mountain and peered over. Nothing except powdered snow was visible. Aria stood beside him and observed the aftereffects. She couldn't hear the screams, but she felt them. Thousands of lives in the villages along the base of the mountain were being crushed. This attack would wreak havoc for miles beyond the base; the icy blast of the avalanche wind and continued subzero temperatures would freeze all life in the surrounding area. It hurt her heart that so many lives would be lost. She left Monte at the edge and returned to be with her family.

"Was that the avalanche?" her mother Reyna asked.

"Yes. It's a snowy hell down there."

"Such a shame we could not save more," her father Cecil commented. Her twin brothers, Tístran and Ölvir, sat huddled under a blanket made of Bengal fox fur. They shook their heads in unison, knocking the snow from their bright white hair. They were disappointed by all of this and blamed Aria for not doing more to save others. They had begged her to take her information to the media, to the authorities, anyone with a voice who could make a difference, but she refused. The air told her not to; the spirits promised to save those deemed worthy.

Though she told her brothers this, they did not care. They did not believe it possible. She hoped to prove them wrong when this was all over, she hoped to find a massive following at the bottom of the mountain that had survived. She had total faith in the air, but still found it hard to envision this occurring. It was hard to imagine an avalanche, arctic freeze, and toxic smog avoiding a few individuals among millions, still she hoped. She needed her brothers to forgive her. They were her heart, her soul, her strength; she needed them by her side in the upcoming days. Having her family nearby was the only way she'd be able to stay strong for everyone else. They were too important to lose—she needed their support.

The snow finally stopped and people began emerging from their tents. Cecil fanned their bonfire, enhancing the flames and attracting the foreign followers of Monte to sit near them. They could not understand one another, but they sat in understood silence. Everyone mourned the death below and wondered what was next in their journey.

Aria, can you hear me? Sahira's thick Indian accent resonated from the rock beneath her feet and into her head.

Yes.

Are you all okay? How is Monte? I meant to speak to both of you right before your avalanche but I got caught up over here. Ours happened only an hour before yours.

It's okay, we are all fine. Did it start with an earthquake?

Yes. The core spirits lent the mountains an assist to make sure the effects were absolute.

I see. How is everyone on your end?

Good. No injuries or casualties outside those lost on the journey up the mountain.

How's Erion?

He's good. Asks about you constantly. Your friends are giving him an earful. Sahira chuckled.

Great. Tell them to stick to my endearing traits.

I don't think there's a thing they could say that would change how he feels for you.

Aria smiled and breathed a little easier knowing she had extra support waiting for her in Switzerland.

I'm glad you're all okay. I'm going to touch base with Monte now. Sahira concluded, then broke their connection. Aria felt her presence tingle down her legs and into the mountain as it left.

The moment Sahira entered Monte's head, his posture perked and his face lit up. Aria watched him from afar and found herself wondering if Erion had the same reaction whenever she called out to him.

She was eager for the day she got to meet him. There was a small window of time when they could have crossed paths at Mont Rose, but the moment came and went. She had to head to Nepal to make it on time and he was still leading his crew overseas from Canada. She asked the air why he needed to leave the safety of his country that wouldn't be affected during this cleanse and they informed her that his journey to the tops of the mountains was critical to the evolution of all air disciples. They'd be stuck at the tops of these mountains for a while and if they did not progress in similar fashions they'd be disconnected and don conflicting anatomies by the time they met. This put Aria on edge. She wasn't sure how the structure of their anatomical makeup could change so quickly, but decided there were a lot of things that no longer made sense.

A few days passed and life at the top of Mount Everest got a little easier. The snow and wind stopped, which made their days more bearable. As for the people, Monte's followers were in decent spirits. Sad for the loss, but happy to be alive. Her parents were supportive of her, but Tístran and Ölvir had not dropped their stubborn objections. They were 25 years old, two years younger than her, and though they were adults there was still some maturing left for them to do. They would not hold their grudge forever. For her sake and theirs, they couldn't.

She spoke to Erion many times, which always made her feel better after arguments with the twins. He soothed her worries, eased her guilt, and reminded her that this wasn't her fault. She longed for the day his words would be accompanied by a loving embrace.

Five days after the avalanches and arctic freeze, the poisonous fog came. There was one spot at the edge of Everest Base Camp that lent sight to the world below, and Aria was standing there when she first caught sight of it. A light breeze circled her head, twirling her long white hair as it spun.

<<*Dear Aria,*>> the air spoke to her for the first time in days. <<*Your voice has reached other disciples of air wishing to be saved. They've embarked across the aftermath of the avalanches and wait for you at the bottom of the mountain in the village of Lukla. We've kept them safe thus far, but cannot protect them any longer. The fog is slow rolling; you have a week to retrieve them if you so desire.*>>

"It took us ten days to get to Base Camp from Lukla," she said aloud.

200

<<You are capable.>>

"At what altitude will we be safe?"

<<In this region, the fog won't rise higher than 17,000 feet.>>

"So we need to get them all the way back to Base Camp. Great. Send them this message: Climb toward Tengboche Monastery. It will save us time if they are already on their way."

<<Surely, dear Champion.>>

The swirling air vanished and the voices were gone.

She looked into the distance and saw the rolling gray fog approaching.

She told her brothers first. Their spirits bolstered and they helped her gather a rescue crew. Together they'd expand their little family of survivors. The quest to save others reinvigorated everyone at Everest Base Camp and strengthened their faith in Aria. They would follow her loyally to retrieve those who sought salvation, and beyond this journey their devotion to her lead would carry them through this time of reckoning.

Chapter 20

Juniper's week in the forest was exhausting. The trees rarely ceased their chattering and they overwhelmed her with information she wasn't ready to digest—the next attack would be devastating floods in South America and Africa. The Amazon and Nile Rivers would overflow, causing landslides and massive damage to all crops and livestock. All life would drown in those regions. Those who survived the flooding would face the onslaught of deadly mesocyclones and tornados from the convective storms raging overhead.

After the fresh water purge, the soil would attack, turning all of Canada, Russia, and the Middle East into death pits. The leftover rain would cover these regions, causing mudslides to wreak havoc in the woodlands and lethal quicksand traps would cover the deserts. There wouldn't be an inch of solid ground left to stand on.

The core was scheduled to attack after the soil. Those who happened to survive the flooding in Africa would be tried again when the volcanoes erupted. They would blast simultaneously and cause ruin across the land. Lava and volcanic ash would singe and snuff every living creature in the area. The moment Africa combusted, Juniper had to be on alert. The core would play a critical role in the strike of the trees. She wasn't sure how yet, they refused to tell her, but she had to have her following safe in the Hoh Rainforest of Olympic National Park by the time Kilimanjaro erupted.

Receiving this information was draining. Not only was it burdensome, but also terrifying. Mankind had never seen natural destruction of this magnitude.

When Juniper returned to work on Friday night, news stories about the earthquakes, avalanches, and arctic freeze killing millions in Asia and Europe was all anyone wanted to watch. Jeb sat at his regular seat watching the television in horror. He glanced over at Juniper every so often in awe, having trouble believing she predicted such a fate. When the crowd died down after the dinner rush, they got a moment to talk.

"How did you know?"

"Do you promise you'll believe me?"

"I'll try."

"The trees told me."

Jeb choked on his beer and looked up at her incredulously. "The trees?"

"Yes. It sounds crazy but it's true."

He took a moment, but did not question the validity of her statement.

"What's next?" he asked.

"The fresh water spirits are up to bat. South America and Africa are next in line."

"Fresh water spirits?"

"Yes, just like the tree spirits. Each element of nature has a voice. I was chosen to listen to the trees; I am their Champion. Other Champions were chosen from across the globe for the other elements. In the end, we are the only hope for the human race. Mankind cannot navigate the perils of nature's turbulence without our guide. Without us, humans will cease to exist."

"I won't lie, this feels absurd, but all evidence leads me to believe you, and I am not one to toy with fate. I'm on your side."

"You're the second addition to my crew. Everyone else seems to be freaked out by me now. Maybe you can help me recruit others. I want to save as many people as possible."

"You got it." He took a swig of his beer. "I'll get them on board."

"Thanks."

Juniper went back to work. Misty and Brett kept their distance. Roscoe showed up right before last call and escorted her home. He stayed with her and updated her on his progress. His father was on board, and though Clark didn't understand any of what he tried to explain, he said he trusted Roscoe enough to follow when the time came. This relieved Juniper immensely. Perhaps Roscoe was the key to recruiting others.

At work the following evening, Carine and Teek were just as distant as Misty and Brett had been. Juniper wondered if they'd been talking amongst themselves, doubting her as a group. It hurt her feelings, but she let them have their space. When the world came crumbling down she'd still be there for them, ready to lead them to safety.

She called Irene on Sunday to follow up on her promise. When Irene answered, her voice was lined with great trepidation.

"How did you know?"

"Something happened to me out here and I've become deeply connected to nature," Juniper explained. "I can hear the voices of the trees. I have been entrusted with the great responsibility to save the human race."

"Trees have voices? You mean to tell me they are alive?"

"No, they are not alive in the way you are thinking. They are alive with the ghosts of humans. I heard my father. He came to me through the trees and warned me of the grave danger we face. Nature does not desire the extinction of the human race, just a cleansing. Destruction of all structures and artifacts created by man and less bodies on earth trying to cause harm. They chose me to champion the cause. I am meant to be our savior."

"You sound delusional."

"How else would I have known about the natural disasters headed to Europe and Asia? Arctic freezes aren't typical there, so how on earth would I have guessed that? I also knew about the tsunamis in the South Pacific, though I only divulged that to Roscoe prior to them happening. I was still unsure at the time."

"Juni, I don't know how you guessed any of it, but it's terrifying and your claims are hard to believe."

"You promised you'd move here if I was right, and I was. I need you to follow through on that promise. Not only is it imperative to your survival, but to mine as well. I need you by my side. I need to be surrounded by people I trust when leading strangers through the new world."

"It's not just me you're uprooting, it's also my kids. You do realize how large a task that is, right?"

"I do, and I promise I'll help the moment you get here. I just need you to *get* here."

"You also realize I can't leave my mother or sister behind. If your claims are true, which I'll have to force myself to believe if I plan to make such a drastic decision based on your tales, then that means they are in danger, too. You may not feel much loyalty to them, but I do. They are my blood, I can't leave them behind."

"Then convince them to come. Just promise me you won't stay behind if they choose not to follow."

"Give me a week. I'll see what plans I can make."

"Please hurry. I don't think we have much time. Massive floods will strike South America and Africa next."

Irene sighed. "I'll do my best."

Juniper sunk into her couch and closed her eyes. Her success felt hinged on the fate of reluctant, half-hearted promises. When Monday morning came, she was ready for a large dose of the forest.

Roscoe, are you ready? Juniper called out, practicing their newly realized telepathic connection. It took a few minutes before he answered.

This is wild.

Meet me at the end of Hurricane Ridge Road.

Roscoe obliged, and after finding her at their meeting place, Juniper led the way through the forest. He was ready to accept the trees, ready to embrace the destiny placed upon him. Juniper warned him he might not hear the voices again, but he remained hopeful. The last time the trees reached into his mind he was spooked. The images filled him with an uneasy sensation; one of dread and horror. Now, he hoped to see what Juniper saw: optimism, survival, hope. Recent facts led him to believe her claims about their intentions were true; the trees were benevolent, they wanted humans to survive.

The duo traveled far and set up camp near Appleton Pass, which was a few miles from the edge of Hoh Rainforest. Juniper was ready to scout a safe location to bring everyone to once the end arrived, and she needed to make sure the path there was easy to navigate. So they spent the week exploring and clearing the trail.

The forest remained silent until Wednesday night.

<<*The fog is rolling through Asia. It lingers as it spreads. It will reach Ireland by Sunday and the floods will begin the moment it touches Tearaght Island.*>>

"How long will the floods last?" Juniper asked.

Roscoe dropped his hedge clippers and looked in her direction.

"Are they talking to you now?" he inquired.

"Shh."

<<*Ten days. Then the water relocates to help the soil reclaim its territory.*>>

"How long before it moves from soil to core?"

<<*Five days. The soil spirits will be quick in turning their land into giant sinkholes.*>>

"And how long until Kilimanjaro erupts?"

<<*Six days from the completion of the soil's chasms.*>>

"So I have 21 days until it's our turn."

<<*Correct. We see your struggle, but remain steady in our faith.*>>

One voice rose above the rest. <<*You will succeed, Little Blossom.*>>

"Dad?" Tears welled in her eyes. "Please tell me it's you."

<<*I have little memory of my human life, but my link to you is ardent. I feel as you feel, I sense your trials, triumphs, and*

trepidations. I have no doubt our bond was significant in my former life.>>

"Is Mom with you?"

<<The memory is hazy, but I recall her choosing the ocean. Every so often I catch a breeze of salty air and imagine a face. Perhaps that's her.>>

"I wonder if she receives subtle moments like that from you."

<<If so, it is unintentional. We do not retain memories from our human lives, but the relationships formed never fade. Even if we do not remember them, the connection lives on.>>

"It makes me really happy to hear that."

<<Stay strong, Little Blossom. You are a light for those who survive the forthcoming dark.>>

"I will, Dad. I promise."

His voice vanished, as did the melodious hum that accompanied him when he spoke, and the forest was quiet again.

"Your dad?" Roscoe asked after a few seconds of silence.

She nodded solemnly.

"I didn't hear them," he expressed.

"I warned you that you wouldn't. They only talk to the Champions. The reason they spoke to you the other day was to convince you to accept your role as my Second. Now that you have, they will leave you be."

"But I want to talk to them."

"It doesn't work that way. The only person you can speak to telepathically is me."

Roscoe's shoulders slumped and he returned to clipping overgrown branches along the trail. He did not argue any further as he understood there was nothing Juniper could do to change this.

"So, three weeks?" Roscoe asked, changing the topic.

"Yeah. The moment Kilimanjaro erupts, it's our turn."

"Did they say *how* it will happen?"

"No, just that I need to be in the Hoh Rainforest with whoever I'm saving by then."

"And what happens if we aren't?"

"I'm not sure."

The grim uncertainty lingered between them as they carried on clearing the path. There was no telling the outcome if they failed, but they both suspected it would be devastating to the fate of the human race. Not only those she planned to save locally, but the other Champions working hard to procure the survival of mankind in their own regions. Juniper was a pivotal piece in nature's puzzle and she could not fail. A direct connection to the trees, for all parties involved, was crucial.

Chapter 21

Mont Rose, Swiss Alps, Europe

The avalanches ended and the arctic freeze had passed. All that remained of this attack was the toxic fog. Sahira Dayal, Champion of the Mountains, kept everyone safe at Dufourspitze summit atop Mont Rose. It was uneven, rocky terrain without large sections of flat land to set up a comfortable camp, but they made the best of the situation. Any lower and they'd be in range of the toxic fog.

Sahira was not connected to the air and did not know when the fog would roll through, but she regulated the mountain's edge with strict patrol. Hours were spent scanning the horizon, looking for signs of the next attack. She attempted to check in with Aria, but hadn't heard from her since she went down Mount Everest with a rescue crew to retrieve survivors.

Erion bugged her daily to see if she received word from Aria, but a week had passed since the start of the rescue mission and neither had heard from her since. It worried Sahira, but she did not relay her concerns to Erion. He was too anxious. Any doubt from her would compound his fear and she needed him to remain strong. He was her partner until the completion of the cleanse. They had to work together until she and Aria were able to switch locations to be with their proper Second. He was tolerable when he wasn't twisted up in his own anxieties regarding Aria, so Sahira did her best to keep him calm.

"The mountains said they're still climbing. They cannot speak to her, but they feel her on their snowy hillsides. She's en route."

Erion's stature remained tense. "I hope she reaches out to one of us soon. I can't do this without her."

"She will. Have faith." Sahira gripped his shoulder and smiled, then walked over to the edge of the mountain.

There was still no sign of the fog and she was growing impatient. She desperately wanted to move on with the process—she was ready to go home, into the mountains of Nepal where she could look down on her childhood home. Badrinath, India was not far from Mount Everest and she was eager to reclaim the life she had before running away to America. She wanted to see her sisters again—she hadn't seen them since leaving India, and while she had convinced them to join Aria in the climb up Everest, her parents had refused. The guilt weighed heavy on her.

<<*Patience, dear Champion.*>> The mountain's voice shook beneath her feet and reverberated up her body.

"When will we be free to leave? I want to see my sisters."

<<*They are safe with Aria.*>>

"I am growing anxious."

<<*You have a long wait ahead of you. You cannot leave this spot until all of nature's battles are won.*>>

"When will that be?"

<<*After the trees strike, there will be one final attack from the core, then prolonged darkness. You must wait here until those shadows fade.*>>

211

"I need to speak to Aria. I need to know that she and Monte are okay. Neither of them have talked to me since they went on that rescue expedition."

<<*You need to worry about the people under your care. Your stay here will be long and you must ensure food, water, and shelter for those you claim as your chosen. You brought them here successfully, but your crusade for survival isn't over. As Champion, they are your responsibility until the end of time. It is your duty to keep them safe, alive, and in accordance with the will of Gaia.*>>

"I know, I just wish we could spread out. I've got all of Aria's followers in addition to most of mine and it's cramped. Our space is littered with tents and bonfires; people can barely walk around without bumping into shelters and each other. I'm shocked no one has accidentally fallen off the mountain yet."

<<*Make it work.*>>

The slight vibration shaking her core vanished along with the voice. Sahira was alone in her leadership once again.

She sat at the edge with her legs dangling over the side. The horizon was calm and steady; no sign of incoming doom. She remained in this spot for hours, anticipating the arrival of the smog, but it never came.

As night fell, she returned to the tent and slumbered peacefully in solitude. The frantic chattering at sunrise woke her.

Sahira left her tent, hurried to the mountain's edge, and peered into the distance. The cause of worry was easily found: a thick line of gray blocked the sunrise and grew larger with each second that passed. By early morning, the sun rose past the smog and illuminated it from above. Swirls of green and purple chemicals entwined throughout the gray, making the sight appear more lethal than imagined. Sahira shivered as death crept closer. Though it grew clearer it never rose higher than 14,000 feet. They were safe where they hid atop the mountain.

The toxic fog encircled the base of Mont Rose within five minutes, leaving the view over every edge blocked by chemical-ridden gray. They could see the fog snake onward to the west, but its tail remained as the head carried on. It merely stretched, letting the back end linger while the front consumed more. The ground below was still. No noise, no movement. The silence of its sudden vacancy roared louder than the avalanches.

Sahira could not bear to watch. The world below was officially lifeless and she grieved in silence.

Her followers watched in muted horror as the fog blanketed the western horizon. Sahira retreated to her tent to be alone, too aware of what came next. The smog would reach Ireland by nightfall and trigger the next catastrophic natural disaster to unfold. It was hard to witness such travesty knowing the terror was far from over.

Chapter 22

Amazon River, Brazil, South America

The water was rising.

Marisabel Rios, Champion of Fresh Water, had moved her following a safe distance from the Amazon River, but she could still see its surge in the distance.

There was no place left to go.

She'd been pleading for direction from the water for days, but the spirits remained silent. The concept of desertion threatened her every waking moment, and the longer they stayed quiet, the greater her fear grew.

Per their guidance, she relocated her people from Manaus, her hometown, to Montes Claros, Brazil, but the water kept rising. Everyone was tired and she wasn't sure how much further she could convince them to follow.

When the landslides began, their temporary shelter in Montes Claros was briskly swept away. She lost five people and these deaths deeply affected the trust she'd earned from everyone else. With no choice but to run, they followed Marisabel.

When they finally escaped the current of muddy water dragging people to their demise, she found a stable spot of land to address those who survived.

"I'm so sorry, but we have to head south again," she shouted over the loud rainstorm that pelted the crowd surrounding her. Her face was wet and her hair was covered in mud. Everyone stood around her, shivering in drenched clothes and wiping grime from their eyes and mouths.

"How much further must we travel?" an elderly woman cried out.

"The weather has only gotten worse. We will perish if we don't escape the radius of this storm," a man added.

"You promised us refuge, you promised us life," exclaimed a mother cradling her baby.

"All you've done is lead us further into harm's way," the woman's angry husband seethed.

The group erupted with frustration and Marisabel tried to swallow the defeat she felt. Though she hadn't failed them yet, everyone around her thought she had; her once devout following was losing faith. They no longer trusted her command and were questioning her leadership capabilities. The shift was crushing.

As they carried on with their complaints, Marisabel looked to the sky in hopes she'd receive some direction. The rain stung as it landed on her face, but the temporary sores were soothed as the water rolled off her cheeks and into her ears.

<<*It's time you lead them to Uruguay. The shores of Punta del Diablo will act as a safe haven until your next quest.*>>

The water spirits had not abandoned her. A smile crept on her face as she absorbed their instruction. They said no more, but that brief moment of acknowledgment was all she needed to restore her resolve.

"Punta del Diablo, Uruguay," she shouted over the bickering amongst her people.

"Uruguay?" the elderly woman objected. "You want us to *walk* to Uruguay in this rainstorm?"

"This rain is slow moving. If we go now, we can get ahead of the storm and the majority of the trek won't be so bad."

"That's almost 3,000 kilometers away!"

"We will move slow and rest. This storm is land-based; walking along the shore will be our safest route. The ocean presents us no harm."

"How long will this take? Won't it be safer to find shelter here and wait out the rain?" a young man asked.

"This is not an average rainstorm. It has been sent with the intent to kill all human life it touches." Marisabel sighed in frustration. "I've already explained this to you: this storm is meant to wipe us out. We've been given the chance to survive. If we don't abide the water's instructions, we will die with everyone else. We can't wait this storm out, we must move onward."

Lightning struck and a mesocyclone began to form. The entire group hushed in fear and Marisabel maintained an expression of eager hope.

The young man shook his head. "Let's go."

With his head down he walked south toward the Brazilian shore of Rio de Janeiro. His family and a few others followed him. Marisabel looked at those who stubbornly remained.

"Will you join us?"

There was a pause before the elderly woman spoke. "Do we have any other choice?"

"I promise I will not lead you astray."

Before anyone else could add their own doubts, a secondary cyclone dropped to earth a few meters from where they stood. The winds tore at the group, knocking many off their feet. A man standing behind her was snatched by the winds and dragged into the cyclone. A rush of pure terror seized Marisabel's heart and the only thing pushing her forward was her will to survive. Fueled by adrenaline, she grabbed a small child and ran. The child cried in her arms, but she kept her cradled and safe in her embrace. The parents followed close behind and Marisabel prayed that others did the same.

The fierce winds ripped at them as they sprinted away from the cyclone, which seemed to be choosing its victims selectively. On any other day, in any other storm, they'd all have died, but somehow they were outrunning a twister. Marisabel thanked the water spirits repeatedly in her head; they were the only reason she and those who followed her survived this heroic dash. It only took a few minutes to escape the cyclone's reach, and once they were in the clear she examined the damage.

The entire town was in ruins. What was once a quaint road lined with shops, restaurants, and a family-friendly street market was now a muddy wreck. There wasn't a single building left standing, or one voice left to cry out through the storm. All those who had not followed Marisabel were lost.

Marisabel said nothing and led those who remained toward the group that had already embarked south. When the two groups reunited, tales of their survival were shared. The first group witnessed the ordeal from afar and the second filled in the gaps of what the others had not seen. Marisabel had saved them; she had guided them along the perfect path to avoid the wrath of the cyclone. No one truly understood how she managed, or what force she had on her side that made them so lucky, but they all suspected it was a bond to an entity much greater than their comprehension. They witnessed firsthand how the cyclone strategically avoided anyone trailing Marisabel and how their loyalty to her saved them from certain death. Their faith in her was restored. They continued following her through the rain, no longer questioning her choices.

The journey was arduous and no one spoke. After a few days of walking they breeched the edge of the storm and found dry land. Though the new climate was a relief, they did not stop moving. The rainclouds were still in sight, growing closer every time they stopped to take a break, and it became clear that they would not escape the storm until they reached Uruguay.

Once their journey became more stable, Marisabel reached out to her Second.

Zaire, can you hear me? she asked in thought. He was located in Egypt, right along the Nile River, and was also tasked to bring his following south. She hadn't heard from him in days and prayed his quest hadn't been as devastating as hers. She waited, but received no response.

Zaire Nzile, this is Marisabel Rios. Feel me calling you, please. I need to know that you're okay.

Another moment passed before Zaire responded, his thoughts reflecting the exasperation he currently felt.

Marisabel, I have missed you. She could feel the pain in his mind's voice.

And I you. Are you okay? How are you holding up?

We are safe underground. We made it to Eshe three days ago,
barely, and have been avoiding the storms since. I lost over a dozen
people in Sudan. A cyclone sprung up unexpectedly and ripped them
from us. It was traumatizing. We ran. I've never sprinted so far in my
life. It was so surreal, my memory of it feels fake. I lost another half-
dozen people to landslides in Ethiopia. It's been terrible.

Is it better beneath the earth with Eshe?

Yes. We are safe from the worst of the storm down here.

I am so glad to hear that. We've had similar casualties, but we
finally made our way outside the radius of the storm. We are headed
toward Rio de Janeiro and once we reach the ocean we'll follow the
shoreline until we reach Punta del Diablo, Uruguay.

I suppose that's where you'll be leaving for Antarctica from?

Yes. I haven't told anyone here about that part of the journey yet.
Their faith in me has been wavering. I have them onboard currently
and I don't want to do anything to mess that up.

They'll follow. Don't worry.

Let me know when you reach Cape Town, and I will touch base
with Coral to see if it's safe for you to begin your journey. I suspect
you'll get there faster than we'll get to Uruguay, and it's imperative
you start the next phase of the journey. Africa will implode the
moment the core strikes and you can't be there, waiting on me.

Let's deal with that when it happens. We still have another week or
two of walking through these volcanic caves before we reach South
Africa. Eshe is Champion of the Core, she will have a good grasp on the
timeframe and if we will be in danger.

So I take it her following is safe from the fresh water attack too?

Yes, but they remained in a deep, underground cave in Djibouti. Eshe is leading us on her own. She will return to her following once we are safe in Cape Town.

Okay, be careful. I eagerly await the day we are united in Antarctica.

The anticipation of that moment keeps me going, Zaire responded. She could feel his smile from across the ocean.

Until then, Marisabel responded before she severed the connection. She returned her attention to the people surrounding her, who were in much better moods now than they were a few days ago. The feeling that encased their journey was perseverance, and its overwhelming presence swallowed every doubt she had regarding their ultimate survival.

Chapter 23

Rub' al Khali Desert, Saudi Arabia

Sofyla Yurchenko, Champion of Soil, was caught in the crossfire of nature's battles ever since the mountains struck. She was warned that Oleshky, Ukraine, her hometown, was in direct line of the arctic freeze and toxic fog, so she and her following fled weeks ago. They'd been traveling non-stop since the earth told her the attack was coming and were now taking careful routes to get to their destination in Saudi Arabia. As they fled Ukraine, they heard the cracking of the mountains all around them. The noise was that of nightmares; it sounded like the planet was splitting in half.

Their trip through the southwest peninsula of Russia was fast as they were all desperate to escape the aftermath of the avalanches. Collectively, they mustered the energy to travel fueled only by their primal instincts to survive. They slowed their pace along the coast of Georgia and through the massifs and plains of Eastern Anatolia. While those lands were tough to navigate, Sofyla was most concerned about their journey through Syria and Jordan.

The toxic fog was still spreading through Europe by the time they reached the Syrian border, and her time to reach her Second in Saudi Arabia so they could continue their journey together was running out. They needed to reach Eshe in the caves of Africa, and though the soil spirits kept warning her to hurry, she knew that getting detained by Syrian rebels was a far worse fate than running late.

Sofyla and her following waited until nightfall before attempting their crusade over the border. By now, the lot were skilled hikers and well versed in keeping a low profile as they traveled. Though she trusted them not to make any dumb mistakes, the uncertainty of what they walked into had her concerned.

As soon as the last of their group stepped over the border, headlights emerged from the darkness accompanied by the sound of gunfire blasting into the night sky.

"Do we run?" her father asked as everyone around her huddled.

"No, that will split us up. Stay by me." Sofyla's confidence was strong and those following obeyed with little hesitation.

I hope you're with me, she thought to herself, praying for Gaia and the soil spirits to hear her.

The vehicles raced toward them, kicking up dust and making the night darker as they neared. And though the sounds of guns being fired had not ceased, they were yet to be aimed at Sofyla or her people.

The armed trucks formed a circle around the group of Ukrainian refugees and armed soldiers positioned themselves between each vehicle. There was no escaping now. The aggressors were dressed in black, wore bulletproof vests, and had scarves wrapped around their faces; Sofyla and her following were being detained by the Syrian Rebel Militia. Her heart pounded as she realized this would not be a negotiation. There would be minimal reasoning with these individuals.

A man jumped down from the largest truck and approached the group. He spoke in a language she did not understand, but she stepped forward anyway, hoping one of them might understand her broken English.

"We are from the Ukraine. We mean you no harm. We are just trying to cross into Jordan."

The leader of this battalion took a step closer and grabbed her face. He shined a flashlight into her eyes, which made her pupils shrink and her eyes pop with color. Her foreign appearance was not welcome.

The man spit on her and shoved her away. He approached Andriy, the largest male of her group, and placed a rifle beneath his chin. He coaxed his captive forward then spoke again in his native tongue.

Andriy shrugged, unsure how to respond to the questions he could not understand and the rebel leader blew his head off.

The women in Sofyla's group screamed and cursed in Ukrainian, and the children cried. Sofyla swallowed her fury, aware that if they fought back, they'd all die.

She stepped forward again.

"We are not here to fight. We just wish to have trouble-free passage through your land."

Furious that the small female addressed him again, the Syrian rebel lunged toward her and struck her with a solid punch. She stumbled backwards, doing everything in her power not to fall down, but she stumbled and the man laughed. She stood up straight and fumed, glaring at him through bloody vision. Her enraged energy radiated and the dusty soil began to levitate—she was channeling the element she championed.

The leader of the Syrian rebels lurched past her and snatched the three smallest children from the group. He lined them up on their knees and his men placed bags over their heads. The children sobbed and begged for their mothers, but their cries were ignored. With a gun pointed at the back of the youngest boy's head, the rebel leader turned to Sofyla and spoke in English.

"You are spies from Ukraine?"

"No."

"Lies!" He shoved the barrel of his rifle into the nape of the boy's neck.

"Let them go," Sofyla commanded, her voice low and menacing.

The man flashed a wicked smile before placing his finger back into the trigger guard.

"Bye, baby," he sneered, but as his finger pressed upon the trigger an enormous sand geyser exploded beneath him. The impact tore his body apart and launched his halved carcass into the night sky. The children were tossed forward from the blast, but remained unharmed.

"Retrieve the children," she whispered to those standing behind her and the mothers rushed forward to help their babies. As they did so, the other soldiers shook off the shock of their leader being blown to bits and regained their stance. One solider stepped forward to stop the mothers from removing the bags, but before he got too close, another sand geyser erupted and blasted the man sky high. His body landed in pieces.

"Anyone else?" Sofyla addressed the men hiding in the dark behind the headlights of their trucks. She was answered with silence. "Let us pass and the rest of you live. If you follow us, I will turn the earth beneath you into quicksand and happily watch you choke."

The soldiers got into their trucks and sped away.

"How did you do that?" her mother asked in astonishment.

"I didn't. It was Gaia and the soil spirits. I told you they mean us no harm."

"Poor Andriy," a young girl said as she fell to her knees beside the lifeless man.

"We must leave him," Sofyla said, sounding harsh but rational. "There is no time to waste. We are already behind."

The group took a brief moment to pray over Andriy and place small mementos on his body, then they followed Sofyla's lead south. Once they were inside Syria, catching public transportation and paying farmers to transport them via horse and carriage to the Jordan border wasn't difficult. Crossing through Jordan was much easier and they bartered with locals for transportation to speed up their trip. They heard rumors of the flooding in South America and Africa as they journeyed, and Sofyla counted down the days until the soil attacked. She had ten days from the start of the floods until the rain moved over the regions commanded by soil. The Middle East was one of those regions and she needed to guide her following and Riad's to safety before then.

After a brief, but emotional unification with Riad in the city of Riyadh, they led their people through the Rub' al Khali desert. She spoke to Eshe often, who was hurrying to help the Fresh Water Second reach Cape Town, then traveling back to the Great Rift valley connecting Yemen to Djibouti so she could help Sofyla cross through tunnels under the Red Sea and into Africa.

The Great Rift Valley spanned the entirety of the Red Sea and connected Yemen's largest mountain, Jabal an Nabi Shu'ayb, to all of the mountains of the East African Rifts via underground caves. They'd travel beneath the Southern Ethiopian Highlands and the Aberdare Range in Kenya, then make the trip into Tanzania where they'd wait out the remainder of the purges with Eshe and her people. It was a guaranteed safe haven, so long as they were able to make it there in time.

They had three days to make it from Saudi Arabia to the base of Jabal an Nabi Shu'ayb in Yemen. The heat and rough terrain was slowing their large group down, and the prospect of making it there on time was not promising.

The days dwindled and they were still meandering through the Empty Quarter of the Rub 'al Khali desert in southern Saudi Arabia when the fresh water refocused its attack to assist the soil. It began with a cool breeze from the west and a heavy rainfall later that night. The precipitation didn't last long, just enough to wet the sand, then the rain carried north toward Russia and they were left to navigate through a hot, dry squall. The loose soil turned into a sandstorm by day three, which made it impossible to traverse. Sofyla was drained and so were her people. The trek was grueling and she no longer had any concept of the distance left to travel.

Eshe, she thought. Her mind was weak from exhaustion. *Eshe, can you hear me?*

Sofyla?

Yes.

Why aren't you here? Eshe asked. *Hasn't the soil begun its attacks?*

Yes, and we are caught in the middle. I see the mountain in the distance, but I don't think we will make it to Ma'rib.

There was a pause.

Reroute to Al Jawf, Eshe instructed. *The caves there are less refined and harder to maneuver through, but they are still connected to the rest of the rift. They aren't as far as Ma'rib and taking shelter there will get you out of harm's way faster.*

Al Jawf, Sofyla repeated, unsure how she was supposed to find this new location.

Head west. If you're as far away as you say you are, it will be the first mountain formation you see on the western horizon. I'll meet you there.

The connection broke and the feeling of sand pelting her eardrums returned. She pulled her shawl tighter over her face and marched forward. People fell all around them as they carried on, succumbing to the harsh fate the elements delivered. As they gave up, their faith in the cause disappeared and the soil no longer saw them as an ally. The moment their auras of loyalty vanished in defeat, the sandstorm covered them in a blanket of death. Sofyla stopped counting as body after body fell victim to doubt. Instead, she focused on rallying those who remained, promising them that the worst was almost over. But the closer they got to Yemen, the worse their conditions became.

A few kilometers south of Najran the quicksand began consuming people whole. One minute they were there, and in a blink they were swallowed. The horrifying sight deterred the following's collective faith. It was a ripple effect; for every one person lost to doubt, another three became crippled by fear and were ultimately lost as well. Sofyla prayed for relief to arrive soon.

When they crossed the border of Yemen, she saw the mountain range more clearly.

<<*Follow the cloudless path.*>>

A vortex of pristine vision appeared before them. It was circular and free of wind. The violent sandstorm raged at its invisible walls, but none of the fury entered their impenetrable tunnel. They were safe again.

Sofyla led them down the long path toward Al Jawf. They caught their breath as they walked through the tube of clean air and refuge. The manifestation of this vortex was a miracle.

It took another two days to reach Al Jawf and when the last of her people entered the safety beneath the mountain, the vortex vanished and the harsh sandstorm lashed at the edge of the cave.

Eshe was there waiting for them. She was tall and exquisite, towering over Sofyla's petite frame. She buried her fellow Champion in a tight embrace at first sight.

"I am so glad you are okay." Her Kenyan accent was thick.

"Thank you for your help. We'd have died without your quick thinking to reroute."

"We are sisters now. I will always protect you."

Sofyla smiled. "And I will always protect you."

"Let's keep moving," Eshe advised. "We have a long and treacherous journey ahead. These caves are poorly sculpted and they won't be easy to maneuver through."

The group followed Eshe through the intricate maze of rocky tunnels, no longer afraid of falling victim to the storm that raged overhead. Sofyla had her sister by her side, and together, they would save everyone.

Chapter 24

Caves of Kilimanjaro, Tanzania, Africa

Eshe led Sofyla and her following to the safe spot where her people hid. It was an expansive cave thirty meters below Mt. Kilimanjaro. As time passed, the heat in their cave grew exponentially. The volcano was about to burst and they could feel the steady rumble of its inferno. By the time Sofyla joined the group, the temperature was unbearable. At fifty degrees Celsius the soil acolytes found themselves in a new hell.

"I apologize for the extreme temperature," Eshe said to an incapacitated Sofyla. "My people have been down here for weeks, adjusting and adapting with the ever-growing heat. I imagine being thrust into this climate is traumatic."

"I can barely breathe."

"It won't get much hotter than this. We are far from the magma chamber so this is the worst it will get. The core made sure we'd be safe. You just need to be strong."

"We will persevere." Sofyla panted and wiped the sweat from her brow. "There's no giving up now."

Eshe's people tended to their visitors, trying to make their uncomfortable stay as bearable as possible. They traveled back and forth between their hiding spot and a fresh water spring they found twenty meters below their cave to deliver water to the weakened soil acolytes. When Sofyla asked why *they* couldn't travel deeper to where the air was cooler, Eshe explained that the people of the core had been easing their way to great depths over months and the pressure of the sudden altitude change might rupture an outsider's eardrum.

The only members of Eshe's family that followed her into the caves were her cousins. Her elderly father, the only surviving member of her immediate family, passed away prior to the purge. It saddened her, but she chose to believe that he had reunited with her mother and brothers, all of whom she missed terribly.

When the core began its strike, the entire cave shook. Volcanoes all over Africa erupted like fireworks, exploding one after another. Due to the supernatural nature of these events, each volcano blasted lava multiple times. With over a hundred active and dormant volcanoes coming to life simultaneously, no one in Africa was safe. The survivors huddled together in their hidden sanctuary and waited out the flare-up. Kilimanjaro still hadn't taken its turn, but once it did their hideout would cool down.

Days passed in the scorching heat of the subterranean cave. They could hear the world above exploding every few hours. They heard the earth's fury echo through the tunnels to where they hid, and felt each aftershock vibrate beneath their feet.

"It's been five days," Sofyla said to Eshe in private. "How much longer until this passes?"

"It will be over soon. On day six, Kilimanjaro erupts, sending this part of the world into prolonged darkness. We have an infinite water supply and enough food to last us a few months. The core prepared us well. We will be okay."

"What comes after this volcano blows?"

"The trees take back the land."

231

"Does the Tree Champion know? Has anyone talked to her?"

"Marisabel has. Her name is Juniper and she was not given as much time as the rest of us to prepare. It remains uncertain if she will prevail."

"Have the trees been helping her?"

"I don't know. I've heard she's the most connected to her element out of all seven Champions, but by being so bonded to nature, she lacks a connection to humanity. Let's pray she pulls through."

"We need her to succeed. It's vital we have direct communication to the foliage and vegetation of the earth when this is all over. I can only do so much with the soil if the growth of new flora is muted to our needs."

"Yes. Though we all play pivotal roles in our endurance as a race after Gaia has reclaimed the planet, she is critical to our ultimate survival."

"I hope she knows her time is up."

Eshe nodded. "Can you stay with the group? I need a minute to assess the damage above."

"Sure, but be careful."

Eshe was quick and agile, dodging random protrusions from the tunnel walls and ducking with stealth beneath the uneven ceiling heights. Her evolution into the core was expeditious; her body and abilities were modifying to fit this element's requirements on a daily basis. She was adapting faster than the other Champions and thriving in her harsh new home. It was critical, considering her element was the most vicious to acclimate with. It would kill her if she didn't become one with fire.

"Spirits of the core, can you hear me?" she asked aloud as she sprinted north toward Kenya.

<<*Yes, dear Champion.*>>

"Can you guide me safely to the top of Chyulu Hills?"

<<*Keep running. It will have expelled its final blast by the time you reach its caves.*>>

Eshe ran with inhuman speed, empowered by the magic of the core. She relished in the abilities her status as a chosen bestowed and wondered what evolutionary gifts she'd be granted in the future.

The route was direct and took only a few hours to complete. The core guided her ascent through the steaming vent, and with careful hand and foot placement, she climbed the jagged wall. The rock was hot to touch, but her skin was calloused enough to endure such heat. She scaled with speed and climbed over the edge of the crater.

She crawled out of the volcano to a dark world smothered in ash. The only source of light was that of the lava erupting from volcanoes in the distance and the magma that still flowed and burnt bright as it slowly turned into indigenous rock. The earth rumbled beneath her and another small surge of lava burst through a secondary cone on the side of Chyulu Hill. The molten rock ruptured through freshly solidified lava and smoldered as it poured over the black rock.

Eshe's heart pounded with adrenaline at the sight. If she had arrived a few minutes later, she'd have been in the main vent, and likely in the path of that residual lava flow. The notion of escaping such danger was exhilarating.

Magma bubbled over the earth below and the buildings that weren't covered in ash were ignited with flames. For a moment she thought of those buried beneath the debris, burning beneath the cinders and choking on ash. Her face contracted with pain as she imagined the horror of such a death. Then she remembered the greater picture. This would stop all the warring in Africa and would bring peace to the world. She and her loved ones could live without fear of violence and terrorism. The age of humans attacking humans could be over if they chose to take this opportunity and craft a better society. There was no need for fighting or lethal squabbling over power, greed, and money. Those issues need not exist if they built their world on a pure foundation, one devoid of desires fueled by ego. Though many innocents died in the crossfire, it was for the greater good. Eshe believed they were on the brink of a better life.

She said a prayer for the fallen and descended back into the volcano. She made the trip in half the time and arrived to a cave of sleeping soil and core acolytes. Eshe found a spot at the edge of the group and nuzzled into the group cuddle.

Tomorrow would be a beast to bear. The explosion of Kilimanjaro would test the backbone of their resolve. It would be loud, uncomfortable, and terrifying, but Eshe had faith in the resilience of those she chose to carry through these wicked times.

Chapter 25

The world was collapsing all around them and Juniper's time was running out. Kilimanjaro would erupt soon and she wasn't sure who would follow her to safety in the woods.

At work, the bar patrons were mystified by the unnatural occurrences across the globe. Many talked about global warming and how our actions caused these catastrophes. Others suggested this was God's doing and he was punishing the human race for its neglectful and immoral behavior. Neither guess was entirely wrong; they just didn't have all the facts. The few times Juniper tried to explain the truth, she lost them at the mention of Gaia. No one believed her when she said Mother Nature was a real entity. They simply laughed and went back to combing the details of their own suspicions.

Roscoe was having more luck than her. With his help, she managed to get her co-workers on board and he was able to convince a sizable group from town to be ready to flee when he gave them the word. She suspected his charisma, charm, and removed connection to the source had something to do with his success. Her spiel was off-putting and awkward since it came from *her*, the *chosen one*. No matter how she worded it, she always sounded deranged.

After all of Canada and Russia turned into muddy death pits and the Middle East transformed into a sinkhole of quicksand, Irene agreed to fly her family to Washington. She needed no further convincing. Her plane was scheduled to land later that day and Mallory and Zoe accompanied her. Juniper hadn't spoken to either of them since Ozzie's funeral, but Irene promised they'd be on their best behavior. They were scared, just like millions of other people in the United States. Everyone suspected it was only a matter of time before these supernatural disasters struck the states and the collective panic was tangible. Mallory and Zoe had their issues with Juniper, but they weren't foolish enough to pass over a chance to possibly survive whatever disaster was headed their way.

The volcanoes tore apart Africa. Five days of lava, fire, and ash, and the explosions continued. Juniper wasn't sure when Kilimanjaro would erupt, but she suspected it would happen soon. She was ready to run, and the few who agreed to follow were prepared for her signal. She'd been spending a lot of time in her backyard, hoping the trees throughout her yard would talk, but they remained quiet. She hadn't heard from them since their last conversation when they told her to be in the Hoh Rainforest by the time Kilimanjaro exploded.

She spoke to Marisabel a few times when she had her feet submerged in Lake Dawn. Marisabel was often out of breath and stressed, but the majority of her people survived the worst of the storms. They were at the shores of Punta del Diablo, Uruguay and boarding a catamaran that would take them to Antarctica when Juniper last heard from her. Their journey was harsh and demanding, which left Juniper feeling grateful that her safe spot was only a trek through the trails she had already cleared. Though the updates from her fellow Champion were terrifying, she also found a strange comfort in their conversations; it reminded her that she wasn't alone in this responsibility.

She didn't have nearly as many followers as Marisabel, but hoped that when the attacks began in Washington, more people would follow out of desperation. It wasn't ideal, these new followers would be unpredictable and possibly unworthy, but it was better than having no one to help rebuild in the aftermath.

After her day shift on Sunday, Juniper went home and enjoyed the sunset on her back porch. No word from the trees, no word from any of the Champions, so she kept her radio on a station that broadcasted 24-hour news.

Roscoe, where are you?

A moment passed before he answered.

I'll never get used to this. I'm with Clark at the office. Are you okay?

Yeah, I'm fine. I just have a feeling it's coming.

Have you heard from the trees?

No. It's been eerily silent on all frequencies. If it happens soon, I'm all alone and I won't be able to help anyone. I'm going to call Irene at the hotel and tell them to come over. Can you round up the others? Even if they won't follow me into the woods now, I want us all to be together so I can lead us there when it happens.

I'm all yours. Clark and I will grab my dad and then I'll give your co-workers a call.

Thank you.

Anything for you, Roscoe promised.

There was a moment of warmth shared telepathically before the connection broke. After all she'd been through, Juniper assumed she'd never love again, but Roscoe was a different breed of man; the caliber of his character was greater than any other person she'd ever met. He was her home.

She called Irene, who agreed to come over immediately, then returned to her back porch to wait. The warm, spring breeze played with her long, brown curls and the smell of fresh blossoms filled the air. It was hard to imagine this place would be in ruins soon.

She tried not to think about it.

Instead, she closed her eyes and imagined herself thriving in the new world. Maybe those who survived would be happier living in simplicity. Maybe they'd realize all the flashy technology, materialistic desires, and shallow narcissisms they'd grown accustomed to only hindered them from a truly fulfilling life. She hoped this devastating change brought out the best in humanity.

Find a flame.

Juniper's eyes shot open and she looked around. The voice was unfamiliar.

Light a candle, strike a match, anything. We need a solid connection.

Juniper went inside and found a Christmas candle at the back of her pantry. She placed it on her kitchen table and lit the wick.

This is Eshe Ahikiwe, Champion of the Core. The voice was much clearer now and her African accent echoed inside Juniper's mind beautifully. *Kilimanjaro will be erupting any minute now. Are you in the location the trees told you to be with your following?*

No, but they are on their way to me. I wasn't sure when the volcano would blow, and I couldn't get enough people to agree to wait it out in the forest. They're still wary.

Yes. I heard you had far less time to cultivate a following than the rest of us. Just promise you'll head to your safe spot the moment Gaia

switches to the trees, even if you're alone. We all need you to survive.
We cannot face the end without you.

I'll survive. You can count on me.

I'll check in with you again soon.

I've been operating in silence lately, so I really appreciate the heads up.

Of course. Take care, my sister.

Eshe was gone and the sudden notion of sisterhood consumed Juniper. She had grown close to Marisabel over the past two weeks, but Marisabel had been in dire straits every time they talked. Hearing Eshe refer to her as a sister put it all into perspective. They were linked. Gaia bonded all seven Champions; as Mother Nature, it made sense her chosen daughters saw themselves as family. This realization renewed Juniper's strength. She had every intention of succeeding, but suddenly, she understood she was surviving for so much more than she ever realized.

She blew out the candle, grabbed the radio from the back porch, and went to the front to wait for the others to arrive. The weatherman reported on the seismic activity forming beneath Kilimanjaro and Juniper's anxiety began to boil over. Her foot tapped against the chipped wood relentlessly, causing her whole leg to shake, and her fingernails were dug deep into her palms. When Irene pulled into her driveway with a carload of people, her clenched fists released to reveal bloody cuts beneath.

"You're here, finally," Juniper expressed, releasing a long-held breath.

"It's only been ten minutes since you called."

"It felt like ten years. We are running out of time."

Juniper hurried to the car and helped Irene unbuckle her kids. There were four little ones, plus her Aunt Mallory and cousin Zoe. She wasn't sure how they were going to get the babies through the woods, but they were small and there were enough adults to take turns carrying them.

Roscoe and Clark showed up next in separate off-roaders. Roscoe's father sat in the passenger seat next to him. Teek arrived in his enormous Hummer a few minutes later with Brett, Misty, and Carine. The large truck was too big for the trails and Juniper worried how everyone would get to Hoh.

"Jeb is on his way with his wife," Brett informed.

"Great. I guess this is everyone?" Juniper asked.

"No, I have a few friends coming. Three guys I graduated college with and their spouses. Also my co-worker Cindy and her husband Carl," Roscoe added. "Those Floridians I offered the free return trip to never came."

"My sister and mom should be here soon," Carine chimed in.

"Yeah, I think all of our immediate families are on their way," Misty said on behalf of herself, Brett, and Teek.

"I'm solo," Clark said.

"No, no. You've got me." Juniper smiled at him, knowing he was thinking of his late wife in this moment.

He winked at her in appreciation.

Her heart filled with hope as the outlook of her success appeared less grim. More people were coming; she wouldn't fail.

Jeb and company arrived in two Jeep Wranglers, followed by the families of Misty, Carine, Brett, and Teek. They came in sedans, which would not be able to traverse the woods.

Roscoe's buddies were on their way with off-roading vehicles. He called to ask if they could tow a few more on their trailer, but they had already left.

"Juni," Roscoe began. "We aren't going to have enough vehicles to get everyone to Hoh. And it would take too long to walk."

Juniper looked into her backyard at the Jeep she never used—it still had its trailer attached.

"If we use my car can we get more?"

"My friend has a whole garage of toys we can use."

"Let's go."

Roscoe ran to the Jeep and got it running. Juniper hadn't driven it in months, so it took a few tries to get the engine to turn over, but she jumped in once it started.

"Clark, you're in charge," she stated. "Keep us updated over the radio and start leading everyone to Hoh. The sedans can make it to the end of Hurricane Ridge Road. If you can lead everyone to that spot, we can scoop up whoever doesn't fit on the off-roaders. Roscoe and I cleared a wide trail all the way to Hoh."

"He showed me already. Get going."

Roscoe sped off toward his buddy's auto body shop—a half hour drive. His friend sent him multiple texts on which dirt bikes and quads were working and fueled, and when they got there they hurried to load the trailer. The shop was next to a crowded general store. Juniper looked around in despair at all the people blissfully unaware of the terror coming their way.

"Do you think we can save them?"

Roscoe shrugged. "Only if they believe the wild claims of strangers."

She nodded and let her hopes of saving more fade to the back of her mind. They could only fit two quads and four dirt bikes on the trailer and as they prepared to leave, a breeze blew Juniper's hair across her face. She looked up to see that the surrounding trees swayed in unison.

<<It's time,>> the trees said in warning and the ground began to rumble.

"We have to go," Juniper said in a panic. "It's happening."

Before they could get back into the Jeep, a huge grand fir burst from the ground and split the general store in half. It grew to 150 feet in a matter of seconds. The devastation was quick and thorough; people were stuck in its limbs and dropped from great heights to their demise. Its vines continued to move with aggression, ending all life caught in its growth.

A mountain hemlock then pushed through the ground with supernatural speed, tearing the highway in half as it grew to enormous height.

The unnatural nature of this attack was perturbing; it was nothing mankind had ever seen before—the trees were taking back their home.

Screams filled the air and people ran from the debris. There were victims, dead and injured, scattered throughout the limbs of the trees. Some shouted for help as they hung to life from the branches and others whimpered in pain, unable to say much at all. The vines that wormed along the branches put these lives to rest with swift strangles.

Juniper raced next door to beg those who survived to listen, but before she could catch anyone's attention, three cedars sprouted beneath the gas station on the other side of the auto body shop, causing the building to go up in flames. Trees were budding and growing at insane speeds everywhere she looked. Their roots snaked through the ground and pulled victims down by their ankles, trapping them and wrapping around their bodies until their lives were stifled.

The highway began to crumble as the concrete broke apart to let the foliage through. And though everyone ran for their lives, they were unable to escape the sudden takeover.

The radio crackled. "I hope you packed what you needed because a huge Douglas fir just grew through the middle of your house," Clark called in.

"I've got my bag with me. Is everyone there?"

"Everyone but you and Roscoe."

"Take them down Hurricane Ridge and into Hoh. Don't stop until you reach the Hall of Mosses, and find a way to make it in one trip. Triple up on the quads, squeeze extra people into the off-roaders. Whatever it takes. We will meet you there."

"Copy."

The earth creaked as the enormous trees tore the ground apart. Those who didn't die by chokehold were sucked into the ground as it disappeared beneath them. A spruce ripped through the auto body shop; its creeping vines seized and crushed everything they touched. When they reached Juniper's feet they lingered, as if sensing her, before moving past. They did the same to Roscoe.

"We can't waste another second. Let's go."

As they drove away, there was a crowd of people huddled in the middle of the highway. They were surrounded as vines and branches slithered toward them. Juniper looked closer and noticed the Wolfe family was among the group.

Roscoe stopped the Jeep and Juniper stuck her head out the window.

"Juniper!" Noah shouted as his mother held him tight.

"We can get you to safety," she called to them. "There's a spot in the woods where the trees are benign. If you follow us you will survive."

"The *trees* are attacking," an elderly man shouted over the eerie noises of the earth cracking. "Entering the forest seems like a bad idea right now."

"You'll just need to trust me."

"We do," Dedrik said without hesitation and led his family toward the Jeep. Though the four Wolfe brothers and their parents obliged, the others weren't so sure.

"Are you coming?" she asked.

There was a pause.

"It's better than dying here," a young man finally conceded with a shrug. He grabbed his sister's hand and led her toward Juniper. They stood on the rear bumper and latched on to the roll bars. The remainder of the group followed.

"Three can fit in the back seat, and two more can ride the rear. Wolfe brothers: If you're up for the ride, we can quickly unload the dirt bikes and quads."

"Let's do this," Wes said on behalf of his entire family. The four brothers raced to the trailer to help unload the bikes while their parents commandeered the quads. Each dirt bike and quad could fit two, and the others did their best to squeeze into the Jeep. Roscoe released the empty trailer and drove toward the forest.

The caravan of motorbikes and quads trailed the Jeep toward uncertain safety, dodging the behemoth trees that sprouted randomly without warning. The Wolfe family followed and created a symphony of revved engines.

"Hold on," Roscoe shouted to the people clinging onto the back of the Jeep before taking a hard right turn off the highway and onto a rough dirt path. It wasn't meant for a vehicle as big as a Jeep, but he did his best to maneuver without crashing. One mile in and he had to stop. He put his hazards on to warn the fast-riding dirt bikers to slow down.

"Why are we stopping?" Baxley shouted as his dirt bike screeched to a stop. "The trees are still freaking out. Look around! It's just as crazy in here as it was in town."

He was right. Trees were still growing at exponential speeds, tearing apart trails and leaving little room for them to travel.

"I'm too slow," Roscoe responded. "This vehicle is too big and it's holding us up. Juni, you need to get on a bike and lead the Wolfe family to safety."

"And what about you and the rest of them?"

"I'll keep moving forward in the Jeep as long as I can. When there's no path left, we will run."

"Fine," Juniper conceded, then addressed the others. "Let's fit as many people on the backs of these dirt bikes and quads as possible. Preferably anyone who will slow Roscoe down when the time comes to run." She needed a bike. "Noah, let me take your dirt bike and you'll travel with Roscoe."

"No," his father, Birk, said as he got off the quad. "Noah can ride the quad. I'll stay behind."

Everyone obeyed and Roscoe was left with nine physically capable people.

"We will stay along the Elwha till we reach Long Creek," Roscoe told Juniper. "We should be able to follow the creek through the valley south of Mt. Carrie and reach Hoh River from that direction."

"Okay. As soon as I reach the others at the Hall of Mosses I will come back with more transportation. Stick to that route so I know how to find you."

Roscoe pulled Juniper in close and kissed her. She did not like splitting up from the one person who meant the most to her. She couldn't lose him now.

She swallowed her tears and got on the lead bike. Her passenger was a small elderly woman named Martha who had already been instructed to hold on tight. She fastened her helmet, pulled in the clutch, shifted to first gear, and sped off. The other riders followed suit. Juniper couldn't look back; she couldn't bear to see Roscoe disappear in the dust as she rode away.

Chapter 26

Martha clung to her waist as she rode with expert agility. Trees sprouted unexpectedly like bombs and she had to be on constant alert. The trails had transformed into minefields and there was no telling when the ground below would betray her. She worried more for her fellow riders; the trees weren't giving her much trouble outside some tricky darting around those already grown. The Wolfe brothers' riding skills were being tested more thoroughly. Noah was almost taken out when a tree began to bud at the wrong second right beneath his front tire. It sent him into a wheelie, which he somehow managed to redirect. The German woman on the back of his bike became pale as a ghost, but the boy kept moving forward like a professional enduro racer.

They zigged and zagged down the trails paralleling the Elwha and followed Long Creek around Mt. Carrie. It was the same path Roscoe planned to take and Juniper was happy to see that it remained mostly intact. If he made it there soon he'd be fine.

They arrived at the Hall of Mosses campsite and were greeted by everyone who had remained with Clark. They all looked unharmed.

"It's a good thing you cleared those paths so thoroughly," Clark said as he gave her a hug. "We'd have never gotten the Jeeps through if you hadn't, and those were the only vehicles big enough to carry the overflow of people here. We'd have needed a second trip if they hadn't fit."

"Too bad we didn't clear a second path south from the top of Elwha. Roscoe is stuck up there now with a jeep and a few others we picked up in Maple Grove. We need to go back and get them. Are you guys okay to ride again?" she asked the Wolfe brothers, who were covered in sweat and dirt.

"Absolutely," Dedrik replied.

"You good, Mom?" Baxley asked, looking to where she waited on her bike.

"You bet," she answered with a wink.

"Great," Juniper said. "Teek, you ride, right?"

"I do. I rode your girly mint bike here," he teased.

"Funny. You're coming with us. Grab one of the extra bikes and a helmet."

"Sure thing, boss."

Juniper did the math in her head. "I'll need you on the extra quad, Brett. Including Roscoe, there are ten bodies. This should be enough. The trails are perilous and I don't want to bring more people than necessary."

With six dirt bikes and two quads, they raced back along the trail they just took. Though it had only been a few hours, the paths were already overgrown and the trails were much harder to navigate. It concerned Juniper that she barely recognized the route. Night was coming and they'd be riding in the dark within the hour. She constantly looked over her shoulder to make sure everyone was still there and okay. By the time they circled around Mt. Carrie, everyone was exhausted. Running on pure adrenaline, they carried on. This was the end of times and they had people to save; there was no giving up now. Everyone grasped the dire nature of the situation and rode into the ruins with selfless courage.

All across the globe, trees grew at unnatural rates, destroying everything in their path. In the suburbs, homes were demolished and the landscape returned to dense forestry. All that remained of previous human existence was the debris of the obliterated structures. The wreckage was far worse in the cities. Skyscrapers collapsed and highways crumbled as the trees shook and toppled the foundations. Millions of people were crushed as the manmade creations fell. The devastation they were experiencing in Washington was happening in multitudes anywhere trees reigned prior to the industrial revolution.

Only Juniper and Teek's motorbikes had lights, which they flipped on once it became too dark to see. Another mile down the creek and the sounds of frantic yelling became audible through the roar of their engines. Juniper raised her arm and slowed to a stop, instructing the other riders to do the same. She turned the handlebars of the Jaden Jaunt to cast light over the area. On the opposite side of the creek her light caught the whites of a dozen eyes. She kept her headlight pointed in that direction as the shadowy silhouettes ran toward them.

Roscoe cried out over the steady hum of the idling engines and the continued growl of combusting earth.

Juniper's heart rate intensified. She dismounted her bike and ran to him.

"You're alive," she said with relief as she buried her face into his shoulder. "I was so worried. The forest is possessed."

"We haven't stopped running since we left the Elwha River."

249

"Is everyone okay?" she asked, looking at the tired faces of those who followed Roscoe.

"Yes. Somehow we all made it this far."

"You must be exhausted. Let's get everyone on a bike and head back."

The night was dark. The only light to guide them was their headlamps and the full moon. The trails were littered with shadows from the colossal trees, so they stayed near the creek where the forestry was less dense and the moonlight shone on the water's surface.

Roscoe rode with Teek since they were similar in size, and Juniper had a teenage girl holding tight to her back. The girl was so tiny it almost felt like Juniper was riding alone.

They were rounding the base of Mt. Carrie when a monstrous cedar rocketed into the sky, separating the group. The earth shook as Juniper hit her brakes and parked her bike. Only three of the Wolfe brothers were still behind her; Noah and Teek were caught behind the tree.

She ran to the other side to see if they were okay and was greeted by the sight of Noah and his passenger falling from the sky.

Their bike was ten-feet high and hanging from the lowest branch, and the boys writhed on the ground in pain. She ran to their side; Teek and Roscoe joined her from the other direction.

"The tree snagged their front tire," Teek explained as Roscoe checked the pulse and pupils of each boy. "It grew so fast it took them up with it. Noah clung to the handlebars as long as he could, but his passenger was latched onto his waist and the weight took them down."

The boys both made noise and could move their toes, which meant they weren't unconscious or paralyzed, but their condition remained dismal. They would not be able to make it the rest of the way on their own.

"We are down a bike," Juniper said, frantic. As the words left her lips, another tree shot into the sky, taking Teek's bike with it. The dirt bike was launched into the sky and landed a few feet from where it had been parked. It broke into pieces upon impact.

"Scratch that. We're down two. How on Earth are we going to get you all back?"

"They are small. We can carry them," Roscoe answered.

"You're going to run again?"

"There's no other choice."

"Fine. I'm running with you," Juniper said.

"Why? There's a bike for you," Roscoe asked.

"I'm not leaving you behind again. I'm staying by your side." Her response was resolute and Roscoe did not argue. He gave her a quick kiss and she ran back to the others to explain the situation.

"I'm not leaving my baby here," Noah's mother protested.

"Laurel, he is in better hands with them than he'd be with us," her husband Birk said, "and he'd only be further injured if you tried to take him back on the quad."

"We can sandwich him between our bodies!" she insisted, volunteering her passenger's assistance.

"This isn't normal riding. We are dodging freakish anomalies at every turn. The likelihood of him falling off is too great. Same with Cade." Birk looked over at the parents of Noah's injured passenger who wanted to stay behind with their son too.

"We don't have time for this," Juniper interjected. "We need both of you at the wheel, taking these people to safety. No one else knows how to ride. We will take good care of your son." She looked back at Dedrik, Wes, and Bax. All were visibly shaken up by their youngest brother's injury. "Can you lead them to the Hall of Mosses?"

"Yes," Dedrik responded.

"Great. Be careful."

The riders stood their bikes upright, closed their kickstands, and took off. The quads followed close behind. The sound of their engines disappearing into the dark amplified how alone the others were. Roscoe and Teek rounded the tree, each cradling an injured body.

The river was lined with rocks, which created uneven footing. One twisted ankle would ruin everything, so they proceeded slowly to prevent a scenario worse than what they already faced.

A few miles in, Roscoe began to lag. He had already run countless miles from Elwha to the middle of Long Creek and he never got much of a breather before finding himself back on foot.

"Let me take him," Juniper insisted. "I can't carry him long, but I can give you a break." Roscoe reluctantly conceded and transferred Cade's small body to Juniper. The boy was a 70-pound 11-year-old and she suspected she could give Roscoe a 2-mile reprieve.

<<Yellowstone is about to erupt. You need to hurry.>>

The voices of the trees caught Juniper off guard; she hadn't heard them in a while.

"What you do mean? I thought the core already attacked."

<<It's the final phase. It's one of four supervolcanoes across the globe to explode. The planet will be rebirthed in the darkness.>>

"Will we be safe in the Hall of Mosses?" she asked, out of breath.

<<Yes, but you should be there already. We can only do so much to help you after the eruption.>>

"Understood." She then hollered to Roscoe and Teek over the explosive creaking of the forest. "We have to hurry!"

They reached the Hoh River five minutes later. The moment Juniper thought they were in the clear, Yellowstone detonated. The earth quivered violently for an entire minute before the ground began to split apart. Giant fissures with bottomless depths ripped across the landscape.

There was no predicting where these death pits would split open and the sound they made as they tore the earth apart was terrifying. Juniper prayed the universe was on their side.

As the ground fractured haphazardly, the sound of the apertures grew louder. The attack was catching up to them as they ran west. Teek ran beside her with Noah in tow, Roscoe was a few paces behind. Juniper turned her head to check on him, only to have the earth slowly disintegrate beneath her feet. Horrified alarm took over her senses as she tried to beat the fissure. Teek was a few steps ahead, leaping over mounds and cracks that formed as the earth crumbled into nothing. Juniper was having a harder time. She was closer to the middle of the fracture and the direction in which the ground collapsed was ever-changing. She tripped with Cade in her arms and felt hot air shoot upward from the newly formed hole. The sickening warmth grazed her back, reminding her to hurry. She picked up the boy and focused only on her end destination. Teek had his arm outstretched, ready to assist her once she was close enough. Two feet from solid ground she lurched and tossed Cade into Teek's arms, but the force of the exchange knocked her down.

She frantically crawled toward Teek, who had both boys placed safely next to him. As the ground beneath her disappeared, she caught Teek's hand. Her body dangled above a cavernous sinkhole. While he pulled her up, she used her free hand to grab the roots at the solid edge of the fissure. She swung her leg, latched it onto the unaffected earth, and pulled herself out of the deathtrap.

The world raced around her in a blur. Her heart pounded relentlessly with fear and adrenaline. She gasped for air and took a brief moment to recollect her wits.

"Where's Roscoe?" she finally asked. All fear of death vanished and was replaced by that of lost love. She looked across the ten-foot wide sinkhole to see Roscoe standing on the other side, a distant silhouette in the moonlight. He did not move or speak, he just stared back in defeat. A swelling surge of nausea filled her body.

"No," she whispered in despair.

"At least he's alive," Teek offered.

"He's all alone."

"He's a mountain man, he knows the forest better than anyone. He will be okay."

"I can't leave him there." She fought the tears that were forming.

"This fracture goes on for miles and there are more forming. We don't have time to wait for him," he pleaded. "We can't stay here."

She took a step closer to the edge.

"You have to go," Roscoe shouted from across the way. Juniper shook her head, not wanting to accept this option.

"I can't leave you."

"You have to," Roscoe insisted.

There was a moment of silence. The space between them felt larger than ever.

I love you, he said telepathically.

I love you too.

The tears fell.

She turned away, unable to watch Roscoe grow smaller as she abandoned him. With angry force she wiped the tears off her face. "Let's go."

Together they made their way back to the Hall of Mosses. Upon arrival, they placed the boys in a safe spot to rest, then she noticed that the group looked thinner.

"Where is everyone?" Juniper's voice was strong and commanding.

"We tried to stop them, but they wouldn't listen," Irene answered.

"When we came back without you, Roscoe's buddies thought you might need help," Brett explained further.

"Their spouses, the Wolfe family, and the parents and sister of Cade went with them," Clark added. "Half of the people you saved in Maple Grove."

"I told you all to stay here," Juniper exclaimed, frustrated that more people had likely perished under her lead. "How many left?"

"Fourteen," Jeb responded.

"Damnit. I can't afford to lose anymore." Juniper stormed off and looked for a spot where she could be alone. They couldn't see her breakdown; they couldn't see her cry. She had to stay strong and confident, but right now she felt anything but capable.

A mossy canopy hung in solitude and she found a secluded spot where she could hide. She might lose her Second, the man she loved, in addition to half of the small following she had mustered by pure luck.

Her mind raced around all those she letdown: Gaia, the trees, her Champion sisters, Roscoe, the human race, and most importantly, herself. She was so sure she'd pull through, that she'd find her inner warrior and succeed without fear. She acted courageously, but the entire process had been riddled with doubt. And even though she was where she needed to be and she met the bare minimum of what was expected from her, it was hard to count her victories when she was surrounded by failure.

Roscoe's face came into her mind. His smile lifted her spirits until his image was replaced by that of his silhouette standing alone on the opposite side of the crater. She could not reach him, she could not help him; they were separated by miles of empty space and unimaginable depths.

Roscoe, can you hear me? she called to him telepathically.

There was no response.

If you're alive, please answer, she wept.

Their connection was lost. There was nothing solid on the other end for her mind to grab hold of. Normally, she could feel him; there was weight on the other side of her thoughts. Now there was nothing. Juniper screamed to drown this reality, refusing to believe he was dead.

As soon as the quakes stopped, she would rally a search crew and find him. Even though he was better trained than anyone to traverse this new, harsh terrain, she still feared for him. There was no telling the dangers that lurked in the forest now that the entire landscape had shifted.

She could feel her Champion sisters calling out to her in her mind, inquiring about the status of her quest, but she did not feel like rehashing her scarce success.

Instead, she rested her body on the wet moss and closed her eyes, praying she might awake to a miracle.

Chapter 27

There were no miracles waiting for her on the other side of her nightmares—only Clark, who had found her hiding spot and watched over her as she slept.

Juniper stretched and let out a yawn. The entire night was filled with earth-rattling quakes and her body ached from nature's rough bed. She emerged from the moss canopy and was greeted by the darkest day she'd ever seen.

"You okay, kid?" Clark asked.

"No."

"Can we talk? You know how much I care about Roscoe too. He's like a son to me, and I'd like to know what happened."

She didn't want to talk about it, but Clark deserved to know. She explained how the riders came to be injured and how Roscoe ended up on the other side of the sinkhole. Clark looked at her for more, but the words were hard to say.

"I had to leave him."

"But he's alive?" he asked. Juniper nodded. "Thank God!"

Clark didn't know about their telepathic connection and she couldn't explain how his presence on the other side appeared to be gone. She kept that fear muted, to Clark and herself.

Clark continued mulling over the story she just relayed. "I suppose Yellowstone erupting explains the black sky."

"Yes. We are safe from the lava and ash here, but the entire world will be dark for a while. As soon as the aftereffects of the volcano stop, we're going to find Roscoe."

"Of course."

"How is everyone back at camp?"

"Rattled. They need you."

"I just needed a moment."

"I understand."

Together, they returned to the main group, who tossed and turned as they stretched awake on their earth-made beds.

The morning sky was blanketed in gray ash. The sun brightened the darkness, but was unable to shine through. The forest felt surreal and movie-like with its drastic shadows and dark contours. Though everyone was awake, they stayed quiet, unsure what came next.

"The tremors seem to be over," Carine said, shivering with her arms around her body. The group was terribly short on supplies, another misstep for which Juniper took the blame.

"Have you spoken to the trees?" Jeb asked. "Any indication what we need to do next?"

The newcomers who remained reacted to this question with furrowed brows.

"You talk to trees?" Zaedon Devereaux, the 22-year old asked with a scowl. He looked at his older sister Genevieve with an arrogant smirk.

Juniper groaned. "Can someone please inform our guests about my situation? And no, I haven't received any new updates, but they told me previously that we must wait out the darkness in our assigned safe spot. It could be weeks, months—I'm not sure, so it's best we make this place as comfortable as possible."

"It's strange knowing that the rest of the country is now vacant of human life," Irene said, cradling her babies at her sides.

"Others must have survived," Aunt Mallory objected. "It's foolish to assume every single life perished in these attacks. There must be some lucky cockroaches out there who dodged the worst of it."

"For the first time in my life, I hope you're right," Juniper said.

"Can we leave to get supplies?" Clark asked. "We wouldn't have to travel far, just into town."

Juniper paused, assessing the dire state of their campsite: no blankets, no shelter, no food. "I suppose the trees will let me know if we've traveled too far out of the safe zone. Plus, we need to send out a search crew for Roscoe and the others."

"So how do we do this?" Clark asked.

"One small search party," Juniper answered. "Clark and I will lead the first, accompanied by Jeb and Brett. We will assess the state of the forest now that the worst is over, and determine the condition of the trails. The rest of you need to stay put. No wandering, no sudden urges to leave. Don't move from this area, no matter how long we take. Is that understood?"

"Got it," Irene answered as everyone else nodded.

"Good. We will be back soon."

They began their hike along the Hoh River, hoping to find supplies and survivors along the way.

Chapter 28

The trails within the park were unrecognizable. There were no remnants of the forest Juniper once called home. If it weren't for the Hoh River, they'd be terribly lost.

"I can't believe the drastic change. It's like we're in an entirely different forest," Clark noted in awe. Just like Juniper, he could once navigate these woods with his eyes closed. It made her nervous; Roscoe was in greater danger than she initially imagined.

"If we follow the river we will get to the fissure that separated us," she informed.

"Let's just hope he stayed put," Jeb said, his voice bleak. They all knew that Roscoe wouldn't sit idle and wait for others to save him.

When they reached the giant crack in the earth, their suspicions were proven accurate. Roscoe wasn't there.

Juniper's heart raced. "Okay. He wouldn't have left the edge of the fracture. He'd have traveled along it until he found a way around. Then he would've followed the opposite side back to this spot and let the river lead him to the Hall of Mosses."

"There's no telling how far this fault goes. It could stretch from Oregon to Canada," Brett said.

Juniper didn't respond. Her breathing quickened as she tried to stay positive.

"We can't jump to worst case scenarios yet," Clark chimed in. "Today we'll head south and see where that takes us. Tomorrow we'll head north. If it means long trips spanning a few days, so be it."

The group nodded and headed south. They walked for five hours before conceding that they needed to head back. The further they traveled away from the Hall of Mosses, the thicker the ash residue in the air became. Not only was it hard to breathe, but the gray sky was turning black.

"Tomorrow's walk north will include a trip into town, which means it'll be an overnighter," Juniper informed the others. "We saw ash today, so I imagine the town is also covered. We will need to dress appropriately; noses and mouths covered." She instructed as they reached the spot where the fault cut the Hoh River in half. Their side was connected to the Pacific Ocean, which was now run dry, and the other side flowed like a waterfall over the fault's edge. Water from the mountain tops had been pouring into the crack for over a day and there was no sign of the crevice being filled. No sign of the water pooling, just a black and empty pit. Juniper hoped the spirits of nature fixed this before it left them stranded without fresh water.

"Have the trees said anything?" Jeb asked.

"No, which means we can search the forest without fear."

They continued their quiet walk along the dried up Hoh River. Juniper hid her anxiety, but inside she was shattered into a thousand pieces. The thought of losing Roscoe was too much.

Roscoe, if you're out there I need to know. She kept her head down so the others could not see her grief. *Please answer me.*

There was no response.

They made it back to the others, who were huddled around a bonfire.

Juniper couldn't be around the others right now, so she retreated to the same mossy spot she found their first night there. It was turning into her private sanctuary within their safe haven. She couldn't see the group, but she could hear their chatter, which only made her feel worse. Roscoe and the others should be with them.

She sat on the mossy rock that faced away from the noise of the group and closed her eyes. Her Champion sisters hadn't stopped trying to break through her mental walls, so she finally let one in.

Hey, Marisabel. She felt closest to her fresh water sister.

Juniper! Where have you been? We've been trying to reach you for days.

I'm sorry. It's been difficult. I am not doing well.

What happened?

I lost my Second and I can't reach him telepathically. Does that mean he's dead? Juniper asked, her voice frantic. It took a moment for Marisabel to respond.

I'm not sure.

I cannot lose him.

Have you asked the trees?

No, and they haven't talked to me since Yellowstone erupted. They probably see me as a failure.

I highly doubt that. You're still alive, and that was the most important part.

I have a following of thirty-four people. How am I supposed to rebuild with that?

I only have seventy-five. I lost two thirds of my following to the flash floods and cyclones. Have you spoken to Sofyla yet? She lost fifty people to quicksand in the Saudi Arabian desert.

Juniper absorbed this new information. She hadn't realized the others struggled as severely.

I'm sorry you lost so many.

We all lost much. Be it our followings or simply the lives we knew prior to being selected as Champions. We've all made sacrifices to adapt to the changing times. We understand your pain, so please don't shut us out.

I'm sorry. I just needed some time to accept my new reality before rehashing it to another.

I get it. Just remember: You are never alone.

Thank you.

How did you lose your Second?

After the Yellowstone supervolcano exploded, the earth began to rip apart. We were carrying two injured boys to safety when the ground crumbled right beneath us. My friend and I made it to safety, but Roscoe got stuck on the opposite side. We went back today to look for him, but he wasn't there. The forest looks nothing like it did before the attack. If it weren't for the river, we'd have never found our way back to the last place we saw him.

I can talk to the water. Maybe they'll be able to help.

I'd be so grateful if they could.

Don't be ashamed to reach out to the trees. I am certain they are nothing but proud.

I thought they would've checked in by now.

They are busiest of all the spirits right now. They have a lot of rebuilding to do beneath the hardened lava, ash, flooded land, and muddy soil.

I hadn't thought of that.

I was told they are having difficulty recruiting the millions who died in the purge. They were hoping to convince the human spirits to be rebirthed as trees, but the deceased are angry and want no part in nature after the massacre.

Juniper understood. *Seems logical.*

Agreed, but we need them to oblige. They need as many spirit-born trees as possible if they wish to rebirth the planet. Trees can grow on their own, but without the supernatural strength of the spirits, they'll never retake the land that's been destroyed.

I wish the trees had told me this.

They would've if they weren't so busy trying to succeed. According to the water, human spirits are rocketing one after another into outer space.

I'm not sure how they'll shift the angry tides in their favor.

They'll find a way.

Sure hope so.

I have to go. Stop blocking us out, okay?

Okay.

And don't lose hope. Roscoe might still be out there.

I'll never give up on him.

Marisabel vanished from her mind and Juniper was alone again.

The next week passed in a miserable blur. There was no sign of Roscoe or the others. They made the trip north into the ash-covered town of Maple Grove and got all the supplies they needed, but never found the end of the fault line. Brett was right: it likely went all the way into Canada. The hope that the south side was shorter remained alive in her heart.

Another week passed with no sight of the fissure's south end. Juniper began to fear that her heart might actually break.

She planned another trip south. This time, they'd spend two weeks trekking along the fissure in search of a spot to cross over. She rallied the small group and led the way. Faces covered with dust masks and goggles, they left the safety of their section of the forest and headed toward Oregon. When they reached the state line, they took a break. The crevice continued south for as far as they could see.

<<Turn around.>>

Juniper was startled; she hadn't heard from the trees in weeks. With practice she had learned how to answer the other Champions using only her thoughts and could now talk to the trees without anyone overhearing their conversation.

We are searching for the others. I lost Roscoe; I need to find him.

<<Turn around. It isn't safe.>>

Is he alive?

<<We cannot answer that. Our main priority is you, not him, and we need you to stay in the safe zone.>>

He won't answer my thoughts. It feels like he can't even hear them.

<<Our main concern is your survival, so you must turn around now.>>

I can't abandon him. I have to keep looking.

<<If you disobey us, we will wreak havoc on those you travel with. You have no comprehension of the danger existing beyond these borders. Do not force our hand.>>

The trees had never threatened her before. In anger she broke the connection and paced the spot where everyone rested.

"Are you okay?" Carine asked, concerned by Juniper's sudden mood shift.

"The trees told us to turn around."

"Why?" Clark asked. He didn't want to end the search for Roscoe either.

"They said if we go any further it'll be too dangerous."

"I'm not afraid of a little danger," Teek said, which elicited a look of disbelief from the others.

Juniper decided not to tell them about the threat as she did not want them to fear the trees, or doubt her bond to them.

"We need to go back," she said, her decision resolute.

"What about Roscoe?" Clark protested.

"We will keep looking for him in the areas that are safe. Right now, I can't risk the rest of you getting hurt."

Her sorrow blanketed the entire group. Though no one wanted to turn around, they understood that she knew best.

"Maybe we can build a bridge over the crevice," Misty suggested, hoping to lift Juniper's mood.

"Yeah." Her voice was void of emotion. "That's a good idea."

They made it back to camp and Clark took the initiative to start building the bridge. Juniper was too heartbroken to focus, though she remained determined to jump in tomorrow. Between the loss of Roscoe and the trees getting angry with her, she felt defeated.

She did not like being threatened, but she also realized that she had pushed the bounds of their patience, so she planned to fix things the next time she heard from the trees—she would not survive if she lost them too.

Chapter 29

The entire group worked hard to maneuver a fallen tree over top of the crevice. After sawing off the branches they were able to roll it at an angle that allowed the top half of the trunk to reach the other side before the weight could drag it into the abyss. Once both sides were touching land, a few made the dangerous walk over the bridge and helped straighten it out. They rolled the trunk one more time into small holes they dug and secured it into place as best they could.

They spent the next month scouring the unfamiliar forest of Olympic National Park. Everyone took turns making the treks except Juniper and Clark, who went on every mission. Despite their continued search, they found no one. They didn't even find any clues in the woods that indicated anyone had been there. No campfires, no footprints, no makeshift shelters. The lack of any human footprints was unnerving.

After endless searches, it came to a point when the others had to make the call. They began organizing a memorial service for those who were lost, but Juniper refused to partake in the arrangements. She was determined to prolong her denial.

Everyone wept during the memorial except Juniper. She stood next to the burning pile of bark and mossy leaves without a tear in her eye.

The days following the memorial were draped in fog; both literally and figuratively. The sky remained gray and the air was moist; the combination was terribly depressing. Juniper was numb. Her thoughts ran in circles inside her hazy mind.

While Clark took the lead in helping the others build a suitable camp, Juniper hid beneath her tree. She made a conscious effort to make regular appearances in the group setting, but struggled to uphold a strong façade. She never lasted more than an hour or two before retreating back to her hideout.

Roscoe, she kept pleading when in solitude. *I need you to respond.*

He never answered, but she never stopped trying.

If you don't answer me I'm going to get mad. Everyone thinks you're dead, and I'm starting to feel crazy. There was a long pause. *Say something!*

There was no pull from the other side, no indication that her thoughts traveled farther than the walls of her skull. She slammed her fist against the rock she sat on, regretting it the moment the impact sent waves of pain through her small hand.

"Juni," Clark said as he approached from behind. Juniper did not turn around to look at him. She needed a moment to compose herself.

"I know you're hurting," he continued. "You can talk to me."

"I'll be okay. We have to stay focused and I need to stay strong."

"You don't need to grieve alone."

She turned to face him. "If I talk about it out loud I'll start crying, and if I let myself cry, I'm not sure I'll be able to stop."

"Fine, but if you keep internalizing it you'll eventually explode. I understand that you're maintaining an air of strength for the rest of the group, but there's no need to try and fool me. I loved Roscoe too and I know that *I* need someone to talk to. We can help each other."

"The pain is too fresh. As selfish as this will sound, I can't listen to you talk about it anymore than I can bring *myself* to talk about it. I cannot fall apart right now. I need to hold it together until our group is thriving self-sufficiently."

"And when will that be?"

"Maybe when the sun comes back."

"If you find yourself slipping, please come to me. I don't want to lose you too."

He departed without pushing any harder. She buried her face in her hands in defeat. Her denial was affecting those who still remained. She had barely talked to Irene since everything fell apart, and Clark was open about how her distance hurt him. Jeb gave her sympathetic looks often, but never overstepped the invisible lines she had drawn. She had to find the courage to make things right. She had to fake her state of mind for the sake of everyone else. They needed her. She led them here and she needed to show them she was strong enough to carry on. They put their faith in her and she couldn't let them down.

Her change in attitude, even if it was a pretense, started that afternoon when she joined the group for a lunch consisting of canned beans and crackers. Their food supply was sparse and they'd need another trip into town soon. Teek and Brett volunteered to collect more supplies and after the endless weeks of searching for survivors in the newly designed forest, Juniper trusted that they knew their way.

Through the chaos of nature's attack, and the consuming grief that followed, Juniper never got to know Roscoe's father.

He was a quiet man who kept to himself, so he hadn't tried either, but she imagined he was suffering silently too. Aldon Boswald sat alone, staring at the bonfire that slowly died.

"How are you doing?" Juniper asked as she sat next to him. Her voice shook him out of his thoughts momentarily, but he did not stay engaged long. He shrugged in response and returned his gaze to the dwindling flames.

"We don't need to talk," Juniper continued. "I just wanted you to know that I love Roscoe, and even though we held that funeral, I'm not convinced that he's dead. I'm holding out hope."

"Well, you better let go. We haven't seen him in two months. Lying to yourself will only make the grief worse when it finally hits you."

Juniper was taken aback. "Don't you want him to be out there somewhere?"

"Of course I do, but wishing for it won't make it happen. I don't mean to be rude, but if he's dead, he's dead, and I'd rather not talk myself into believing otherwise. It won't do either of us any good."

"Alright then. I'll leave you alone."

His grief had manifested into anger and there was nothing she could do to change that. She left his side and sat with the others around the campfire. They kept the mood light despite the gloomy circumstances they faced. Everyone was hungry, tired, and scared, though they collectively hid their sour moods in order to preserve some semblance of peace. Juniper feared it was only a matter of time before their true dispositions would rise to the surface and tear the group apart. For now, she listened gratefully as Noah recalled happy memories of the motocross races he and his older brothers had won.

Juniper retired to bed early. Though spending more time with the others was a nice distraction, it didn't erase her suffering. Forcing a smile was draining and she needed time to be morose in private.

Her grief while isolated was relentless. It seized her from all angles and took her breath away. Her thoughts fell into dark pits, making the rest of the world disappear. The intensity of her sorrow sent her into fits of delirium and when she escaped these terrible moments of disorienting heartache, the crushing weight of her grief grew heavier.

Roscoe, where are you?

The more she spoke to no one inside her mind, the worse her condition became. She was losing her mind and refused to let anyone help. She faked sanity brilliantly during the day, and slipped back into hysterics at night. Clark suspected she was struggling, so she kept her distance from him. She didn't need his help; there was nothing he could do.

Making it worse were the dreams. Roscoe came to her often, alive and unharmed. He held her tight and whispered his love. She awoke each morning crippled by the nightmarish dreams. They left her debilitated with false hope, and it often took hours to convince herself those moments weren't real.

The last time she experienced such paralyzing grief was when her parents died. Roscoe was the first person she let in since—the first person she loved since their passing—and fate took him away from her too.

Another round of taunting dreams left her under the spell of a relentless shiver. With heavy circles under eyes and a deafening migraine, she wrapped herself in a blanket and shuffled from her secluded spot to join the group.

Everyone looked worn. Those whose families were intact were weathered physically, and those who grieved in private, like Juniper, looked torn apart from the inside out. She took a moment to remind herself she wasn't the only person buried beneath emotional pain.

She sat next to Noah and Cade, who were now orphaned just like she had been at a young age. She told them about the death of her parents when she was a little girl, hoping it might help them cope. Even if they never talked about it again, she suspected they might find some comfort in her presence knowing she had survived a similar grief. It was important to remind them they weren't alone.

After comforting the boys, she realized she wasn't taking her own advice. Though she saw the hypocrisy, she felt she was too deep to backtrack and let anyone in on her bordering madness. She couldn't drag someone else into her mess; she needed to save herself. Once she found solid ground, she'd approach Clark or Irene, but for now she had to tackle it on her own. She pulled herself from the depths of depression before, and she had no doubt she could do it again.

Chapter 30

Don't give up on me.

Juniper snapped out of her slumber. Awake, she desperately tried to remember her dream, but all she could recall was Roscoe's final plea.

He spoke to her, she was sure of it, and it wasn't a figment of her imagination, it was him. He was alive somewhere, calling out to her while she slept.

Talk to me, she begged. *I'm awake. I'll remember what you say.*

There was no response and the other side remained vacant. She buried her head into her hands and strained her memory. She was with Roscoe in the dream, he held her like he always did, but his words weren't whispers anymore. They were loud and clear shouts. When she tried to remember what he said his voice became muffled and camouflaged by static.

Since nobody else knew they talked to each other telepathically, there was no one she could confide in. She stood and paced the area beneath her private canopy of moss.

The day passed and she went to sleep with hopeful excitement. Remaining mindful of her dreams, hoping to retain them all, she never slipped into a deep slumber. She woke up the next day without a visit from Roscoe.

It continued that way for the rest of the week. By Friday, she was visibly agitated.

"What's going on?" Clark asked, sitting next to her and eating directly from a box of cereal.

Juniper hesitated, but decided to tell Clark her secret. He shoved a handful of Fruit Loops into his mouth as she divulged.

274

"Roscoe and I can communicate telepathically."

"What?" A half-chewed piece of cereal flew from his mouth.

"Ew," she said, brushing his breakfast debris off her lap.

"Sorry." His mouth was full. "You caught me by surprise. Why didn't you tell me that before?"

"It was our secret. It felt special to keep it private."

"I get it, but he's been missing for months. Have you heard from him?"

"I'm not sure. I tried persistently from the moment we were separated, and I kept trying even after the funeral, but never heard from him. I was driving myself crazy attempting to make contact, but a few nights ago I think he finally found a way to reach me. I heard him in my dreams."

"Your dreams?" Clark asked with skepticism.

"I know it seems unlikely, but I've been dreaming about him for weeks and he never said more than sweet generic whispers. Then suddenly, he started to scream. Every night, he came at me shouting, demanding my attention. He begged me not to give up."

"Juni, you were sleeping. How do you know it was real?"

"It felt different than the previous dreams. Those were my subconscious toying with memories, whereas this was a real moment. He was there."

"Okay, I'll play along. If it was him, what now?"

"We start searching again. If he's alive we need to find him. The fact that I can't talk to him as easily as I used to and that he can only reach me when I'm sleeping is a bad sign. He probably needs our help."

"I'm all for helping you, but if you try and get the others to follow they'll revolt. A few have already expressed doubt in your ability to lead and you don't want to fan that flame. They all think he's dead. Let them continue thinking that. And if we find him, they'll be pleasantly surprised."

Juniper nodded, absorbing all of his advice. She was happy she confided in him. Without his guidance, she would've rallied a search crew for the man they believed was dead. She didn't want them to think she was crazy, so Clark's insight was invaluable.

They agreed that taking Jeb and Irene was the safest bet. Jeb had proven his loyalty. He was the first to believe her when she tried telling everyone the truth about the trees, and he hadn't questioned her since. Irene loved Juniper no matter what. Once Mallory and Zoe agreed to watch her kids, she accepted their invitation to make the trip into town for supplies.

An hour into their walk, Juniper told them about her dreams.

"You two can talk telepathically?" Irene asked, flabbergasted.

"We could. Now the connection feels broken. I've only been able to hear him in my dreams. I don't know what it means. Is he injured? Dead? Maybe he's just really far away," Juniper theorized aloud. "I have no idea. I just know we need to keep looking. If he's hurt, we need to help."

Both Jeb and Irene were inclined to believe he hadn't survived, but they kept their thoughts to themselves and agreed to support her in this quest.

"We are getting supplies though, right?" Jeb asked.

"Yes. I just want to look for Roscoe on the trips to and from town. We will go off-trail and take different routes back."

"Just don't get us lost," Irene requested.

"I won't."

The trip normally took four days, but their detours turned it into a weeklong voyage. There was no sign of Roscoe or the others and when they returned to camp, everyone was on edge.

"What took so long?" Jeb's wife exclaimed as she ran into his arms. "We were so nervous something bad happened."

"Sorry, my love. We tried a different route, hoping it would be faster, but obviously it wasn't. Didn't mean to make you worry." He kissed Alice's forehead.

Irene ran to her kids, who buried her in a group hug. Juniper directly retreated to her private corner.

When night came, she had hopes of hearing Roscoe, but all attempts to remain alert during her dreams failed due to exhaustion. She fell into a deep sleep and lost all control of her subconscious.

Roscoe appeared.

Juniper tensed and tried to hold onto the moment, but as soon as her awareness returned, he began to fade. He was shouting at her but his words were muffled. She begged him to talk louder, and though his facial expression and body language implied he was trying, she still couldn't hear him. Trees began sprouting into life between them and Roscoe's image became buried in shadows. He reached his arm through the barricade of trees, but his hand vanished before she could grab it.

The distress forced her awake. She sat up covered in cold sweat and tried to swallow the tears that welled, but there were too many. They fell and the loss of control was overwhelming. She forced her mind to focus on her breathing and was able to take a few deep breaths to suppress the looming panic attack. The tears slowed and she wiped their trails off her cheeks. The nightmares were winning.

Juniper refused to wither into an old, pathetic version of herself. She was allowed to grieve, but she wouldn't let it get the best of her. Never again.

She wrapped herself in a blanket and shuffled through the dark to where Clark slept. He set up his bed near Jeb and Alice, but they were far enough apart that she wouldn't wake them all.

"Clark," she whispered. He rustled a bit before turning and squinting up at her.

"Juni?" he mumbled with concern, "You okay?"

"No. I don't think I am."

Clark sat up and forced his eyes open. After a minute of adjusting he addressed her again.

"What's wrong?"

"He's haunting my dreams."

Clark leaned in and let Juniper hide in his embrace.

"It's because you miss him. It's normal. You'll be okay."

"The lack of sleep is driving me mad. I swear he's really there and trying to talk to me, but then I take a step back and assess my mental state and realize I am exhausted. My emotions are on the fritz. I'm having trouble drawing the line between real and fake. It's maddening. I'm so afraid I'm going to lose control and let my mind slip back into the dark place I escaped from years ago."

"I won't let that happen. You're safe with me; you just need to keep me in the loop. If you shut me out, I can't help."

Juniper nodded and his solace eased her nerves. He wasn't afraid of her fears and was ready to tackle them alongside her without judgment. His selfless support gave her the comfort she desperately sought. As she surrendered in Clark's embrace, she realized she was looking at her sorrow all wrong.

She was strong enough to scale the depths without help; she was capable of rescuing herself just fine. She had done it before, many times over, and was accustomed to going it alone. But it wasn't about being her own hero, it was about letting others in. She didn't *have* to go it alone. She could allow those who cared about her to assist in her recovery, and in the process, help them recover too.

There was nothing safe about tackling the darkness alone. One slip and she'd be gone. She had too many close calls before, moments of such despair her world went dark and she had no desire to find the light. No will to make her world bright again. After years of traversing the shadows alone she finally realized that there was nothing wrong with reaching for a hand to hold while navigating the darkness. Having a guide toward the light did not mean she was weak, it meant she was smart. Letting an outsider see her monsters and allowing them to help her tame them was an act of true courage. Coping on her own took strength, but allowing herself to be vulnerable in front of others was the real triumph.

"Thank you."

"You're family. I'll always be here for you."

She believed him, and when she returned to her mossy patch she was able to get a good night's rest for the first time in months.

Chapter 31

She began to let go. Her heart held onto hope for a miracle, but she understood she couldn't force it. Roscoe visited in her dreams often, and though it hurt to wake up from these encounters she cherished these reveries. Seeing him while she slept kept his spirit alive.

Though the dreams were nice, she finally started to come to terms with the fact that these encounters were figments of her subconscious and nothing more. She still hadn't heard his voice while awake and she had to conclude that their telepathic connection was broken because he wasn't on the other end. It was painful to accept this reality, but she forced herself to stomach the apparent truth.

Her new outlook and demeanor was well received by the group. She was coherent, motivated, and pleasant to be around again. No one said it, but they were happy to have their leader back.

<<*You seem well,*>> the trees remarked after a long stretch of silence.

Juniper sighed, disinterested in talking with them.

As well as I can be.

<<*We are proud of you. You have shown courageous strength.*>>

Did I save enough people?

<<*Yes.*>>

Juniper looked at her small crew and wondered how that was possible. It was a sensitive subject and she decided not to press the issue.

Marisabel, Champion of Fresh Water, told me about your struggle to recruit the recently deceased. Are you having better luck now?

<<We've experienced slow improvements. We hadn't anticipated the bitter nature of the departed human spirits.>>

I could've predicted that. Next time, seek counsel from the one human you speak with.

<<We did not mean to ostracize you, but you had more pressing matters to focus on.>>

I get it. Juniper wasn't ready to rekindle her friendship with the trees yet. She was angry they didn't help her find Roscoe and the others, and she wanted them to feel her disappointment.

When does the darkness end?

<<In a few months. When the ash clouds clear, you will awake surrounded by Gaia's glory. All will be born again.>>

Then what?

<<Then you persevere. You find a way to rebuild and repopulate in a manner respectful to nature.>>

Fantastic.

The trees rustled in silence for a moment, whispering amongst themselves. Juniper heard their chatter but could not make out what they said.

<<We sense your dissatisfaction with us. We hope you don't truly believe that we abandoned you.>>

It's over now. There was no sense pointing out their selfish behavior. She needed Roscoe, but the trees only needed her. Starting an argument over a matter long gone was futile. She needed the trees to have her back and she didn't think it wise to pick a fight with the only source keeping her alive.

<<In time it will all make sense.>>

Juniper refused to reply.

<<We cherish you, dear Champion.>>

The trees lingered a moment, waiting for a reply, but all Juniper could muster was a fake smile. The trees sensed her hesitance to return the sentiment and granted her the space she desired. They were gone and she was alone, festering in aggrievement.

Another struggle she'd need to let go. There was no room for animosity in the end of times and she'd have to find it in her heart to forgive the trees. It was the only way to stop her disappointment from turning into bitter hatred. She intended to lead her people into a healthy, prosperous life, and a toxic relationship with the trees would spoil everything. In time, these wounds would heal.

It was a cold day in the forest, and despite the lack of fresh air, a clean breeze flowed past them at all times. There was no justifiable explanation for a stream of quality air under these conditions, yet it was always there. It reminded her that there were forces beyond her that controlled their fate; that they played tiny roles in their survival during the aggressive death and rebirth of nature. Here, Gaia protected them, and there was no telling the state of the deconstructed terrain beyond the forest.

She received telepathic visits from her sisters often. Marisabel, Coral, Eshe, and Aria talked to her the most. Building strong bonds with her fellow Champions was therapeutic. Having their love and support made everything hurt less.

They were scheduled to have their first group meeting that afternoon, so Juniper found a quiet spot in the woods where she could attend uninterrupted.

She waited for the pull.

An icy wind blasted Juniper and Aria swept her up and carried her thoughts to the meeting place.

I'm not sure why I can't connect to the meeting place on my own, Juniper commented.

It takes practice. You'll get the hang of it, Aria reassured her.

Thoughts flew by in a blur as they reached the spot where the others waited. It wasn't a real location, just a place in their subconscious where they all could materialize. The space was stark white and she was wearing an outfit she'd never seen before.

The green gown was covered in emeralds, tourmaline stones, and jade beads. The dress shimmered with gemstones along the bodice, and the dark green tulle skirt draped over her legs with a drizzle of beads and stones near her feet. The sleeves were capped and clung by the points of her shoulders, and the neckline plunged to the middle of her ribcage. Her long brown curls hung loose and she wore a crown of bark and leaves. When she looked down at herself, there was a glowing sheen of green outlining her silhouette. She looked over at Aria in question, her green eyes brighter than ever.

"These are our auras," the Air Champion explained.

Aria spun in a circle and her long, chiffon skirt danced in the wind. The top of her dress was sheer fabric bedazzled in intricately placed diamonds, and she wore a white bandeau beneath. Her white hair was tied into an up-do and had lace and feathers strewn throughout. Her blue eyes held white speckles that danced like snow as she smiled.

Juniper looked around at her sisters, all of whom looked stunning. They each took their place in the circle and held hands.

To Juniper's left was Marisabel. She wore a dress that was light blue and Grecian-inspired. The sleeves were silken fabric that acted as both the shoulder straps and chest piece. The belt of the gown was tight and attached was a mermaid-styled skirt that was tight around her hips then flowed like water to the floor. The color complimented her olive skin tone and dark brown hair. Juniper smiled at her and Marisabel's aura gleamed through her blue eyes as she squeezed Juniper's hand in friendship.

Sofyla, Champion of Soil, stood on her right. Her yellow gown was a classic combination of chiffon and lace, with brown highlights in the stitching. The back was open in a low-V to the top of her tailbone, and the neckline went up to her collarbones. The long sleeves were made of finely stitched lace and connected to her middle fingers like rings. Her sandy hair was long and straight, and her hazel eyes were as captivating as quicksand.

Juniper was in awe. She thought she might never get the chance to put faces to the names since they were spaced so far across the globe, but here they were. Her sisters stood beside her in thought, as exquisite and as graceful as she imagined.

Once all the Champions connected by holding hands, their auras linked and a being of light descended into the middle of the circle. It was Gaia. Her naked silhouette was illuminated by starlight and the colors of a celestial death storm. The varying shades of greens and blues, with splashes of bright pinks and purples, were breathtaking. She didn't need a face, for her body emoted every sentiment known to mankind. Her figure was a swirling nebula of wondrous grace, and her appearance left them all in awe.

<<*Dear daughters, I am sorry I did not connect with you sooner, but it was necessary to see your dedication before I let you in. The war is over and I could not be more proud. You survived and saved many others along the way. As you know, I do not hate humans, I just could not tolerate the manner in which they evolved. I know there is good in you, and I am thrilled to watch you cohabitate with nature and the other creatures of Earth with respect and dignity. You are humanity's second chance.*>>

"*Mother Earth,*" Sahira Dayal, Champion of the Mountains began. She stood between Aria and Eshe. Her dress had an enormous, a-symmetrical scalloped tiered skirt made of gray organza. The bodice had a square neckline with butterfly sleeves and flashes of silver swirled within the fabric as she moved. Her dark, brown hair was tied into a large bun with a gold ribbon. As metallic as her outfit appeared, it didn't outshine her stone-colored eyes. "*I am grateful to be one of the chosen, but I'm still having trouble sleeping knowing that so many were slaughtered.*"

<<*I understand your struggle, but you could not have done anything to prevent it,*>> Gaia responded. <<*As the elements told you, it was either save yourself and those you could gather, or fall victim like the rest. You all chose wisely, as your participation guarantees the human race a chance to endure.*>>

"What happens now?" Coral, Champion of the Ocean, asked. She stood to the left of Marisabel and wore a gown made of shiny purple beads and gems. The neckline was scooped and the straps were thick by the chest and grew thinner as they reached her shoulders. The back was cut into an even deeper scoop to the low-hanging belt line. She wore a gold belt with a purple and pink pectin Raveneli shell as the buckle. The scalloped, A-line skirt was symmetrical and the circular edges were covered in beads. She was of Indonesian-Chinese descent, so her skin was light and her hair black. Her connection to the ocean colored her sapphire eyes. *"Are we to live in Antarctica forever?"*

Marisabel's eyes widened in question. She too was stuck on the icy continent and was hoping to lead her people to warmer climates soon.

<<*It need not be that way. I think you'll be best suited to stay there, but that choice is yours when the time comes. For now, you must remain. Your elements will tell you when it's safe to relocate.*>>

"What if we cannot rebuild before our human lives cease? We are all in our late twenties and early thirties, which only gives us another thirty to forty years to accomplish what might take centuries," said Eshe, Champion of the Core. She wore an orange ball gown made of silk that had a skirt layered in red, orange, and yellow feathers. The effect set the dress aflame. Her dark hair and skin contrasted her fiery aura beautifully and made her glow as bright as lava.

<<*I'm glad you asked that. I've come with a gift.*>>

Gaia placed her hands into the nebula of her stomach and extracted seven orbs of light. The colors inside each swirled with luminosity. She placed an orb in front of each of the Champions and it hovered in the air near their hearts. With a wave of her arm the orbs propelled into their bodies. In unison, the Champions tilted their heads toward the sky as Gaia's gift entered their hearts. It had total control over them as its light spread through their minds, bodies, and souls. They stayed connected with firm handholds, but their bodies shook with aggressive force. All Juniper could see was white as her body digested the strange endowment. It lasted so long, she began to worry that her body might reject the gift and that it would kill her instead.

When the sensation ended, the sisters regained their senses with deep breaths and varying expressions. Eshe, Sofyla, and Coral looked offended, Aria and Sahira appeared traumatized, and Marisabel wore a look of terrible alarm. Juniper wasn't sure how to feel. At first, the gift felt like the arrival of death, but now that it was over, she felt more alive than ever.

"What was that?" she asked.

<<*A gift of eternal life, for you and your Seconds. As you are in this moment, you will remain.*>>

Juniper's heart sunk. This gift could have saved Roscoe.

"We will live forever?" Eshe asked, her look of offense morphed into wonder.

<<*If you take care. It's a gift of eternal life, not immortal life, and you are still vulnerable to most of mankind's weaknesses. I've granted you immunity to disease and the ability to heal faster, but not safety from fatal injuries.*>>

"Why not grant us immortality?" Coral asked.

<<Because I want you to live safe and humble lives. Slipping into states of recklessness, conceit, and superiority would be too easy without the fear of death. I trust you now, but time changes people and since you'll have so much of it, I need to guarantee that you stay modest.>>

Though it made sense, and they should be grateful to have received any form of extended life, the expressions on some of her fellow Champions suggested otherwise. There was a feeling of disappointment among them, and an even more subdued notion of annoyance. Those who felt anger hid it well, but the energy was still present. Gaia sensed it too.

<<In time you will understand my reasoning, and I hope you all find gratitude in your hearts. I believe I chose wisely when selecting each of you, and I hope this role of power has not changed the women behind the Champions.>>

Juniper scanned the faces of her sisters to see if Gaia's supportive warning changed their energy. The few who previously wore scowls absorbed her words and reminded themselves they had no reason not to smile. They were the luckiest women on earth. They were chosen by Mother Nature to endure the end of times. They were chosen as the Champions of the human race and given the gift of eternal life. This reminder went unspoken but was felt by all. The mood lifted and the sisterhood was alight with positivity again. Their auras brightened and the light illuminating the circle pulsed with a steady glow.

"Thank you, Gaia," Juniper said as the energy shifted. "We are grateful for your gift."

<<*You are very welcome.*>> She could not see Gaia's smile, but she felt it. <<*Keep faith, my daughters. Together we will live in harmony.*>>

Gaia rose into the air and Her being of light exploded like a supernova. Her pieces of fiery color rained over the Champions and dissolved before touching their heads.

They released hands and stood in silence for a moment.

"*Who was sulking after she explained her gift of eternal life?*" Eshe demanded. "*It made us look ungrateful.*"

"*It was me, I'm sorry,*" Sofyla confessed. "*I just needed a moment to remind myself of my luck. I was still wrapped up in the overwhelming feeling of receiving the orb and my mind wasn't absorbing anything clearly. I am grateful, and I didn't mean to exude negativity.*"

"*It's okay,*" Juniper jumped in. "*We are still human.*"

"*No, it's not okay,*" Eshe retorted. "*Yes, we are still human, but we need to hold ourselves to a higher standard. We need to be above the petty human emotions that preyed upon us in our former lives. They are what led us to this fate and we cannot let Gaia down by repeating old habits.*"

"*Fine,*" Juniper continued in defense of Coral, "*but we also shouldn't be attacking each other as we learn how to operate in our roles as Champions. We are family; we are bonded by something beyond any of our previous realms of reality. This is strange, and crazy, and we are still adapting. Still learning. Gaia is an entity far beyond our reach; our elements come and go as they please, and our followers have no clue what it's like to carry this burden. We are all we have. If we don't show unconditional support and love, we will drive a wedge between the sisterhood.*"

"She's right," Aria chimed in.

"Yes, she is right," Eshe huffed. *"But that doesn't mean we shouldn't push one another to be the best versions of ourselves possible."*

"Agreed. Let's just show mercy in our approach," Juniper suggested. Eshe's expression was of defiant surrender and the argument was over.

Being together as a whole unit for the first time was telling and the Champions were establishing their roles amongst each other. Juniper was content in the role of mediator. She was an empath due to the struggles she'd endured throughout her life and felt she'd contribute greatly in this facet. Eshe was the fire and passion propelling the group forward. Coral embodied the unpredictable currents of human emotion and kept the others grounded in their humanity. Aria was a breath of fresh air that lightened everyone's spirits. Sahira provided the stone-hard reason they'd desperately need. Sofyla was as soft as sand with a mischievous flare that kept their shared energy playful, and Marisabel was strongest of them all as she was the link that kept them all bound. She had formed solid relationships with each of them and her presence was a comfort to all, even when she did not say a word.

"It's time to go," Sahira reminded them. *"We have people waiting on our attentive lead."*

Juniper didn't have anyone waiting on her. While the others told their followers why they'd be mentally absent for a while, no one in her following knew she was vacant from her body right now.

Eshe disappeared in a flash of flames and Sahira followed closely behind, leaving a trail of gray dust. Coral and Marisabel held hands as they departed. They disappeared like paint on a canvas that had been left in the rain. Sofyla's image exploded with a burst of sand, leaving only Aria and Juniper in the white room.

"Ready?" Aria asked and Juniper nodded. She felt Aria seize hold of her thoughts and did everything in her power to hold on to the feeling of the room. She hoped that savoring the ambiance of the meeting place would help her return on her own next time.

They soared through their shared subconscious and Aria tossed her down a side hallway to where her body waited at the end of the corridor.

Juniper sat up and gasped. She was back in the forest beneath her mossy canopy and no longer dressed in an elegant gown. Her hair was a knotted mess, her skin was covered in dirt, and her clothes were the same she'd been wearing for months. Back to normal.

Juniper smiled despite the unpleasant return to her meager reality. There was a place where she could meet with her Champion sisters, a place where they could talk to Gaia directly. She closed her eyes and felt the gift of eternal life echo in every heartbeat. She held her hands in front of her face and opened her eyes. Energy radiated through her fingertips. She picked up a sharp rock nearby and pricked her finger. The wound stung as she watched the blood roll down her finger. It moved slowly down her skin, across the span of her palm, over her wrist, and down her arm. When it reached the middle of her forearm she felt the cut heal.

An enormous grin emerged on her face. Gaia entrusted her with eternal life, and she planned to make Her proud.

Chapter 32

Juniper and her following persevered through the days of prolonged darkness. For her mental health, Juniper let go of Roscoe. His memory remained vivid in her heart, but the hope that he might still be alive diminished. It was no longer healthy to wish for his return; doing so was a detriment to herself and those she was tasked to protect. The pain lingered, but she carried on.

The dreams in which he spoke to her ceased. She missed his nightly visits but understood his absence was for the best. The less she saw him in her sleep, the easier it was to let go.

A week passed and Juniper began to feel like her old self again. There were moments where her grief snuck up on her unexpectedly, but she was able to function between them. She spoke to Clark often and their conversations kept her on the right path. She eventually let Irene in too. Having their support was her greatest tool in healing.

As a group, they often talked about what happened. Everyone struggled with survivor's guilt. Juniper expressed her dismay that she couldn't save more and the majority of the group consoled her, reminding her that she did her best. There was no way to stop the end, even if her emails had found their way to the right connections to warn the masses. The best she, or anyone else, could do was survive and move forward. There was no changing the past, so they agreed to live full and meaningful lives on behalf of those who were lost. They'd keep humanity alive and build better lives for everyone who remained. It was all they could do.

Eventually, the group made peace with all they endured; the indirect guilt, remorse, and confusion settled and they became united in gratefulness. With the worst behind them, they began working hard to make their living arrangements as comfortable as possible.

Teek's parents were the chefs of the group. They found ways to make the bland food taste better. Misty's brothers finished the shelter with the help of Jeb, Brett, and his sisters. They nestled a wooden roof between a tight set of trees and covered it in moss and leaves to prevent rain from leaking through when the weather came back. The walls were made of braided vines that would shelter them from harsh winds and animals, once they returned. For now, the shelter was mainly used for warmth. The body heat of everyone huddled together warmed the small space and kept them healthy. Catching a cold would be dangerous now that they had no access to medical help.

The Devereaux family was the most resistant to their new way of life. They often whined and complained about their discomfort, unconcerned that everyone felt just as bad, or worse. Zaedon Devereaux was young, tall, and strong, but he did not want to help with any of the manual labor. His response to any requests for assistance was annoyed sighs and eye rolls. Genevieve was also young and capable, but acted weaker than she was and insisted she hurt her wrist while helping with the shelter. She milked the fake injury and spent her days napping and eating. Their parents were even worse.

Phineas constantly talked about rebuilding the world so that it resembled what had been destroyed. Despite Juniper's continued reminders that they were not saved in order to repeat old mistakes, he insisted that they should construct new cities and roadways. He wanted to explore the continent in search of structures that were spared and suggested returning to unsustainable energy sources to begin the process. Juniper could not stress enough how terrible the idea was and prayed that no one else in the group supported his suggestions. His wife, Claudia, was unable to let go of her materialistic tendencies. She went on one trip into town and came back with a suitcase full of clothes, jewelry, and impractical shoes.

"Any updates from the trees?" Clark asked. He sat next to Juniper and warmed his hands over the bonfire.

"I've been wondering the same thing," Jeb chimed in.

"Not much. They are busy trying to rebuild the world. I did experience the first group chat with my fellow Champions, though."

"Telepathically?" Clark asked.

"Yes." She decided not to mention there was a subconscious meeting location buried in her mind. It would be too hard to explain. She relived the visual often, though, and imagined herself being showered and dressed in her luxurious green aura gown again. "The scenarios they are enduring are similar to ours. It's nice to be reminded that we aren't alone. There are others out there surviving just like us."

"That *is* a comforting thought," Jeb said. "Makes me feel less isolated."

"Yeah," Clark agreed. "Thinking we were the only ones left on the planet was depressing. I'm happy to know there are other groups spread across the globe."

"Maybe we can link up with them one day," she suggested with a shrug. If this was possible, she hoped it happened soon. Though she would live long enough to see that day, the others might not and they deserved to live in a large and loving community.

"That would be nice." Clark smiled. He was happy to see Juniper thriving again after her breakdown.

"Do you think everyone will stay after we're allowed to leave this forest?" Jeb asked.

"What do you mean?"

"Well, right now, we have no choice, but once we are allowed to travel, do you think some might venture off on their own?"

"I hope not," Juniper answered. She never considered this possibility. She glanced at the toxic Devereaux family, who were currently complaining about the bland meal they were served. They'd be the first to jump ship. "Do you think so?"

"I wonder about a few," Jeb replied.

"If some left, do you think others would follow?" Juniper was suddenly feeling very disconnected to the underlying pulse of the group.

Jeb shrugged. "Some days I think yes, others I think no. I guess it will depend on where you plan to lead us next."

"I haven't thought that far ahead. I don't even know how long we will be stuck here or what the trees will tell me to do once the darkness ends."

"I would start thinking about it if I were you," Jeb advised. "If you don't have a plan, the majority will likely follow someone who does."

Juniper clenched her teeth in aggravation. He wasn't wrong.

"As much as I don't want to lose anyone, I cannot control their loyalty. If certain individuals decide to leave and go their own way, so be it. I'm done trying to convince anyone to follow. I've already proven myself."

"I understand. I'm just informing you of what's being discussed in whispers. I don't want it to come as a shock if that day arrives."

"Would you abandon me?" Juniper asked, suddenly doubting everyone.

"Of course not," Jeb protested. "I don't have a death wish."

"That's exactly what leaving would be. I don't suspect they'd survive long without me. The world is still in a state of volatile rebirth, and I imagine it will remain this way for quite some time."

Jeb shrugged. "Leaving your side would be foolish."

"So is returning to dirty and antiquated sources of energy."

Both men nodded in agreement.

Juniper shook her head and glanced at the Devereaux family again. She didn't need Jeb to tell her who was behind the whispers, but she did wonder who was listening. To prevent their negative energy from manipulating others, she'd need to take stronger action against their behavior. She thought gossip would tear the group apart, but while she was biting her tongue, others were planting seeds, and she realized that letting the whispers fester was the only poison she needed to fear.

She retired to her sleeping quarters for the night, too tired to address the problem now. The ash clouds wouldn't be clearing anytime soon, so she had time.

A few hours into her sleep Roscoe's image returned. He was louder than ever. She tried to push him out of her dream, but he wouldn't leave.

WAKE UP.

Juniper tossed beneath her blankets as she tried to rewind her dream and start over.

JUNIPER, HELP ME.

Let me go. She made an attempt to seize control of her dream, but the claws of his reappearance dug deep. His image was stained on the backs of her eyelids.

Unable to rewind and redo the dream, she tried to fast forward instead. Roscoe continued to scream. She ran from him and her surroundings became blurred. Though she was gaining distance, his voice never decreased in volume. When she stopped, out of breath, he stood before her, staring down on her as she panted.

I'M NOT DEAD.

Yes, you are. Leave me alone!

She began to run again. This time, Roscoe did not follow. She sprinted through the woods, faster than a speeding train, and emerged in an open space. There were no more trees, but she kept running. Without warning, the ground disappeared beneath her and she was freefalling into a fissure. She screamed and woke up from the nightmare.

Tears streamed down her face from fright.

After weeks of peaceful slumber, Roscoe's reappearance came as a shock. She was shaken and unsure why her subconscious was playing evil games. Unable to fall back to sleep, she stared at the sky beyond the trees and waited for the blackness to shift into a lighter shade of gray.

When the sun began to rise beyond the ash clouds, the world brightened. She guessed it was approximately six in the morning, so she stopped feigning sleep and got up. Instead of heading toward the bonfire to warm up, she walked a little deeper into the woods in the opposite direction. She needed a minute to clear her mind before greeting the others.

A few feet beyond her mossy sanctuary was a small ledge and acres of sterling alpine trees. They were tall, thin, and tightly spaced. The ground they covered was flat, but it was impossible to see to the other side due to the dense forestry. This part of the forest was foreign; she'd never seen it before. It was one of the many new additions to the woods after the attack and Juniper wished she had a camera to capture the stunning view.

She carefully stepped down the ledge and faced the long rows of trees. It reminded her of a funhouse at a carnival. There were so many trees placed in such close proximity that their appearance felt like a mirage. It didn't feel real and it was impossible not to go cross-eyed when trying to focus on one spot. She took a step forward and her entire vantage point shifted. The change felt like a hallucination. She blinked her eyes a few times to readjust her vision before taking another step. The scenery shifted again and she began to think something greater than the woods was playing tricks on her. Stationed between two thin trees she placed her hands on their trunks and realigned her balance.

Then a noise came from the distance—the cracking, crunching sound of twigs and leaves. Juniper's brow furrowed and she tried to listen closer. The footsteps were headed toward her, so she ducked behind a tree and held her breath. If the animals were back, they'd be hungry, and she did not want to be their first meal. The noise continued to grow in volume as it approached. It sounded close enough to see, so Juniper peeked around the tree to catch a glimpse.

The moment her eyes narrowed in on the source she lost control of her senses. She stepped out from behind the tree and stood in the open space. Her breath was gone and the tears that wanted to fall were frozen in place. The sounds of the forest were replaced by the numbing hum of her thoughts whizzing in circles at exponential speeds. Her heart rose into her throat and threatened to choke her with the sudden reemergence of hope. She tried to speak, but the words came out as hollow breaths. A tingling sensation ran down her arms and she lost feeling in her fingertips. With eyes closed she shook her head, afraid this was another trick of the trees, but when she reopened them, the sight was the same. She tried to pinch herself awake, but she wasn't asleep. This was real; it wasn't a dream.

Roscoe stood a few feet in front of her, alive and smiling.

Chapter 33

Roscoe was covered in dirt, blood, and ash. Despite his tattered condition, he grinned and ran toward her. He buried her in a hug and Juniper collapsed in his embrace.

"Is this real?" she asked, afraid to feel too much in case this moment was stripped from her.

"Yes. I've been trying to reach you."

"I heard you in my dreams."

"It was the only time I could reach you."

"I thought I was going crazy."

"Sorry. I'm not sure what happened to our connection."

"I thought I lost you." She looked up at him with tears in her eyes.

"I'd never leave you." He grabbed her face and kissed her. The reunion was surreal, but perfect. Juniper couldn't believe he was back.

"Are you okay?" she asked. "You have blood all over you."

"I'm okay now." He pointed at an injury on his leg. "This one kept bleeding. No matter how many times I wrapped it up, the blood kept pouring. It got so bad I thought I wouldn't make it. Then one day all my gashes and wounds healed." He shrugged.

Juniper gasped, then smirked. "I'll explain why later." Peering over his shoulder she saw another unexpected sight. A crowd of people stood twenty feet from them, patiently waiting and watching their happy reunion.

"Who are they?"

"They were looking for you."

"Me? I don't know who they are."

"When we got separated I tried to find the end of the fissure so I could walk around it and get back to you. I walked north and before I could find the end point, the trees called out to me."

"The trees? I thought they only spoke to me."

"They said I needed to help you. I left the forest to find everything covered in ash. I couldn't go anywhere until I found protective gear," he explained, pointing to his strange wardrobe as he continued, "hence the old lady scarf and dollar-store sunglasses. It was the best I could find. The trees then led me over the Hood Canal Bridge and instructed me to steal a boat from someone's backyard so I could row across the sound. The trees told me to keep my sights on Mount Stickney, and sure enough, a few days later I was greeted by new arrivals. They're from all over the country. They said they heard your voice before the trees attacked. They were trying to get to Olympic National Forest but got caught up in the attacks along the way. The trees intercepted and had them rerouted. There may be more out there, still traveling and trying to reach you."

Juniper's brow furrowed, then she remembered the message she sent into the universe weeks ago.

"Yes," she nodded, "I did call out to like-minded spirits. I never thought it would work though." She smiled and looked back at the crowd.

"Well, it did, and the trees helped me find them. They led us back the long way, since we couldn't all fit in the row boat, and then safely guided us here."

All of Juniper's anger toward the trees vanished now that she realized they didn't abandon her or Roscoe. She hadn't heard from them because they were too busy helping Roscoe survive.

She felt bad that she had jumped to conclusions, but was grateful to be wrong.

"So, they all came because of me?"

"Yup. When I greeted them in Gold Bar they asked me how to get to Olympic National Park. When I asked how they knew to go there, they said that Juniper of the Trees spoke to them. You saved far more people than you realized."

"I'm in shock."

"So was I. I think it's wise we search for other survivors in the upcoming weeks. I imagine many of those who heard your call are still traveling."

Juniper nodded, noticing a few familiar people in the distant crowd. "Is that the Wolfe family?" She scanned the faces. "And your friends, and all the others who left?"

"Yes, the trees led me to them once I returned with your new followers. They were near Lake Cushman."

"All the way down there?"

"Yeah, they got really lost."

"I'm glad they're okay. Noah and Cade are going to be thrilled."

"Let me introduce you to the others," Roscoe suggested. He took her hand and led her to the crowd. They stared at her with mixed emotions. Some were in shock; others wore expressions of awe.

"This is Juniper," Roscoe announced to the group. They shuffled toward her expressing sentiments of elation, gratitude, and wonder. She was taken aback by their admiration, but overwhelmingly appreciative. Not only for their kindness, but for the fact that they listened to her message and believed in her.

The trees spared them, knowing they were headed to Juniper. Their faith in her kept them alive and she was honored. It would be a tall task to feel worthy of such reverence, but she had every intention of living up to their hopes.

The world as they once knew it was gone and death draped the landscape, but somehow they were still alive. It did not diminish the weight they felt for those who were lost, but it did give them a sliver of hope. They could survive, and they would. They'd carry on with strength and create a world worth fighting for.

Juniper led the sizeable crowd back to the Hall of Mosses. The unpredictability of people in large groups used to give her anxiety; there were too many personalities, opinions, and conflicts. Hiding in the forest, away from humanity, was the only place she felt safe. But she was different now. She had grown and healed; she now saw her old fears in a new light. There was no safety in isolation; no life in her self-made quarantine, and this large group gave her comfort instead of unease. For the first time in years she felt present, like she was truly inhaling the wonder of the current moment. Gaia chose her and the trees helped her reach this moment of bliss. The inner warrior she had lost over the years, the courage she had been trying so hard to reclaim, had returned.

She was a Champion, not only of nature, but of herself. Her vision was clear and together, she and her people would endure. Though she had herself to thank, her gratitude for this miracle also belonged to the trees. She glanced toward the treetops with a smirk and felt the magic of the trees envelop her heart. Out of hiding and into this brave new land, she came alive.

Thank you for reading *Hall of Mosses*—I hope you enjoyed the story! If you have a moment, please consider rating and reviewing it on Amazon and sharing your thoughts via social media. All feedback is greatly appreciated!

Amazon Author Account:

www.amazon.com/author/nicolineevans

Instagram:

www.instagram.com/nicolinenovels

Facebook:

www.facebook.com/nicolinenovels

Twitter:

www.twitter.com/nicolinenovels

To learn more about my other novels, please visit my official author website:

www.nicolineevans.com